My Husband's Mistress 2:

Renaissance Collection

My Husband's Mistress 2:

Renaissance Collection

Racquel Williams

www.urbanbooks.net

Urban Books, LLC
300 Farmingdale Road, NY-Route 109
Farmingdale, NY 11735

My Husband's Mistress 2: Renaissance Collection

ISBN 13: 978-1-64556-199-6
ISBN 10: 1-64556-199-2

First Mass Market Printing June 2021
First Trade Paperback Printing July 2020
Printed in the United States of America

10 9 8 7 6 5 4 3 2 1

Distributed by Kensington Publishing Corp.
Submit Orders to:
Customer Service
400 Hahn Road
Westminster, MD 21157-4627
Phone: 1-800-733-3000
Fax: 1-800-659-2436

My Husband's Mistress 2:

Renaissance Collection

by

Racquel Williams

Acknowledgments

First and foremost, I want to give all praises to Allah. Without his continued blessings, I wouldn't be where I am today.

I want to shout out to all my readers and supporters, old and new. Thanks for rocking with me on these releases. I'm forever grateful.

Shout out to my support system. Y'all already know, I appreciate the support.

Shout out to my authors at Racquel Williams Presents. I appreciate all the support y'all have given me.

Shout out to my homies on lock. Please remember, one day, the struggle will be over.

Shout out to my test readers. I appreciate the brutal honesty that y'all provide.

Shout out to my promoters. I am grateful to have y'all.

Shout out to everyone that supports the movement. I am definitely blessed.

Chapter One

Hassan Clarke

One of the things I dreaded in life was getting locked up. I'd never been in a cell before, so you know I was mad as fuck that I got locked up. Destiny almost gave me a heart attack when she said the police wanted me. The first thing that came to mind was the shit that popped off with Corey. That was until the officer said I was charged with assault and battery. Instantly, I knew it was Imani. I was shocked that her ass would press charges against me—ungrateful-ass bitch. After all I did for her and her bastard child, this was how she repaid me.

I tried to talk to the officers, but they weren't trying to hear me. Instead, they took me to Central Booking near Sherman and Sheridan Avenues. I went in front of the magistrate and was given a bond in the amount of twenty-five grand. I felt relieved because that was chump change. I was also booked and fingerprinted like one of these criminals out here.

The worst part was when one of the cell mates noticed me. Instead of him keeping his mouth shut, he walked closer.

"Ain't you that attorney? Umm . . . I can't remember the name."

"Yes, that's me," I said as I hung my head in shame.

I knew it was only a matter of time before everybody and their mama knew I was locked up. I was ready to go. I didn't want to spend another second in a jail cell. I patiently waited to get a bond. Even though Destiny and I were beefing, I was pretty sure that she'd make sure I got out of here soon.

I sat in the dingy-ass jail cell, waiting to hear my name called, but it never happened. Minutes turned into hours. It was damn near night again, and no one came to bail me out. I was transferred that evening to Rikers Island. I couldn't believe this shit. I was a prominent member of the community, and here I was, getting treated like I was a common criminal.

"They're going to pay. All these bitches are going to pay," I said out loud.

"Nigga, what you mumbling about?" this crackhead-looking motherfucker said.

"Nah, homie, it's best you mind your own business," I snapped.

"Nigga, you better watch yo' mouth. I don't know the kind of niggas you're used to dealing with, but around here, you got to show respect, boy."

I was tempted to punch this nigga in his mouth, but I kept my peace. After all, I was a defense attorney, and I knew the law inside out. There was no way I was going to fuck up my chance of walking out on bond. Not over a bum-ass nigga that probably has nothing to lose.

When I got to Rikers Island, I was processed, given a name badge, a mat, and some sheets. I walked into the unit that I was assigned to, and, boy, did reality set in. There were a bunch of burly looking dudes posted as soon as I walked on the floor. I tried not to make eye contact. I just walked to where my cell was located. I dropped my cot on the floor and looked around for the nearest phone. It wasn't hard to spot, but a long line of people stood there. It didn't seem like I would be getting on the phone anytime soon.

It was dinnertime, and I passed on it, not because I wasn't hungry, but because I wasn't trying to eat that shit. I stayed back on the unit while the majority of dudes left for the mess hall. I didn't waste any time. I hurried and jumped on the phone. What's crazy was that in the midst of the cell phone frenzy, I barely remembered numbers because everything was stored on my phone. So I couldn't call anyone except Destiny and my mama. I didn't have any money to put on the phone, but after talking to a dude that stayed back on the unit, he decided to let me use his credit. In return, I would put money on his books when I bonded out.

The first number I dialed was Destiny's. The first time, the phone went straight to voicemail. I hung up and then dialed her number again. I listened as she picked up. The recording informed her that this was a jail call, and she could press five to accept.

"What do you want?" she immediately asked.

I was thrown off by her nonchalant attitude. This bitch knew where the fuck I was, and this how she was acting?

"Yo, did you call Leon, and why the fuck my bond ain't posted?" I yelled into the phone.

"Listen to me, you bastard. Don't you call my phone, acting like I owe you shit. You need to call one of your nasty-ass whores to come and bond you out."

I wanted to fly through the phone and squeeze the life out of this silly bitch, but I remained calm.

"Yo, what kind of shit you on? I understand that you're upset, but now isn't the fucking time for your selfish rants. I'm in fucking jail, and I need you to get some money, get a bondsman, and come get me out ASAP," I calmly said.

"And you're not listening. I'm not doing shit else for you. You got your ass in there, now you figure a way out. Please don't call my fucking phone anymore."

That bitch hung up in my ear before I got a chance to respond. "Ha-ha," I chuckled to myself. If this bitch only knew how much I despised her. I wished she would do us both a fucking favor and kill herself.

I rubbed my hand over my head. I had to figure a way out of here. Next, I dialed Mama's number.

"Hello, hello," she answered frantically.

"Hey, Mama."

"Hassan, what the hell are you doing in Rikers?"

"Long story, Mama. Imani had me locked up on some bogus charges."

"What kind of charges, and do you have a bond? Lord, Charmaine goin' whup that ass."

"Chill out. You know these phone calls are recorded. Anyway, I have a bond, but I left my wallet and everything in the house. I asked Destiny's dumb ass to bond me out or call my partner, but she acting dumb and shit."

"So, what you want me to do? You want me to go get your wallet from the house?"

"Nah, I 'ont want you going over there, getting into it with her ass."

"Boy, ain't nobody worried about that ho. I need to get you out of there right away."

Before I could respond, the phone cut off. I think the credit ran out. I hung up the phone and walked back to my bunk. I felt a little better now that I'd heard my mama's voice. I no longer felt alone, and I knew she would do whatever it took to get me out of here.

Chapter Two

Destiny Clarke

This man had to be the dumbest person I've ever met. Here he was with a great career, and he went and caught a case behind some pussy. Pussy that didn't even belong to him. Boy, I tell you, these so-called men do not think with their heads. They think with their cocks, and because of that, they are always getting caught up in some bullshit.

From the minute the police showed up, I knew his ass did something he had no business doing. I waited for a few hours. Then I called the jail and found out he had a string of charges, including assault and battery. "Damn fool," I chuckled to myself after I hung up the phone. I tell you, pussy is a powerful weapon.

I called Mama's phone. I needed someone to vent to.

"Hey, Mama."

"Hey, baby, how you doing?"

"You ain't goin' believe what I'm about to tell you. The police locked up Hassan."

"Say what?" she asked in astonishment.

"Yes, this morning. I heard a loud banging on the door, so I jumped up. It was the police with a warrant for him. I called the jail and found out he had numerous charges, including assault and battery."

"Assault and battery? I 'ont know much 'bout the law, but ain't that when you hit on somebody?"

"Yup. I think it's the whore that he's been sleeping with." I had to be careful around Mama. I didn't want her to know that I'd met Hassan's other woman.

"He's a bigger fool than I thought. You helped him to make a life, and he's throwing it all away behind a trick. I tell you, they should lock him up and throw away the damn key."

"Yea, I was shocked at first, but that's what his arrogant behind gets."

"I'll be happy when he's finally out of your life for good."

"Me too, Mama. Anyway, I got to go. Love you."

"I love you too, baby."

As soon as I hung up, the phone started ringing again. It said unknown, so I was a little reluctant to pick up. Nevertheless, I answered and immediately realized it was Hassan calling from jail.

I should've hung up on him, but my curiosity got the best of me. What surprised me the most was the bastard questioned why he wasn't bonded out yet. See, he really thought I was just a dumb bitch, and I can't blame him, because I put up with his shit for years. The only thing was, Hassan didn't know that I was no longer that scared bitch that he married. I was as cold as an ice cube in the freezer. By the time our conversation ended, I knew he had an idea of who he had turned me into.

I knew I was getting stronger every day. The old me would've been down at the jail, bonding out my husband, screaming and hollering. But not today. I've grown to realize that the fool never loved me, and I was done playing the dumb bitch.

***

I decided to go through Amaiya's closet and bag up the clothes she could no longer wear. I planned on selling the house after the divorce was final. Too many memories of Hassan in the house; plus, I needed a new start away from it all. Then I heard the doorbell ring.

"Who the hell's trying to sell me something now?" I said out loud.

I put the bag down and marched down the stairs. I looked through the peephole and noticed it was Hassan's gorilla-looking mama banging on my door. I turned around, went into my living room, and grabbed the mace out of my purse. I didn't invite this bitch over, so I could only guess she was here to start trouble.

I walked back to the door and unlocked it. "What is it you want? Your son is not here." I looked at her with my left hand akimbo and my right hand in my pocket, holding my mace.

"I'm here to see your ass, bitch. You know damn well where my son is at, and you're playing stupid." She pushed me out of the way with her big ass and entered my home.

"You can't come up in my shit. Like I said, you fat bitch, your motherfucking son is not here." I balled my fist up and struck her in the face without thinking.

I waited all my life to get this bitch. I will never forget how she disrespected me.

Whap! Whap!

That bitch slapped me a few times, knocking me off balance. I stumbled a little but maintained my balance. I used all my strength, leaped toward that bitch, and pushed her ass down. As soon as her big ass hit the ground, I jumped on top of her and started punching her in the face nonstop.

"Bitch, don't you *ever* come up in my shit and disrespect me," I yelled as I punched her in the face.

"Fuck you, you stupid-ass ho." She hawked up a bunch of phlegm and spat it in my face. Then she grabbed my hair and started pulling it. I was starting to lose because this human gorilla was using her weight against me. I knew that I couldn't let her hold me too long. I reached into my pocket and grabbed my mace as I sank my teeth into that bitch's arm so she would let go of my hair.

"*Aargh, aargh,* you dirty bitch. You bit me," she screamed out in agony.

She loosened her grip on my hair, and I pulled away, then sprayed the mace into her eyes.

"*Aargh, aargh,* you bitch. I'm going to beat the brakes off you," this pig-looking bitch said.

I didn't let up any. I emptied the remains of the can in her face, all while blocking out the horrible sounds of a gorilla screaming bloody murder.

"You see, bitch, you should've killed that bastard when you was pregnant. If you did, I wouldn't have to deal with his bastard ass. Now, get your ass up out of my shit before I throw you out."

"Fuck you. I told my son you wasn't shit. All you are is an uppity-ass ho."

"Yea, well, it takes one ho to know another ho. You and your family are nothing but parasites. Bitch, you need to thank me, because, without me, y'all would be eating Ramen noodles seven days a week. Now, get your dirty, stanking ass out of my shit before I get yo' ass locked up," I said as I grabbed her arm.

I used all my might to push her fat ass out the door. The bitch barely resisted. She was too busy trying to wipe the mace out of her eyes and nose. As soon as I got her out the door, I slammed it shut and leaned against it. My nose and eyes were also burning. I didn't hesitate, though. I walked to the downstairs bathroom and thoroughly washed my face.

After that, I walked over to my window and peeped outside. The bitch's car was gone. I was tired, and my head hurt from that bitch pulling my hair. I flopped down on the couch. I was too old for this shit, but I knew trouble had a way of showing up on my steps. I was tired of all these bitches and this bitch-ass nigga trying me. Never in my life had I ever had to act like a fucking animal until I married this bum. *When will it end?* I thought.

Chapter Three

Imani Gibson

I had mixed feelings when I learned that they locked up Hassan. I was angry that he beat me up, but I didn't want him in jail. I mean, what the hell was I going to do without him? Tears welled up in my eyes as the thought of loneliness kicked in. Not only did I lose my baby, now I knew for sure that he wouldn't mess with me anymore, not after all this. Tears flowed from my eyes as I closed them. I had no idea why my life had to be so hard. All I ever wanted was to be loved, and I thought Hassan was going to be the man that loved me. I was so wrong. All I've been getting lately from him was pain.

I was finally discharged from the hospital. My cousin came through to pick me up. We grew up together but split up once we got older. I had no one else to call when I got admitted to the hospital.

"Hey, *chica*, you ready?" she quizzed.

"Yea, let's go." I sat in the passenger side of her Chevy Impala.

The sun was beaming down, and it made my eyes hurt a little. I was still in pain from the beating I took. The doctor prescribed Percocet for the pain. I wondered what I should use for my mental pain.

"Girl, did you hear what happened to Corey?"

"What Corey?"

"Corey, from Edenwald. The one you was cool with."

Oh Lord, here we go with this shit. What the hell that fool done got himself into? I thought.

"Nah, you know I been in here. What happened?"

"Nah, this happened before you went to the hospital. Some dude walked up on him and shot him multiple times."

I stared at her trying to see if she was playing.

"Are you serious?" I asked in shock.

I knew I didn't fuck with him, and I wished he'd just disappear for good, but that's still my baby daddy. This news was very disturbing.

"I'm dead-ass serious. Yo' ass don't watch the news? It was all over NBC and TV One a week and a half ago. They said he was in critical condition."

This shit just never ended. I knew Josiah wasn't done with all his questioning. I had no idea what I would tell him if Corey didn't make it.

"Do they know who shot him?"

"Hell no, bitch. Let me find out y'all had something going on. You look like you 'bout to cry."

I wished this bitch would shut up. I knew she had no idea that Corey and I fucked around and that he was Josiah's father. There was no way I was going to put my business out there like that.

"Nah, we were friends. I'm just shocked to hear this. I wonder if Hassan heard about this."

"What the fuck you worried about that bitch-ass nigga for? Look how he beat you up. Josiah told me everything. I'm happy you got his ass locked up 'cause he ain't no

man. He's a pussy, and you need to leave his ass alone,"
she yelled.

"I'm grown. I know what I need to do," I snapped.

"Girl, bye. You getting upset over a nigga that takes
you for a punching bag. You need help," she said sarcastically.

"You know what? Just drop it. It's my fucking life, and
if I choose to stay with him, then I'll do just that."

That was the end of the conversation for me. It was
taking everything in me not to jump on this bitch while
she was driving. Who the fuck did she think she was
talking to? It was *my* pussy, and I'd do whatever the fuck
I wanted to do with it. I remained quiet for the rest of the
ride. As soon as she pulled up, I got out of the car.

"Do you need me to come in with you?"

"Hell no, bitch. I don't ever want to see yo' ass again,"
I said as I walked off.

"You know what, Imani? Grow the fuck up," she yelled
as she pulled off.

I stuck my middle finger up, walked up the stairs, and
opened the door. I was happy to be home. I hoped Josiah
wasn't home, because I'd had enough of everyone's opin-
ion of my fucking life. *Can a bitch just live?* I thought.

The first thing I checked was the camcorder that was
in my room. It was still in place. I locked my door, sat on
the bed, and started watching it. Everything was on there,
from Hassan professing his love, to him fucking me, and
also him beating me up. It was painful as I watched how
he beat me as if I were just a ho in the streets. I started
crying again as I saw my own movie in black and white. I
looked into his eyes, and all I saw was hate and anger. I
wondered when it changed.

I picked up the phone and dialed Destiny's number. I had everything she needed on tape. First, I needed to delete the part where he was hitting me because I didn't want that bitch to see how he was treating me.

"Hello," she answered.

"Hey, how you doing?" I asked.

"Good. I meant to call you. Was it you that got Hassan locked up?"

"Nah, that wasn't me. Might be one of his other bitches," I lied.

"Oh, OK. Do you have anything for me?"

"Yes, I have it all for you. Do you have the rest of my money?" I cut straight to the chase.

"Sure, I got it. I'll call you and let you know when we're going to meet up."

"A'ight," I said before hanging up the phone.

I was happy the bitch was keeping her word. I was broke and had tons of bills that needed to be paid. I didn't plan on staying here. As soon as I got the money, my son and I were leaving. Starting over fresh might not be a bad idea, after all.

After Josiah left for school, I decided to visit Corey in the hospital. I hoped his ass wasn't on all that bullshit of us being together. He needed to accept he was just a fuck—nothing more, nothing less. I parked in the hospital parking lot and sashayed off into the building.

"Hello, sir. I'm here to see Corey Griffin."

"What's your name, and can I see your identification?"

"Sure. My name is Imani Gibson." I handed him my driver's license.

"OK, ma'am. He's in room 102B."

I took my ID and walked off. They were acting like they had this nigga under high security and shit. I took the elevator up to the second floor. His room was the first one on the right. I walked into the room and noticed his sister sitting by his bed.

"Hello," I said as I walked closer.

"Hey, may I help you?"

"My name is Imani. I'm a friend of Corey's," I nervously said.

"E-manyi . . . That name sounds familiar."

"Hey, Mani." Corey opened his eyes and spoke with difficulty.

"Hey, Corey. How you doing?" I stepped closer to his bed.

"Sis, this is Imani, Josiah's mama."

"Oh, OK. Corey told me he had a son with you. I would love to meet my nephew."

I didn't know how to respond. I wasn't here for all that. I only stopped by to see how he was doing. I didn't respond. Instead, I smiled at her.

"Corey, how you feeling?" I said as I smiled at him.

"I'm fucked up, B."

"Corey, do you have any idea who did this to you?"

"Nah, but I'm thinking it's your boyfriend. He's the only one I got beef with," he said in a weak tone.

"Boy, what you talking 'bout? Hassan wouldn't do no shit like that to you," I said.

I was kind of furious that he would think Hassan tried to kill him. I knew Hassan had his ways and all, but he wouldn't go as far as to try to kill somebody.

"Like I said, my gut is telling me his pussy ass had something to do with this. With God's help, when I get outta here, I'm going to handle that nigga myself."

"Corey, stop it. Don't be getting yourself riled up," his sister interrupted and rushed to his side.

"I ain't come up here to hear all this 'bout Hassan. I just wanted to know how you were doing."

"Imani, or whatever the hell your name is, my brother is in here fighting for his life. I don't know what's going on between Hassan and my brother, but I plan on letting the police know about it. So if you know anything about who shot my brother, it would be best if you start talking." She stared me down.

"Listen, chick, I don't know anything, so I don't care what you tell the police. I only stopped by to check on a friend, but I see I ain't welcome up in here.

"Corey, I hope you feel better soon. I'm out."

"Aye, Mani. Can you bring my li'l man up here to see me? I want to see him."

I turned to him. "Corey, Josiah don't need to get involved in any of this. He has no idea you're his father, and I don't think the first time y'all meet should be up in here."

"Excuse me, don't you think you've caused my brother enough pain by keeping his child away from him all these years? What kind of woman are you? You have a man that loves you and his child, but you prefer to play a side bitch to another woman's husband, lying to that nigga, making him think he's the daddy. Enough is enough already. All my brother wants is to be a father," she spat at me with anger in her voice.

"This is between your brother and me. I didn't fuck you, so you have no business with me. Your brother knew what the deal was from the beginning, so he can stop playing the fucking victim. I'm done explaining myself to you, so get the hell out of my way before I move you my-damn-self."

"Bitch, I wish you would, but you get a pass this time because my brother is here fighting for his life. The next time we meet, it won't be so friendly—"

Before she could finish her sentence, Corey started coughing, and his machine started beeping.

Beep! Beep! Beep!

A nurse rushed in, and then the doctors followed.

"Code blue, code blue! Please get out of the room," a nurse yelled as they gathered around his bed.

I walked out of the room, even though I wanted to stay and see what was going on. I decided to leave, not because I was scared of his dumb-ass sister, but because I knew I didn't belong there.

As I walked to the car, I whispered a prayer for Corey and then started to ponder on what he said to me. Why would he think Hassan did this to him? Was there any truth to this? *I have to find out one way or another,* I thought as I pulled off.

Later that night, I heard that Corey passed away. I felt sad about his passing because I knew he was part of my son. I felt guilty because I kept my son away from him for his entire life, and now, he would never get a chance to meet his father. "Oh God, how do I clean this mess up?" I screamed out in anguish.

I've been through a lot in my lifetime, and I just needed it to end. I wished, at times, my mama was still alive, so I could lie against her shoulder and tell her about e'erything that was going on in my life. I felt so alone. I held my head and continued crying my heart out. At least Corey was out of his misery and didn't have to worry about this wicked world anymore. . . . I wondered, how would Hassan feel if I were no longer here. Would he miss me? Or would he move on with his life and replace me? So many questions that I needed answers to.

Chapter Four

Hassan Clarke

I had my hopes up after I talked to Mama. I was confident that she would get me a bond. But that hope soon disappeared when two days went by, and my name wasn't called for bond or an attorney's visit.

I knew I didn't have any other choice but to call my office collect. It took everything in me to do that because I didn't want to involve my firm in the situation. I knew it wasn't a good look. But I swallowed my pride and dialed the number.

"Mr. Clarke, is that you? What the heck is going on? We've been trying to reach you."

"Yes, Shari, it's me. It's just a little misunderstanding that will be cleared up soon. Is Leon in?"

"OK, I understand, and, yes, he's here. Let me transfer you."

"Thanks, love."

I anxiously waited as Leon came on the phone. I didn't care about being embarrassed. I needed to get out of this hellhole.

"Hello, Has. What's good, man?"

"Man, you ain't goin' believe this bullshit. I'm over here in Rikers."

"What the heck are you talking 'bout?"

"Man, long story that I can't even get into right now. I'm charged with assault and battery on Imani. I have my first appearance at 10:00 a.m., and I need you to be there."

"A'ight, bet. I'll be there."

"I 'ppreciate it. I'll see you then."

After I got off the phone, I felt a sense of relief. I walked back to my bunk and lay down. I didn't socialize with these bum-ass niggas up in here, telling their jail-house lies. Most of them were hardened criminals who didn't deserve to see the streets again. But who was I to judge shit? My pockets were on swole because of dudes that broke the law.

That bitch Imani lay heavily on my mind. We've been through so much shit together that I would've never guessed she would go as far as pressing charges on me. That bitch was dead to me. I put that on my life.

I closed my eyes and tried to doze off, but sleep wouldn't come. I was ready to get up out of here and file for divorce. After that bullshit Destiny pulled, I planned on not giving that ho a dime. I don't give a fuck 'bout no alimony or child support. For all I care, that bitch can sell her pussy to feed her fucking daughter. I knew it sounded cold, but there was no love in my heart for that bitch, and the fact that Amaiya was part of that bitch, I didn't give a fuck about her either.

"Ha-ha," I chuckled as a thought popped into my head. I knew exactly how to get that ho back. When I filed for divorce, I was also going to file for custody of Amaiya. That would drive Destiny over the edge. I hoped it would drive that bitch to suicide. With that thought, I was off to sleep. . . .

***

By 4:00 a.m. the next morning, the guards were hollering for people that have court. I was eager to get out of here because I knew I wasn't going to be back in this dungeon. I packed up my cot, gave my bunkie dap, and strutted to the front where the guards were waiting to transport us to the court.

On the way to the courthouse that I was so familiar with, I whispered a few words to the man above. I was confident that my partner had me, but just in case, I needed extra cushion. I stayed quiet the entire ride, but the niggas' mouths beside me seemed to have a severe case of diarrhea. One nigga said, "I can't wait to get out so I can fuck the shit out of my girl." Another fool stated, "I can't wait to hit them streets. Oh boy, it's on and popping." I shook my head and closed my eyes. I really didn't have any plans. For now, I only wanted to get out.

The bus arrived at the courthouse early, and we were placed in a holding cell. I hoped Leon was on his way down here. I needed to run my case by him before I went in front of the judge.

"Clarke, you have an attorney's visit," the tall, lanky guard said.

I got up and walked to the front.

Two minutes later, he escorted me into a room where Leon was waiting.

As soon as he saw me, he stood up. "Hassan, my man." He gave me dap.

At that moment, I felt a little ashamed that my colleague was able to see me like this.

"All right, what the hell happened? I need to know everything, so I can go in there and fight for you."

Even though I didn't want him in my business, I had no choice but to keep it real with him. But I left out a few things which I didn't think was his business.

"I warned you from day one, that girl was trouble."

"Yea, well, there is something else. I didn't meet her at the job. Imani and I been screwing around for years, even before I started law school."

"Man, I don't know what's going on, but this is a felony you're charged with. You already know this don't look good for you. My goal is to get you out on bond, and the rest, we can figure out." I could tell by the tone of his voice he was annoyed.

He left, and I was returned to the holding cell. Reality started to kick in. I worked my entire life to get this law degree, and all it took was a minute to jeopardize it. I knew I wasn't going to give up that easy. The bottom line is, it was my word against hers. I knew it would be hard, but I had to come up with ways to discredit her story. There was no way I was going to prison—especially not behind a bitch that I took care of.

"All rise. The court of the Criminal Division is now in session. The Honorable Judge Braxton is presiding."

"Be seated," Judge Braxton said.

I've heard those exact words over a hundred times, but this time, it was surreal. I hung my head down in shame as I sat on the other side of the law this time.

"Your Honor, first on the docket, docket number 66421-53. The State of New York vs. Hassan Clarke.

"Defendant is charged with one count of First-Degree Assault. . . ."

I didn't hear anything else until I heard my name mentioned.

"How do you plead, Mr. Clarke? Mr. Clarke, are you with us?" the judge said, interrupting my thoughts.

"Not guilty, Your Honor."

"Court date is set for September 12, 9:00 a.m. Mr. Clarke, you are ordered not to go anywhere near the complainant or contact her in any way. If you violate this order, your bond will be revoked immediately."

"I'm about to post your bond. So sit tight. You'll be out in a few," Leon assured me.

I nodded my head to acknowledge him. I was sick of this shit already.

I felt relieved because I had no intention to return to Rikers. I wasn't a criminal, and I didn't belong among those hardened criminals. *I'll be happy when all this bullshit ends,* I thought.

Chapter Five

Destiny Clarke

There was something about this man that kept tugging at my heart. For years, I haven't had sex or thought about being with another man. I took my vows very seriously, even though I knew I was faithful to a man whose cock was community property.

I tried to ignore the way I was feeling, but at night, I would lie in my bed, wondering what it would feel like to have a good man, one that knew how to treat a woman that had been broken. The thought of him sent chills up my spine. Yes, I'm talking about no other than Private Investigator Spencer.

My heart was a little reluctant, but I decided that going out to dinner with him wouldn't hurt anything. Plus, it would help take my mind off some of the shit that was going on in my life. Without further hesitation, I dialed his number.

I got cold feet and was about to hang up when his sultry voice said, "Hello, there."

"Hi," I could barely say.

I felt like I was in high school, and he was my crush. Butterflies took flight in my stomach as I tried not to breathe too hard into the phone.

"How is the beautiful Miss Destiny doing this evening?" he asked.

Oh Lord, this man was putting his charm on me. I had to catch myself. I didn't want to come off as thirsty. I was too old for that giddy-headed shit.

"I'm fine. I just called to see if the offer was still on the table, I mean, the dinner offer," I said nervously.

"Yes, the offer is definitely still on the table. I would love to take you out and show you a good time if you would allow me to."

"Hmm, OK, I'm available tomorrow evening."

"Alrighty. Is 8:00 p.m. fine with you?"

"Yes, that's perfect."

"Text me your address tomorrow, and I'll pick you up about a quarter to eight."

"OK, I'll see you then." I hurriedly hung up the phone.

My pussy was thumping, but I tried my best to ignore it. There's no way I was going to fuck him on the first night. I learned that from messing with Hassan. I wasn't in any rush to get fucked, not after all that I've been through. The next time around, I'd be more careful, and I wouldn't be so desperate for love. Sometimes, I wondered had I taken it slower with Hassan, would I have seen him for the snake he was.

I caught myself drifting into misery every time I thought about happy times. I always managed to end up thinking about him and how badly he did me. I needed to let go of him and all the bad things he did to me. However, it was hard because of the scars that he left on me. The thought of having herpes invaded my mind. How could I date someone when I was infected with a disease that couldn't be cured? How do I tell my next partner that my pussy is infected, and he can't suck on my clit because he might catch that shit in his mouth?

I picked up my phone because my first thought was to call Mr. Spencer and cancel our date, but I changed my mind. It wasn't like we were fucking. It was only a dinner date, I reminded myself.

I was up bright and early. After Amaiya went to school, I decided to run to the Galleria out in White Plains. I hadn't been out on a date in over fifteen years, and I wanted to look my best. I walked into Macy's, which was my favorite store. I knew I could find something sexy and comfortable there. After looking around, I decided on a nice pair of Levi's jeans and a nice top that showed a little cleavage. I had no idea where we were going, so I didn't want to overdress. This outfit was perfect for whatever setting he chose.

After I left the mall, I decided to stop at my hairdresser on Gramatan. It had been awhile since I'd sat in a chair at a salon. I wanted a touch of color. I was tired of looking like plain Jane and wanted to spice my look up a little bit. I also got my nails and feet done. I had to admit, I looked damn good when I was finished.

After dropping off Amaiya at Mama's house, I headed home to get dressed. I felt nervous and excited, all in one. I thought about calling him to cancel but quickly abandoned that thought. This man had helped when I needed him. The least I could do was show a little bit of gratitude. I texted him the address and got dressed.

Along with the outfit I bought, I put on a pair of Michael Kors heels. There was something about heels that made a woman sexier and enticing. I looked myself over in the mirror and smiled. Tonight, I looked and felt like a million bucks. I cut the light off and sashayed downstairs.

It was seven forty-five on the dot when my doorbell rang. I glanced at the time. *I love a man that knows the time,* I thought before I opened the door.

"You smell good. What are you wearing?" he asked, showing all twenty-four of his pearly whites.

"Uh, umm, it's Dior J'adore, and thank you," I stuttered.

"Let me get that for you," he demanded as he opened the door for me.

I wasn't sure if this was him just putting on for me, but he was giving me the royal treatment.

I sat comfortably in my seat as he drove and listened to the sweet melody of Luther Vandross singing "Always and Forever." The mood was right as I closed my eyes, dreaming of an always and forever kind of love.

He took me to an Italian restaurant on Boston Road in Portchester. The restaurant was elegant, and the service was on point. I could tell by the patrons that it catered to the upper class. The lights were dim, while smooth jazz played in the background. I sat across from Spencer as he stared into my eyes.

"Is something wrong?"

"No, ma'am. I'm just taking in your beauty."

"Really?" I smiled at him. I wasn't sure what I should say.

The waitress walked up to us and took our orders. I wasn't sure what I wanted, so I got Pollo Sorpresa, which included crusted chicken breast sautéed in white wine with pounded Parmesan cheese, and asparagus with lemon sauce. I wasn't big on Italian dishes, but I didn't want to seem like I was picky. There was total silence as we ate. I would do anything to find out what he was thinking. After we finished eating, he paid, and we left.

On the way back from dinner, we chitchatted but about nothing too serious. My body was screaming at me each time he opened his mouth. I swear, he should be on somebody's record singing.

He pulled up to my house a little after 11:00 p.m., but I wasn't ready for the night to end. I was enjoying his presence and his positive attitude.

"Well, thanks for gracing me with your presence, lady."

"This is so not like me, but do you want to come in for a little while? Amaiya is at my mom's."

"Are you sure? Where's your husband?" I sensed the uneasiness in his voice.

"Don't worry. This is my house, and that bastard is in jail."

"All right, I'll come in for a few. Please tell me you have some gin," he joked.

"No, I don't have gin, but I do have red wine."

I opened the door, and we walked in. I made sure I locked the door behind me and walked into the living room, with him in pursuit.

He sat down while I walked into the kitchen to pour our drinks.

"Here you go," I said as I handed him the glass.

"Thank you. This is a beautiful home you have here."

"Hmm, yes, I guess so. It used to be my home, but it seems more like a prison these days. After the divorce, I think I'm going to sell it and buy something smaller for Amaiya and me."

"Really? Where do you plan on moving to?"

"Not sure. I really don't want to go far from Mama. She's getting older, and I need to be around, you know."

"I understand that. Sometimes, I wish I had my mother around." He took a sip of his wine.

"What happened to her?"

"She died a few years ago from ovarian cancer. I swear that lady was everything to me," he said before taking a big gulp.

"I'm sorry to hear that. Well, I'm sure she's smiling down on her baby boy."

"Yea, I hope I'm making her proud. Anyway, it's no secret that I'm digging you."

"Are you? I hadn't noticed," I joked.

"Well, let me cut to the chase then. From the moment you walked into my office, I wanted to ask you out. However, it wasn't the appropriate time. I tried to get you out of my mind, but there's just something about you that grabbed me and wouldn't let go."

"So tell me, Spencer, do you always date your clients?"

"No, not always, but then again, I don't get too many sexy, brilliant, and sassy women in my office."

"Ha-ha, good one."

"I'm dead ass, though. You are a beautiful woman, Destiny."

"You know I had a rough marriage, and, truthfully, I don't think that I'm ready to date so soon."

"No rush, but I would love the chance to show you how a queen should be treated."

His words sent chills up my spine as he took my hands into his and stared into my eyes.

"I know you've been through hell, but don't let one bad apple mess it up for the rest of us."

Before I could respond, he put his hand over my lips. "Shh . . ." He leaned in and kissed me. I wanted to pull away, but my heart wouldn't let me, so I started to kiss him back.

"So, this is the nigga you fucking now, huh?" Hassan's voice startled me.

Spencer jumped up, and I stood up beside him.

"What are you doing here? I told your ass I want you out of my shit."

"Fuck you, bitch. So, nigga, what the fuck are you doing here in my house?"

"The lady of the house invited me in."

"Nah, fuck that. This is *my* motherfucking house, and you, my nigga, is trespassing." He stepped toward Spencer.

"Yo, bro, be easy. I 'ont want no trouble. As a matter of fact, I was just leaving."

"Nah, nigga, fuck that. Ain't nobody leaving 'til I find out what I want to know."

"Hassan, you need to grow the fuck up. This is *my* house, and I invited him here. So, if you have a motherfucking problem, you need to address *me,*" I said as I stepped toward him.

"Ha-ha. I see you a weak-ass nigga that hides behind a bitch," Hassan spat with venom in his voice.

In a split second, Spencer punched him in the jaw. Blood spilled out of the corner of his mouth.

"Nah, nigga, you done fucked up. Do you know who I am? I'm Hassan, the attorney," he said as he wiped the blood away.

He lunged toward Spencer, but Spencer backed up and pulled out a Colt .45 gun.

"Like I said, I was leaving. Now get out of my motherfucking way before I splatter your membranes all over this carpet." Spencer aimed the weapon at Hassan's head.

"Nigga, fuck you and take this bitch with you."

"That may not be a bad idea. Destiny, go ahead and grab a few items so we can go."

"Fuck you, you stupid bitch. That's why you ain't bond me out. You was too busy sucking this nigga's dick."

I was going to answer him, but instead, I shook my head and walked off. On my way up the stairs, I whispered a prayer to God. I didn't want Spencer to kill this fool. I might hate him, but he's my daughter's father, and I had no idea how I would explain this to her.

I grabbed a night bag and stuffed a few pieces of clothing inside. Then I hurried back downstairs. I walked past Hassan, who was still mumbling shit about who he was going to kill.

"Bitch, you're dead to me, you hear me? And let your little boyfriend know, the next time he shows his face 'round here, he'll be dead," he yelled after me.

I turned around, took a few steps toward him, and then spoke. "Don't you wait up for me, honey. I'll be fucking and sucking on his cock tonight, and I'm pretty sure he will be sucking the life out of my clit." I winked at him and walked through the door with Spencer behind me with his gun still in his hand.

Chapter Six

Hassan Clarke

I was happy to be out of that dungeon. I swear I had no idea that Rikers Island was that terrible. Leon was there to pick me up to take me to the office. I called Tanya to pick me up from the office, hoping she wasn't still upset about that baby situation.

"Hey, babe," I said as I sat on the passenger's side.

"Don't, 'Hey, babe,' me. Where the hell have you been? I've been calling you nonstop for days but got no answer."

"Man, I was in jail."

"Lol. You're too fucking funny. Of all the lies you could come up with, you chose this one. You know what, Hassan? I'm tired of your bullshit. Neither my baby nor I deserve this shit."

"Baby? So, you're keeping it?"

"My child is not an 'it,' and, yes, I am having my baby. I just told my mom and dad that I was pregnant, and they are so happy. This will be their first grandchild."

So, this bitch has completely lost her mind. I thought I made myself clear the last time that we were together that I don't want any more children—and definitely not from a white bitch.

I was tired, and I needed a shower. I tried to tune this bitch out, but she just kept on talking about a fucking baby.

"Listen, Tanya, do what the hell you want to do. I don't want no more children. Shit, I don't want the one I got now. All y'all bitches getting on my nerves with this baby shit. Y'all just want to trap a nigga, fo'real."

"You know, you don't have to be so cruel toward your child and me. I've always been good to you. Shit, I stuck with you through everything." She started to cry.

Oh, man. Here we go. Why do I always end up with these emotional-ass bitches? I thought.

I breathed a sigh of relief when she pulled up at the house. I didn't hesitate to jump out of her Jeep. I sped up the driveway but stopped in my tracks. A late-model Mercedes-Benz was parked at the foot of the driveway. I looked around but didn't see the owner, so there was only one explanation. I slowly put my key in the hole and turned the lock, careful not to make any noise. Then I tiptoed inside and saw the living room light was on. I walked toward the living room . . . and that's when I saw that whore sticking her tongue down some nigga's throat. I wanted to rush over there and beat that nigga and that bitch's ass for disrespecting me like that. This was *my* motherfucking house. How bold was that bitch to bring that bitch-ass nigga into our home?

I interrupted them by addressing that ho. You should've seen her face. I saw the fear in her eyes, and that alone gave me satisfaction. The bitch-ass nigga was a different story, however. The nigga signed his death warrant when he punched me in the motherfucking face. I could've fought him, but the only thing that saved him was that pistol. See, I knew it was time to get me a gun because he was the second nigga to pull a gun on me and didn't use it. I made a mental note that we would meet again, and the next time wouldn't turn out good for that bitch-ass nigga.

After that ho and the nigga left, I took a shower. I was feeling horny as fuck. I wanted some pussy. After all, that was the first thing niggas want when they're released from jail. *Who should I call?* I thought. Tanya popped up in my head, but, fuck, we got into it earlier. But that didn't stop me from calling her phone.

"Hello," she answered angrily.

"Damn, babe, can you please stop being so angry with me?"

"What do you want, Hassan?"

"I want you, babe. I want to apologize to you for the way I treated you earlier."

"Whatever."

"C'mon, you know I don't like it when you act like these ghetto bitches. The Tanya I know has class."

"*You* make me act like this. I don't like the way you started treating me after I told you I was pregnant."

"C'mon, babe, let me make it up to you," I pleaded.

"All right, but if you continue treating me like shit, I won't have no choice but to leave you alone."

That was music to my ears. That was my cue that she was no longer pissed off at me.

"Well, you can please come to see me. I want to suck on that pussy to show you how much I care for you."

"Hmm. Sounds interesting, but my stomach hurts, so you can't go all the way in. Where are you?"

"I'm at home, where you dropped me off."

"Oh, hell no. I'm not going over there. I don't want no problems with yo' wife."

"Tanya, grow a backbone; plus, she's not home. She went out with her boyfriend."

"All right, if you say so. I'm telling you I don't want no drama around me. I don't want to lose my baby."

About an hour later, Tanya pulled up in the driveway. I opened the door for her. Without hesitation, I picked her up and carried her upstairs into our bedroom. I laid her on her back and pulled her pants and drawers off. Then I dived into her pussy, sucking on that clit like I was starving. The aroma from her pussy juice sent me into a frenzy. I stuck my tongue deep into her sweet pussy as she moaned and groaned.

"Oh, daddy, give the dick to me," she begged.

"Relax, babe."

I used my teeth to nibble on her pussy, while I stuck my fingers inside.

"Daddy, please, fuck meeee," she cried as she exploded in my mouth.

I used my tongue to lick up her juices. Then I lay on my back.

"C'mon, baby, ride daddy's dick."

She got on top of me and straddled the dick. That's the beautiful thing about Tanya. She knew how to take the dick like a pro. I knew every inch was touching her insides. She didn't ease up. She slid all the way down, using her pussy to swallow my dick. I loved the way she bounced on my dick. I pulled her down to me and placed one of her C-cup breasts in my mouth and sucked on it like I was a baby hungry for milk.

"*Aargh, aargh,*" I groaned in ecstasy.

This bitch's pussy was the real deal, and I've had good pussy my entire life. The way her walls gripped my dick made me feel like I was in heaven. I grabbed her tightly as I dug deep inside of her.

"Daddy, daddy, give me that dick, pleaseeee."

"*Aaaargh,*" I yelled as I busted inside of her.

I hugged her tightly as my limp dick eased out of her. The pussy was so good, I wanted to go another round, but I was tired and felt drained.

"I love you."

"Love you too, babe," I said.

Shit, I was telling the truth. I loved her pussy. I didn't love her. She just wasn't the kind of bitch to settle down with. She was too weak, and I knew I could have my way with her anytime I wanted.

I was tired now and needed sleep. She, on the other hand, seemed to be relaxed.

"Aye, you know you can't spend the night, right?"

"So, you only call me over here to fuck and leave?" she shot me an evil look.

"C'mon, Tanya, you know damn well if that crazy bitch catches you up in here, all hell goin' break loose. You must've forgotten how she behaved the last time you were here."

"Hmm . . . Whatever, Hassan. You stay on that bullshit. You need to go ahead and tell her about our baby and us. 'Cause if you don't, *I* will tell her ass."

I leaped toward her and grabbed her arm. "Listen to me. If I were you, I wouldn't do that shit. I promise you, you will regret ever fucking with me," I said through gritted teeth.

"Let go! You're hurting me." She tried to snatch her arm away.

"Tanya, I'm dead-ass serious. Now, get your things and leave before I do something I might regret."

"Whatever, Hassan. I swear I'm done with you. My baby and I don't need you. I fucking hate you," she cried.

I was too tired to argue, and my mind was not on Tanya or the baby she's talking about. For all I care, she could kill herself along with the baby inside of her.

After she left, I took a long, hot shower. My mind was still on Destiny and the pussy-ass nigga she had in my house. That bitch disrespected me in the worst way, and to make shit worse, she left with him. This ho was acting like she wasn't married. All kinds of emotions flowed through me, and some of them scared me. I never considered myself a killer or thought I could ever kill someone. However, tonight, I knew for sure I wanted to kill that bitch I married. Put her out of her misery for good.

It was my first day back at the office. Needless to say, I knew a lot of work was waiting for me. I arrived earlier than anyone so that I could get a head start on the workload. I stepped off the elevator and walked to the office that was on the west wing. I unarmed the alarm and walked into the office and was surprised to see the receptionist was already at her desk. Any other time, I would've flirted, but considering everything that had happened, I decided to lay off.

"Good morning, Boss Man," she said and smiled at me.

"Good morning, my dear Shari." I kept it brief.

I was about to open up my office door when Leon stepped out of his office. "Aye, Hass, let me talk with you real quickly."

"I didn't even know you were here this early, my man." I followed him into his office. "Is everything a'ight, man? You don't look too pleased."

"Sit down, Hassan. I've been up all night, trying to find the words to say to you, and there's no easy way to say it."

"Say what?"

"Hassan, I think you need to give up your partnership at the firm. This case you got going on is not only shedding a negative light on you, but it's also shedding a negative light on the firm, on me, and our clients."

"What the fuck are you saying to me, my nigga? This firm is mine. I built it with my paper and my sweat. What gives you the power to tell me you want me to give up *my* partnership? I'm the motherfucking boss in here. Don't you know that? I'm the reason why you're eating so well," I yelled at this nigga.

"You need to calm down. You're not thinking about the future of this company. You've been arrested for first-degree assault on a female. It's not a good look for the company. Imagine when the word gets out that you were arrested for beating up your girlfriend. The press is going to have a field day with us."

"Leon, I guess you didn't hear me the first time. This is *my* company, and I am *not* leaving it—plain and simple. You hear me? Now, you can take your ass and get the fuck out of my shit."

"You know you can be a real asshole sometimes. I warned you about that chick, but, no, you didn't care. Now, look at you. You're about to lose everything over a chick that's not even worth it. I don't know what's going on with you, but I think you need to get it together—fast. Look around you. You're losing everything you once loved. You're sinking fast, and I refuse to sink with you. Now, please, excuse me. I need to find me a new firm. Also, your wife has an interest in the company, so I'll see how she feels about it."

I stood there looking at this nigga with fire in my eyes. All I saw was jealousy and envy. I knew he wanted my position, but it was fucked up that he was trying to kick a nigga while he was down.

"You know what? You're one jealous motherfucker. You want my life *and* my position here at the firm."

"Hassan, let's be real. You don't have too much of a life. You run around here like you the man, but, bro, you look like a damn fool. You have a good woman, but you fucked it up for a hood bitch. Didn't you know once you started making money, you needed to stop fucking them broke bitches? But let you tell it, you got all the fucking sense in the world. Ha-ha, you can have that shit, bro. We're done here."

I didn't respond. Instead, I walked out and into my office. This nigga done bumped his head somewhere . . . either that, or he was a plain ole fool. This is *my* company, not his, and definitely not that bitch Destiny's. This was *my* idea, and I busted my ass for years, building it from scratch. I will *not* walk away from it, and no one else will reap the benefits.

I sat at my desk, listening to the messages from clients. I could barely concentrate on the task at hand. That nigga really had rubbed me the wrong way. I should've punched him in the mouth when he brought up that dumb shit. That nigga had no idea who I am.

My cell phone started ringing. I looked at the caller ID and saw it was Big Dre.

"What the fuck is this nigga calling me for?"

"Hello. I thought you wasn't going to call me on the phone."

"Shit, nigga, fuck all that. I've been trying to call yo' ass for days now."

"Well, I couldn't answer the phone. I was busy."

"Busy? Nigga, did you see the motherfucking news?" he yelled.

"News? Why would I need to see the news?" My anxiety level skyrocketed.

What the fuck is this nigga talking about? I thought.

"Nigga, you know what the fuck I'm talking about."

"No, I don't know. As a matter of fact, if you need an attorney, I'm willing to be your attorney, Mr. Brooks."

"What the fuck! You acting like you ain't hired me to off that nigga. Now you acting brand-new and shit. I'm telling you, pussy, if I go down, *you* going with me. I'm pretty sure there's a district attorney that would love to give me a deal if I gave him a bigger fish to fry."

That statement got my attention fast. This old fake-ass thug was talking about snitching on me. I tell you about these streets niggas that claim they go hard, but all it takes is a charge, and they'd start singing like a bird.

"Yo, what do you want from me?" I said in an aggressive tone.

"Shit, it's hot right now, and I need to be ghost. I need fifty grand by the end of the week."

"What the fuck! I ain't got that kind of money lying around."

"Maybe not, but I know you got it somewhere. Shit, you might need to hit that wife of yours. She's got a few coins," he chuckled.

"We're getting a divorce."

"Listen up, fuck nigga. I 'ont give a fuck where you get it from. You have until Friday evening to get it to me." Then he hung up.

"Fuck," I whispered as I rubbed my hand over my face.

I couldn't believe that this fuck nigga was blackmailing me. Where the fuck does he expect me to get fifty grand from without raising an alarm? I was also curious to find out what he was talking about. What was on the news that had him so spooked? God, I prayed my name wasn't mixed up in this shit. I couldn't go to prison—I just couldn't.

Chapter Seven

Destiny Clarke

The first night that I spent with Spencer was peaceful. He took me to his home. At first, I was a little reluctant because I really didn't know too much about him. For all I knew, he could be a rapist. It was late, and I was tired from everything that had happened earlier. I was still shocked that Hassan popped up at the house like that.

I took a quick shower and changed into my pajamas. Then I lay in the bed beside him, inhaling his masculine scent, which made me gasp for air. It's been awhile since I was this close to a man, one that I was attracted to, physically and mentally. I relaxed as he lay behind me with his arms wrapped around me. I lay there thinking of how great it felt, wondering if this could possibly mean happiness. Neither of us spoke. Then I peacefully dozed off. . . .

Spencer dropped me off at my house in the morning. Hassan was gone, which was great. I had such a great night and didn't want to deal with his bullshit. I thought back on last night, and it was perfect, even though sex wasn't involved. The mental part of it was all I needed.

Spencer and my relationship grew stronger over the next couple of weeks. I still hadn't slept with him, and he didn't pursue me on that level, even though we slept in the same bed on the weekends when Amaiya was at my mother's house.

I ain't going to lie. I was ready to feel him inside of me. At first, I didn't want to rush into anything. But fuck Hassan. The truth is, he wasn't worried about me when he was fucking them bitches, so why the fuck I should worry about his ass? Just because he's a man doesn't mean he can get away with dogging me out. I wish he had walked in on Spencer digging my guts out. I would've loved to see his face.

One evening after dinner, Spencer and I went back to his house. We were sitting on the couch, drinking and talking. He leaned in and started kissing me. He began rubbing my legs. Then his hand slowly traveled up my dress. My body trembled as he found his way between my legs. I wanted him badly. Fuck that—I wanted him *now*. He pulled my underwear aside and gently massaged my clit. My pussy was already moist and ready for him to slide in. He eased up off the couch and kneeled in front of me. I knew exactly what he was about to do. . . .

"Stop! You can't do that," I blurted out.

"Baby, I want to. You want me to. Let me please you like I know I can," he pleaded.

"It's not that. I d-o, do want you," I stuttered.

"So, what's the problem?"

I took his hands in mine, and then I spoke. "I don't want to scare you away, but I have herpes. . . ." I held my breath after the words left my mouth.

"You're joking. You're just trying to scare me off," he laughed.

"Seriously, A few months ago, I found out I had it. Hassan infected me."

There was a long pause between us. . . .

He squeezed my hand. "Babe, I'm so sorry. Man, I want to kill that nigga for all the shit he put you through. Man, oh man." He shook his head.

My heart was racing because I didn't know if he was going to break it off with me. I knew that this was a chance I was taking, but I didn't have a choice. There was no way I was going to infect him or put his health at risk.

"Babe, get out of your thoughts. I know you're wondering if I'm going to leave you. Hell no, I'm a grown man, and you're the woman that I want. There is nothing or no one that can get in the way of that. I 'ont know too much about herpes, but I guess there are ways to get around it. We're goin' figure it out together. I want you, Destiny, not just physically, but mentally."

I wiped away the tears as this man spoke from his heart. Just when I thought I was damaged goods because I had an STD that couldn't be cured, this man was willing to accept me.

"Dry them tears. You're a beautiful person inside out, and I can only hope you will give me the chance to treat you like you deserve."

I couldn't find the words to say anything, so I remained quiet and just let the tears flow.

That night after we got all the emotional stuff out of the way, Spencer carried me upstairs. He slowly stripped off my clothes. I watched as he took off his clothes. My eyes popped open when I saw the little six-inch cock he pulled out.

Lord, what is he going to do with that little thing? I thought. It was even worse when I saw him pull out a Magnum condom. I thought Magnums were made for big cocks. I couldn't say another word. I just lay there.

I closed my eyes as he massaged my breasts. His touch made my body tremble. I wanted him. I had no idea why, but I did. I was wet and bothered and wanted to be fucked. I was nervous because I didn't know how it was going to work out with his little size. He spread my legs apart and slid his erect cock inside my hungry pussy.

"Oh-oh," I groaned out in ecstasy.

He slowly slid in and worked the middle like a pro. In that instance, the size didn't matter. He pounded my walls as I dug my fingernails into his back. I had multiple orgasms back-to-back. I felt like my brain was coming out of my head the way juice was spilling out of me.

"*Aargh, aargh, aaaargh,*" he groaned as he busted.

I couldn't move. I felt like all my energy had evaporated from my body. I lay there for a few minutes, thinking. I actually enjoyed this. He made love to my mind and my body, and I loved every second of it. This was something that I could get used to, but, first, I needed to divorce that bum-ass nigga. Just the thought of him dimmed my happiness for a brief moment. I quickly snapped out of that foul mood and focused on the happy times that were ahead of me. I just hoped this was real, not that fake-ass love shit. You know how dudes are usually the sweetest when they want to fuck, but they quickly have amnesia after they get you right where they need you to be. . . .

I took a quick shower, put on some lotion, and got back into bed. I rubbed his chest as I rested my head on him. Whatever this was, I wanted to take my time so it could last were my thoughts before I dozed off.

Imani Gibson

I was happy the weekend was over. Today was Corey's funeral, and even though we didn't end on good terms, I still wanted to pay my respects. I got up and walked to Josiah's room and peeped in on him. He was lying on his bed, playing on his phone. I knocked on the door before I pushed it open.

"Can I talk to you for a minute?" I said as I sat on the edge of his bed.

"What's up?" He looked at me like I had interrupted him.

"Well, I know that I haven't always been the best mom to you, but I did my best and made sure you never went without. What I'm trying to tell you is that my decisions were not always the best, but as your mother, I had to make moves so we could be all right."

I paused. . . . I had to gather my thoughts.

"Ma, get it over wit'. All this sentimental stuff I ain't tryin'a hear all that," he said.

It took me by surprise. Why was Josiah acting like this?

"Boy, what I'm trying to say is that I'm sorry I lied to you about who your father is. I only wanted what's best for you. The truth is that Corey was your real father, and he got killed the other day."

"You lied to me because you're a fucking whore. You didn't do shit for me. You did it because you wanted to hold on to that bum-ass nigga. Now, you're telling me that my real father is dead. So, I'll never get a chance to talk to him or bond with him, because your dumb ass lied. I fucking hate you. I wish you wasn't my mom."

I sat there frozen as the words that came out of my son's mouth pierced my soul. How could he say these things to me? I gave him life. Everything I did, I did for him. Tears filled my eyes and eventually flooded my face.

I reached over to touch him. I wanted to let him know that I was sorry. Sorry for robbing him of the chance to meet his father. Now, it will never happen.

"B-babyyyy—"

"Don't touch me. You know when I was young, I looked up to you. You was everything to me, but now, I see that all that shit was a fantasy. You messing wit' that woman's husband, and you letting that nigga beat on you, and you *still* fuck with him. I swear, I can't wait until I'm eighteen. I'm going to move far away from you."

I continued crying. I tried to talk, but the words wouldn't come out. After a moment, I got myself together, and then I spoke.

"First of all, you not goin' be up in my shit disrespecting me. Regardless of what you might think, I am *still* your fucking mother. And for the record, Hassan was my man before that bitch got her paws on him. So, before you start speaking on some shit that you have no idea about, get your fucking facts straight," I spat.

He stood up and stepped toward me. "Are you saying you want me out? Just say the word, Mother."

I slapped him in the face. "Don't you fucking try me, little boy."

"Bitch, that's the *last* time you will put your hands on me ever, I swear." He stormed out of the room and walked out the front door, slamming it behind him.

"Noooo," I dropped to my knees and screamed out.

Within a couple of months, I lost everything in my life. First, Hassan, then my unborn child, and now Josiah. He was all I had left. I got up and ran to the door to see if he was outside, but he was gone. My baby was gone.

After the incident with Josiah, I didn't feel like going to Corey's funeral. I had to push myself, though. At one point, we were cool, and this was the last time I would ever see him. I bought myself a nice black dress with some heels. I knew I had to be on my A-game because Corey's other hoes might be there. I knew news traveled fast, so the fact that we had a baby together was public information.

I walked into the packed church and felt all eyes on me. I took a deep breath and continued walking up to the front so that I could take one last look at him. I don't know why my eyes filled with tears as I stared at the dark, swollen figure in the casket. He had little or no resemblance to the Corey I knew. I figured the bullets from the gunshots did him like that. I wiped my eyes, turned, and walked away.

Throughout the entire service, you could hear screams, especially when the pastor was telling all those lies about "how great of a man he was." Don't get me wrong. I don't think he was a bad dude, but he was far from the great person they were painting him to be. I couldn't take any more of this, so I got up to leave. I tiptoed out with my head hung down low until I reached the front of the church.

"I have no idea why you would show your face up in here. You ain't welcome."

I lifted my head and noticed Corey's dumb-ass sister, blocking my path.

"Listen, bitch, I came to show my respect to a friend. You need to chill out. You wouldn't want to create a scene at your brother's funeral."

"You know what? You put my brother through so much shit—even on his deathbed. You have no shame to come up in here. You are not welcome here, so get the fuck out. I regret that my brother didn't live longer, so he could find out that you wasn't nothing but a whore."

"You silly bitch, I ain't did shit to him. I gave him some pussy, and he fell in love. Shit, I heard you on females. I promise, if I gave you this good pussy, you'd be sprung too. Now, let me get out of here before I show my ass."

"You nasty ho. You fucked my brother and his boy, and just so you know, yes, I like *clean* bitches. Not a thirsty-ass ho like you. Now get yo' ass on before I get you thrown out." She walked back into the crowd.

I was furious that this bitch felt like she had the right to speak on some shit that she had no idea about.

"Rest in peace, Corey," I mumbled, then walked down the steps and out into the pouring rain. I didn't run for shelter, nor did I care about my newly sown in Malaysian weave. I took off my heels and walked slowly in the rain as it pounded down on my head. My tears mingled with the raindrops. I had no idea what I was crying about. I just knew that I was tired of all the shit that was going on in my life. I was ready to start over.

Chapter Eight

Destiny Clarke

The divorce papers were filed, and my lawyer informed me that Hassan was going to be served this week. We had so much evidence on him from the pictures that Spencer gave me to the evidence that the forensic accountant found. That bastard had money stashed away in different accounts in different countries. I couldn't believe that after I helped him to get on his feet, he would hide some money from me, and how dumb was I for thinking that he was playing fair. Now, it all made sense. I used to wonder where all the money he made from the firm went. Now, I had the evidence in front of me. I was going to court with full ammunition against him. My lawyer was asking for half of everything he got while we were married. Also, he asked for alimony. It's only fair that I get what belongs to me. After all, it was *my* money that helped him.

After I left the lawyer's office, I stopped at the fish market and grabbed some fresh whiting. I hadn't cooked in a while, and Amaiya called me out on that earlier. To be honest, I used to love cooking for Hassan, but now that we're done, I hated to even go into the kitchen. My daughter brought me back to reality, though. She was more important, and even though she often fixed her own meals, once in a while, Mommy got to throw down in the kitchen for her.

It was a warm day outside, so after I finished cooking, I decided to do some spring cleaning. I started with my room. I was ready to turn over a new leaf, so getting rid of everything that belonged to *him* was first on my list. I decided to play some music while I cleaned. I was really feeling upbeat. After all, this saga was about to come to an end, and a new chapter with Amaiya and Spencer was about to begin.

I was tired of the dull comforter that was on the bed, so I went into my closet and pulled out my lavender comforter. Then I pulled off the dirty sheets and threw them on the floor. I was about to put a fitted sheet on the mattress . . . when a small pink item caught my attention. I moved closer and picked it up. It was a pink rhinestone earring. I brought it to my face and closely examined it.

"You bastard," I yelled out as I dropped it.

I don't wear that cheap shit, so I knew off the top that it wasn't mine. I bought all Amaiya's jewelry, so it definitely wasn't hers. Unless my husband was a faggot, it sure as hell wasn't his. The only other scenario is this bastard had a bitch up in my bed. I got sick to my stomach, just imagining him and one of his whores in my bed, which *I* fucking bought.

Quickly, I grabbed my cell phone and called him. He pressed *ignore* on me, but I called right back.

"I'm in the middle of something. What the hell do you want?" he yelled.

"I don't give a fuck about what you're doing—you dirty, low-down bastard. You had your whore in my fucking bed," I screamed.

"Destiny, baby, you're really losing it. I didn't have anyone in your bed. You need to quit with all these accusations," he calmly stated.

"Hassan, fuck you. I'm holding your bitch's earring in my hand, so I got fucking proof. Trust me—I'll be sure to give it to my attorney." I clicked *end* on him.

I sat on the bed, still staring at the earring. Why was I so shocked? I knew for years that he was cheating, but I turned a blind eye, hoping and praying that he would change. He didn't. Instead, it only got worse. At the moment, I wasn't feeling too strong, and I started to cry. I knew he was cheating, but this earring confirmed that he was not only cheating, but he had that whore in *my* house and in *my* fucking bed.

"Mama, what's wrong?" Amaiya rushed over to me.

"Hey, baby." I quickly dried my eyes.

"Ma, why you sitting here crying, and whose earring is this?" She snatched the cheap piece of metal out of my hand.

"I have no idea."

I was tired of lying and making excuses for this bastard.

"Mama, listen to me. You need to file them divorce papers so you can move on. You're so much better than him, and you deserve better. I know you worry about me and how I'm going to take it. Don't worry, Mama. I know how badly Daddy treated you, and you deserve to be happy. I'm a big girl. I can handle it," she said as she squeezed my hand.

I had no words after what she said. I gave her a long hug and rubbed her back. That was all the confirmation I needed. I really felt guilty that we were splitting up because I wanted my daughter to have both of her parents. I could see now that she was stronger than I thought. I was ready to see what the future held for us.

"Ma, I love you."

"I love you too, babe. Now, go ahead and wash up. I cooked your favorite fish." I smiled at her.

"All right, Ma, I'm starving." She dropped the earring on the bed and walked out of the room.

I picked up the earring and wrapped it in a piece of tissue, then stuffed it into my drawer. After making my bed, I vacuumed the floor. I love the smell of clean linen. *If only Spencer were around to share the bed with me,* I thought as I walked downstairs to fix my daughter's plate.

Hassan Clarke

"Mr. Clarke, there's a person by the name of Johnson here to see you."

"Thank you, Shari. Does he have an appointment? I don't recall having him on my schedule."

"No, sir, but he said it's urgent, and he needs to talk to you."

"Thank you. I'll be out shortly."

Johnson . . . This must be a new client or something, I thought.

I got up from behind the desk and walked out to the front. I saw the stranger but didn't recognize him.

"Hello, I'm Attorney-at-law Hassan Clarke."

"Hello, I'm Johnson. Please consider yourself served." He handed me an envelope, turned around, and walked away.

I turned and saw Shari looking at me. Quickly, I clenched the envelope and walked into my office.

I sat down and ripped the envelope open. "Bitch!" I yelled. Destiny was divorcing me and asking for half of my earnings *and* alimony. Over my dead fucking body! She could get the little change that's in the bank account, but that's all that bitch was going to get her measly hands on.

I was in the middle of contacting a divorce attorney when this bitch beeped in on my line. I pressed the *ignore* button, but she called right back. I was in no mood to talk to this ho, but she caught my attention when she mentioned something about an earring. I tried to play it off, but I knew the earring belonged to Tanya. She was the only woman that I had in her bed. The funny thing is that I don't recall her earring coming off. I held the phone away from my ear. There was nothing that bitch was saying that I wanted to hear. After she finished bitching, she hung up the phone.

I dialed Tanya's number. I knew she did that, being on some spiteful shit.

"Hello," she answered.

"Aye, B, the other night when you were over at the house, did you lose an earring?"

"Nah, why?"

"'Cause Destiny just called me, talking about I had a bitch in her bed."

"And, so what if you did?"

"What the fuck you mean? I told you I was about to get a divorce, and I couldn't afford for it to get out there that I was cheating."

"Well, that sounds like a personal problem. Don't you dare call me, checking me about another bitch."

"Tanya, you're starting to piss me the fuck off. I told your hardheaded ass to chill out. I have enough fucking problems in my life," I yelled into the phone.

"I don't know who you yelling at, but you need to lower your voice. I'm sick and fucking tired of the way you treat me. You treat those black bitches like they are queens, and because I'm white, you treat me like I'm a doormat. I'm done dealing with this bullshit. I guess I'll see your ass in child support court. I don't care who you fucking, because you *will* take damn good care of my baby."

I then removed the phone from my ear. I was sick of all the fucking bickering. After about five minutes, I clicked *end*. I had no idea if she was still on the line. Truthfully, I didn't give a fuck.

"Oweiii. . . . What a fucking day," I uttered to myself.

I sat back in my chair, and for the first time in my life, I felt despair. I've always known how to get myself out of situations, but this time, I felt like I was drowning. None of these bitches had any idea that I'd beat their motherfucking ass.

I grabbed my phone and briefcase. I had a 2:30 p.m. meeting with my lawyer. I wished this shit would just go away, but for now, I had to deal with it. That bitch Imani fucked up by getting me locked up, and with that, she fucked up my life. This charge was serious. I'm an attorney, so I knew damn well this shit might not turn out good for me.

I parked and walked into Baxter & Associates. I knew the brother because we worked on a case together. I knew firsthand that he was a beast in the courthouse. I hate to brag, but I was *that* nigga, and these other law-yers were no competition when it came down to handling a case. *Shit, I may come off better defending myself,* I thought, but I quickly dismissed that idea.

"Hello, may I help you?" the cute little Puerto Rican broad said.

"Yes, I have an appointment with Jamal Baxter."

"Sure, please have a seat. Mr. Baxter will be out shortly."

Within a few minutes, Jamal walked out into the waiting area.

"Hassan, my man, come on in." We exchanged daps, and I followed him into his office.

"I'm sorry that we had to meet under these circumstances. I was reviewing your case and was kind of curious about why you didn't use your partner for it. Your firm is well known to be one of the best," he chuckled.

"Well, I decided not to involve the firm in my personal affairs. Furthermore, you're a beast in the courthouse, and I need someone with that experience," I lied.

"Sure, I understand. OK, so I need you to tell me everything that went down. You know that's the only way I can effectively provide counsel. I am not charging you anything, 'cause I consider you family. All I ask is that if I ever need any kind of help that you extend yourself the same way I did."

"Damn, bro, *that's* what I'm talking about. You ain't got nothin' to worry about. I got you."

I sat in the chair, and this time, I told the story exactly the way it went down. I trusted him, and I knew he would do his best to get me off these charges.

"Have you spoken to Miss Gibson since the incident?"

"Nah, I'm done with that bitch. Excuse my language."

"Well, it might be a good idea to go talk with her to see if she'll drop the charges."

"Man, this bitch got me locked up. I ain't got shit to say to her, dawg."

"Listen, bro, get out of your feelings. I need you to think like an attorney right now. This advice that I'm giving you is the same advice you would give to me if the roles were switched. This is a domestic violence case, and most times, the so-called victim recants their story. The DA will drop the case because it's so much harder to win a case without a complainant. Think about it."

He was making sense. I had plenty of cases dismissed because the women dropped the case or didn't want to cooperate with the authorities. What bothered me was the fact that I had to talk to that bitch. After I got locked up, I vowed one night while I was in that cell that I would never see or talk to that bitch ever again. I had no feelings, and my heart was as cold as ice whenever I thought about her and her fucking bastard.

"Man, I swear I had no intention of ever speaking to her again," I said as I sank in the chair.

"I understand that, but it ain't like I'm asking you to fall in love with her. You're a smooth talker, so finesse her a little and get her to drop the charges. Man, your career—and your freedom—depends on this."

The word "freedom" rang out in my head, and I quickly understood what he was trying to say to me. I knew I had no other choice but to make up with her.

"I got you. I'm on it ASAP," I confirmed.

We talked a little longer about what strategy he was going to take if Imani didn't drop the charges. It felt strange because I was on the other side of the table this time. But I knew that I had to humble myself because I was not the lawyer in this case. I was the client.

I got up to leave, but Jamal spoke. "Aye, bro, please don't do anything stupid while you're out on bond. I don't want this to blow up bigger than it is."

"I got you, bro." I opened his door and walked out, thinking about how I was going to get at Imani. I knew that bitch had a slick mouth and might come at me sideways. I knew I'd have to use everything in me not to beat her ass for getting me locked up in the first place. I stepped out in the humid weather, straightened my tie, and walked to my car.

I am Hassan Clarke. I can do this, I thought.

Chapter Nine

Destiny Clarke

Today wasn't a good day for me. I woke up this morning feeling sick with flulike symptoms. I thought it was the flu, but I didn't have a cold. I did have a bad headache, a mild fever, and a runny nose. My body felt weak, and when I went to use used the bathroom, I noticed I had a big bump with blisters on my pussy. That's when it dawned on me. I was having an outbreak from herpes. I sat on the toilet seat and cried. I knew I had it, but reality finally hit me in the face. I was hurt, but I was also angry. I couldn't get the wicked thoughts that I had for Hassan out of my head. I wanted him to feel everything I was going through . . . all the pain and the embarrassment.

I took a hot shower and some of my pills. The rest of the day was spent in bed going over my account and making a note of everything that I needed to do. I also called a realtor. I decided to sell the house and move into something much smaller. In another year, Amaiya will be going off to college, and then it would only be me.

Spencer wanted me to spend the night with him, but I declined. I just wasn't in the mood to be around anyone, especially when I knew I couldn't sleep with him. I knew if I explained it to him, he would've understood, but I chose not to. I felt ashamed and decided to tough it out. I recalled the doctor telling me that stress could trigger an outbreak, and I believe it because lately, I've been stressed out to the max. Hassan has put so much strain on me mentally and now physically. Some days, I wanted to throw in the towel and say fuck it, but I knew I deserved better. I didn't want to be with a liar, a cheater, and an abuser. That man had put me through too much shit, and I would never allow him to even breathe on my pussy—ever again.

I got a phone call early in the morning. It was Hassan's bitch, Imani. She sounded like she was drinking or smoking some shit. Whatever it was, that whore sounded desperate. She wanted her money. Even though I couldn't fully understand what she was saying, I managed to make out that she was ready to meet with me. I sat up in bed with all kinds of thoughts running through my head. I thought about telling her that I didn't want what she had, because, honestly, I didn't trust that bitch. Besides, fifty grand was a lot of money to give away to a person. Hmm. . . . Whatever she had, I needed proof before I handed over my hard earned cash to that two-dollar whore.

I got out of bed and talked to Spencer for a little while. I told him that I had to meet with Imani, and being the protector that he is, he told me not to go. I wanted to listen, but I also needed the video of Hassan. I refused to let him walk away with a firm that I helped build and money that I put into his pocket.

I grabbed my purse and my keys, but I turned back and walked into Hassan's room. I needed to grab something.

Imani Gibson

After I left Corey's funeral, I couldn't forget what he said to me the day I visited him in the hospital. He believed Hassan was the one who got him shot. Then his sister insinuated that I knew something about it. I knew one thing . . . I didn't know anything about no murder. I wondered if Hassan could say the same thing.

I was tempted to call and ask him. Shit, I wanted to see why he was not at his childhood best friend's funeral. I remembered how close they were, and his absence made me question if there were any truth to what Corey said. Did Hassan get that boy killed?

"Oh my God," I yelled out. If Hassan did this, he did it because I lied to him about Josiah, and he found out about Corey and me. Guilt swept over me. I hoped this boy didn't lose his life over a bitch that would never love him.

"God help us all," I mumbled.

I watched as my son walked into the living room. I never really looked at him the way I did today, and I saw the resemblance to his dad, his *real* dad. I think I was in denial for so long that I had convinced myself that he resembled Hassan. I was so wrong. The older he got, the more he started looking exactly like Corey. I kind of felt guilty, but then again, a bitch had to do what a bitch had to do. Josiah didn't appreciate what I did for him, but in the end, he would thank me. We lived a great life off Hassan's dime, and Josiah never went without.

***

I was in the grocery store on White Plains Road, picking up some milk and cereal, which was all I could afford these days. I swear, I needed to get my hands on some money fast. Either that or find me a dope boy who I can throw this bum pussy on, suck the black off his dick, and lock him in. Shit, he 'ont even have to love me. Just him paying these damn bills would be good enough for me.

My phone started to ring. At first, I ignored it, but it kept ringing. I dug down into my purse and grabbed it.

"Hello," I yelled in frustration.

"Mani, it's Hassan. Please don't hang up."

I froze in the aisle. . . . Then I looked around to see if he were behind me.

I cleared my throat. "Umm, what the fuck you want? I have nothing to say to you," I lied.

I was beaming with happiness inside. I thought I would never hear his voice again. I thought he was done with me, but I guess I was wrong.

"Babe, listen to me. I'm so sorry for what I've done to you. I swear, I didn't mean to. It's just that I snapped after I found out you cheated on me," he cried.

I wanted to believe him, but common sense was telling me not to.

"Hassan, what do you want from me?"

"Babe, I don't want anything. I want you, that's it. I can't live without you. I swear, I'd rather kill myself than to live without you," he bawled.

I just lost a friend. I damn sure didn't want to lose him also.

"Babe, please let me come over there and see you. Please," he pleaded.

"Man, come on, but if you start acting crazy, you got to go. I'm not going through this anymore."

"Babe, I swear on my mama, I will never treat you like that again."

I didn't believe a word that was coming out of his mouth. I knew it was all game, but I decided to let him come over anyway. I ain't goin' to lie. I wanted him to suck on this pussy and then beat it up. I hated to go this long without fucking. Plus, I was hoping that he would throw a couple of stacks on his son and me. I didn't care what anyone else said.

I took a quick shower before he came. I also turned on the camcorder so that I could record him some more. I couldn't wait to see that bitch's face when she sees her husband's head buried in my pussy. I'm doing this for the money, but also to show this bitch how much her man wanted *me*.

In no time, I heard the door banging. Josiah hadn't been here in days, so that was good. The last thing I needed was for those two to go at it again. I opened the door, and he walked in.

"Hey, beautiful," he said and planted a kiss on my cheek.

I didn't respond. I smiled at him. Even though I was kind of happy to be in his presence, I was still angry at the way he beat me down. I tried to coach myself to loosen up. I needed some money from him, and acting like this wasn't going to help the situation.

"Do you want anything to drink?"

"Hell yea. Pour a big glass of whatever you got."

I took out his Hennessy Black and poured him a glass and also put a dose of my special "medicine" in it. I was careful not to put too much in his drink. I didn't want the nigga falling out . . . just enough to get him where I wanted him.

"Here you go," I smiled at him.

He downed the first glass and asked for a second, then a third. Damn, whatever was going on with him, he was stressed out. I sat on the couch beside him, pretending like I was drinking the Heineken.

"Aye, babe, you know, I-I-love you, girl," he stuttered.

"Really?" I asked and got up and unbuttoned his pants.

I stripped all my clothing off and got on top of him, straddling him. I squeezed my walls together and slid all the way down.

"Damn, babe, that shit feels good."

"Really? Show me."

As this bum stroked me, he started talking and stumbling over his words, and out of the blue, this nigga started crying. What the fuck kind of shit was this? If I wanted a bitch, I would've got one with a pussy. I continued riding him and rubbing him down.

"Hassan, let me ask you a question."

"Ask me anything you want, ma. Your wish is my command," this drunken bastard mumbled.

"Baby, listen," I said as I grinded a little bit harder on his stiff dick. "Why didn't you come to Corey's funeral? I know you were mad at him and all, but he was yo' boy." I grinded harder and squeezed my pussy muscles together.

"Babe, fuck that nigga. I'm happy that nigga dead. As a matter of fact, I got that nigga killed. Yea, let's see how he motherfucking feels now. Who's laughing now?" he bragged.

I almost died when he uttered those words.

"Boy, stop playing. You ain't do that shit," I quizzed.

"I put that on my mama. I had that fool Big Dre body that nigga. Babe, enough about that dead nigga. It's about us. Me and you now."

I wanted to get up, but I couldn't. I needed some money from him, so I didn't want to upset him at all. I hurriedly grinded on him so he could bust faster.

"Damn, baby, take your time. I know you miss the dick, but don't break it off."

"I just miss you so much, daddy," I lied.

I was happy when I felt his dick hardened. I knew he was about to come. I immediately jumped off him. Any other time, I would've been eager for him to bust inside of me, but not this time. I was shaking inside. I knew he wasn't lying because he wasn't the kind to brag about things that he did not know about.

I grabbed a towel out of my drawer and wiped between my legs. I wanted to go to the bathroom to clean up, but I was afraid to leave him in the room. I was concerned that he might find the camcorder. He was a murderer, and God knows what he might do to me if he found out that I had his full confession on camera.

After sex, he lay back on the bed, staring at the ceiling.

"Aye, I need you to drop the charges against me. I can't do no time, and I might lose my license."

"What? Is that why you called me, so I'd drop the charges? Wow! I should've known there was something behind your sweetness," I said, feeling aggravated.

"Nah, babe, it ain't like that. Mani, I want you in my life. I'm getting a divorce, and I'm ready to put a ring on your finger."

"Hassan, I ain't no fool. You haven't called me in a while. Then out of the blue, you asked me to drop the charges. You beat the hell out of me. You should've seen my face, and you left me for dead." I busted out crying.

I was feeling hurt, thinking back on how badly he had beat me. I swear I didn't want to drop the charges, but I still loved him. I was confused and didn't know what to do. . . .

"Hassan, I need some money to pay the bills. I'm getting evicted, and Josiah and I don't have nowhere to go."

"I ain't got no money. Shit, call one of them niggas you be fucking."

"What? There you go again. You don't give a fuck about me, but you asking me to drop charges. Hell no. You man enough to put your hands on me, then you man enough to face the time. Now, please, get the hell out of my house," I demanded.

"You putting me out? My money pay for this shit," he chuckled.

"Nigga, I only kept you around because you was paying to fuck. You ain't paying no more, so you need to get yo' ass on," I gritted on him.

"Ha-ha, you fucking slut. I fucking hate you. Your ass better get down to the DA's office and drop those charges, or you and your bastard will be next on my list." He spoke with conviction.

"Get out. You think you was doing me wrong? Nah, baby boy, I had you. Believe that."

I walked out of the room and opened the front door for him. He bucked at me on the way out, but I didn't flinch. "Go ahead and do it."

He walked through the door, mumbling all kinds of bitches under his breath. Hassan thought he was the man, but I was *that* bitch. The one he would soon wish he had never met.

The last few days were hard for me. I kept coughing and coughing. I went to the doctor, and he gave me

some more medicine. I let the doctor know that the medication he had me on wasn't working. I hoped it wasn't
another case of pneumonia. It had been years since I
had a severe case of pneumonia. The chills were getting
worse, and I couldn't stop coughing. To make matters
worse, I hadn't seen Josiah in days, so I had no one to
help me to the bathroom or to make me a cup of soup. I
thought I was going to die, alone and heartbroken.

After a week of being ill, I finally started to feel better.
I had to act fast. I only had two days before I was evicted
from the apartment. I called Destiny so that I could turn
over the video and get my money. I was going to move
and start over. I had no idea if Josiah was going with me
because I hadn't seen him in a while and when I called
his phone, he wouldn't pick up. I swear I was tired of
dealing with his ass. I tried my fucking best, but just like
every nigga in my life, his ass turned out to be a piece
of shit. I wasn't going to waste another minute worrying
about his ass.

I twisted and turned all night. My life was spiraling
downhill ever since I met Hassan. I thought I had met
Prince Charming, but come to find out, he was a fucking
ho that cheated on me over a million times. He did the
unthinkable when he gave me that disease. I hadn't
forgiven him since then, but I didn't tell anyone. I didn't
want everyone in the Bronx to know that I was sick. I
thought we were going to be together forever and take
care of our son. But shit got crazy after that fool Corey
showed up. I cried until my head started to pound.

Before I knew it, it was morning. Instead of making
breakfast, I went to the kitchen and put the bottle of
vodka to my head. I didn't stop even though it was
burning my empty stomach. I needed something to

stop the pain. I ran to my room and grabbed my phone. I searched through it and found Destiny's number. I wanted my money from that bitch. Maybe I'd go away, far away from here. I remembered I had some cousins out in ATL. I wondered how it was out there. There was only one way to find out.

Chapter Ten

Destiny Clarke

I arrived at the bank and walked in. There was a big crowd for a weekday, but I remained in the line. I promised this whore I was going to give her fifty grand if she taped Hassan and her having sex. I knew it was a desperate move on my part, but I wanted every bit of evidence when my attorney and I walked into that courtroom. I knew that bastard had firsthand knowledge of the court system, and he would use it to bully me. I wasn't going out without a fight. I busted my ass for all those years to make sure that bum could get a degree and make something of his life in hopes that he would provide for his daughter and me. He did quite the opposite, though. He cheated, bought his whore lavish gifts, and hid his money in secret accounts. I was not being a bitch. I was only going after what was rightfully mine.

The teller glanced at me when I told her how much money I wanted. I stared that bitch down. Shit, it's *my* money. Nah, I didn't take it out of our joint account. I took it out of the account that I had opened for my daughter. See, Hassan wasn't the only one with a plan. The only difference is that my money was in Amaiya's name and can't be touched unless it's for me or when she gets to the age of twenty-five.

The teller handed me the money, and I carefully stuffed it into my Michael Kors bag. Then I walked out of the bank and went to my car, making sure I looked around. Crooks are everywhere, and God knows, I wasn't going to give up my life earnings easily. As soon as I got into the car, I grabbed my Obama phone and dialed Imani's number. She picked up on the first ring and sounded like she was sitting there waiting on my call. That didn't sit too well with me. I mean, was that whore sitting on her ass waiting on me to call so she could spend my fucking money?

I decided to meet her at her house. I didn't want that whore back at my home; plus, I couldn't be too careful. On my way to her house, my mind was blank. No thoughts were there, so I just stared ahead of me. I wanted this to be over with so that I could move on with my life. No one person should have to go through all this bullshit, especially over a sorry-ass, two-timing nigga, at that.

I was careful to park on the side. I didn't want to draw any attention to myself. Who knows, Hassan might be lurking around. The last thing I needed was for him to see me going in or coming out of his whore's house.

I slightly banged on the door. She immediately opened it. I stepped inside the apartment that smelled like a stinky pussy. This was the second time that I smelled that same scent coming from her. Whatever it was, that bitch needed to get help ASAP.

"Hey, I'm happy you made it. Sit down. I see you're a woman of your word."

"Yea, as humans, we don't have anything but our word," I smiled slightly.

I didn't sit. I didn't plan on staying long.

"Do you have my money?"

"It's all here. Where's the video?" I asked as I patted my purse.

"Hold on." She walked to the back of the apartment.

I got nervous then. I wasn't thinking straight, and I wasn't sure this bitch wasn't up to no good. I thought about leaving, but my feet wouldn't budge. My blood was boiling as I thought about what could be on the video.

"Here you go, honey. I told you Hassan's ass couldn't stay away from me for too long," she bragged. The smirk on that ho's face irritated me to my soul.

I took the camcorder from her and reached into my bag to grab the money. But instead, I grabbed Hassan's gun. I pointed it straight at that two-dollar whore's head.

"What the fuck are you doing?" she asked with her eyes popped open. "You trippin' and shit," she giggled nervously.

"You didn't think I would trust you, Imani, did you? I know your kind. You thought you was going to fuck my husband, wreck my marriage, and take my hard earned money. No, bitch, you were wrong. I worked too fucking hard to make a fucking life to let a broken-down whore like you continue tearing me down. I warned you to stay away from him, but you thought it was a game. How dare you think that my pain is a silly game." Tears welled up in my eyes as I let this whore know how much pain she and that bastard inflicted on me.

"Bitch, you still tripping over that nigga? I thought we were way past that."

"We are, and that's why I'm here standing with a gun."

"You lying-ass bitch. We had a deal. I held up my part, and now you renege on your end? I really need the money to get a place for my son and me. You're a woman.

You should understand what I'm going through. How can you be so cruel?"

"A woman would work or sell her pussy to take care of her hungry bastard. There's a difference. You're a money-hungry whore that thought you were goin' come up off my hard work and sweat. Fuck being a woman right now. As a matter of fact, I'm a mad bitch right now. I told you the first time you called me to tell me about that bastard of yours that I don't give a fuck about that illegitimate little monkey. You should've killed his ass when you found out that you were pregnant. You thought I was a fool, but, no, I'm far from a fool. I waited for this moment. The last time wasn't right, but this time, it's just you and me. I've lived for the moment when I would see you beg for your fucking life—the same way I begged my husband to leave your ass alone."

"Please listen to me. I *will* leave Hassan alone. I'll take the money and never look back. You can have him, I swear. Please, just give me the money and go," she pleaded.

"Ha-ha. I don't like this version of you. I prefer the whore that called my phone to brag to me that my husband was fucking her, and you two were having a baby together. I bet it was funny to you that day, huh? But to me, it meant my husband violated our vow."

Pop! Pop! Pop! I squeezed the trigger three times. One time, I missed, but the other two hit her in the chest.

Everything else happened in slow motion. I watched as she fell to the ground. She stared at me, and in her darkest moment, she mumbled, "You're as dead as me." Then she started to cough, and blood spilled out of her mouth. She took a long, deep breath, and then her body stiffened.

I trembled with fright as I realized what I had done. I stood frozen, staring at her lifeless body.

Lord, what have I done? I thought.

An inner voice responded, "I 'ont know, but your ass needs to get up out of here."

I snapped back to reality real fast. I looked down at the bitch and knelt beside her to check her pulse. She was dead! I placed the gun back in my purse, slid off the little pair of cocktail gloves I wore, and stuffed them in my purse. I took a glance at my surroundings, turned around, and walked calmly out of the apartment. I was careful to hold my head down until I got to my car. Then I removed the scarf from my head and pulled off.

As soon as I got off her street, I started to feel ill. I pulled over and vomited a few times. After I emptied the breakfast I had eaten earlier, I held on to the steering wheel for support because I was shaking so hard. It took me a few minutes to get myself under control before I pulled off again.

I drove to Hunts Point, where I deleted her number and carefully wiped the Obama phone off. I pulled up and grabbed a rock so I could smash the phone into tiny pieces, then kicked the little pieces under the trash and debris.

God, I needed a drink and a fucking cigarette, and I didn't even smoke. I saw a cop car fly past me, and I panicked, even though it was going in the opposite direction. I drove the speed limit to the house in fear that I might get pulled over with the firearm.

I pulled into my driveway and let out a long sigh of relief. Quickly, I looked around to scope out my surroundings. No one was out, and Hassan's car wasn't in the driveway. I grabbed my purse and walked quickly into the house. I ran straight to the kitchen and poured a glass of wine. I downed it in seconds and followed up with another glass as I stood at the counter and waited for my nerves to settle a little. Finally, I put the bottle back on the shelf. I didn't plan on getting drunk because I had shit to do, and my mind had to be focused.

My phone kept ringing, but I ignored it. Now wasn't the time to be talking. My adrenaline was rushing, and my mind was in overdrive. I walked upstairs and headed straight for Hassan's room. . . .

That night was very hard for me. I vomited most of the night, and I was shaky and worried. Every sound I heard made me jump. No one knew that I knew her or that we had ever met, but I was still on edge.

I couldn't get those last words that she spoke out of my head. I wondered what she meant when she said, "*You're as dead as I am.*" What was she trying to tell me as she took her last breath? I racked my brain all night until I fell asleep. I was mentally and physically drained. . . .

I had a great sleep last night. I was so tired that I slept all night. When I first woke up, I realized that I was still in my bed and not a jail cell. I jumped out of bed in an upbeat mood. *Finally, that whore is out of my life for good,* I thought with a smile.

"Hey, Ma, you a'ight?" Amaiya asked as she walked into the kitchen. I was sitting, having a cup of coffee.

"Yes, sugar. Your mama is feeling great. How are you feeling?"

"Tired from basketball practice yesterday."

"Well, you know that comes with the territory."

"Ma, can I spend the night over at Laurie's house?"

"Hmm. . . . Who's going to be there?"

"No, Ma, no boys will be there, and, yes, I will give you her mother's number so you can call and check up on me like I'm four," she joked.

"Well, see, you already know the process. Once you get older, you will wish that I checked up on you, missy."

"Bye, Ma, see you later."

"Bye, baby. Love you." She was already gone through the door.

I walked over to the door and made sure it was locked. Then I went upstairs to my bedroom. I was eager but nervous to see what was recorded. I turned my TV down so I would be aware if someone entered the house. Then I sat on the carpet and turned it on. . . . Tears fell like a waterfall as I watched my husband's real-life movie. It seemed surreal, but it was Hassan in the flesh, fucking and sucking on his whore. As if that weren't bad enough, this sorry-ass nigga I married had the nerve to be talking shit about me. As I listened to his words, they pierced through my soul. I could only imagine what he said behind my back, but hearing it was more hurtful and cold.

I watched as his whore looked into the camcorder, smiling as if she were happy that I would see my husband pounding her. He was such a fucking liar. I remember him telling me he never ate no pussy other than mine. Really? That nigga's head was buried between her legs. I was angry and pissed the fuck off. The tears just kept coming. I wanted to take a break but decided not to. I needed to finish it. I had no time to waste if I wanted to get this bastard out of my life for good. I thought all that was bad, but to see him beating her ass made me cringe.

There was a long pause. I thought it was the end of the recordings. . . . That was . . . until I heard Hassan's voice talking. His whore was riding his cock, and he was talking. I'd had enough, I thought—until I heard a conversation about murder.

Murder! Did I hear right? My lawyer husband was on tape confessing to getting somebody named Corey murdered. I rewound the tape and listened again. This fool was lying there getting fucked and placing himself in a murder case. I quickly cut off the tape and leaned against the bed. Just when I thought shit couldn't get any worse—it just got worse.

Hassan Clarke

I had to get money out of my account to give that nigga Big Dre. I thought about not giving that punk-ass nigga a dime, but I was terrified he might run his mouth if he got caught. I decided to meet him at the corner of the A&B West Indian Grocery on Westchester Avenue. I tried to be careful because I didn't know if the police were already involved, and if this was a setup. I parked and walked over to the vehicle, where he told me he'd be waiting. I hated that I was sitting so close to this snake-ass nigga.

"Yo, you got my money?" this slime-ball nigga asked.

"Yea, it's right here. Yo, how do I know this the last time you'll come at me about some paper?"

"Nigga, I told you, shit is hot as hell right now. I need to get away. Ain't nobody worried about coming back at you 'bout no money."

"I 'ont believe shit you say. First, you ain't want no money, but here you are, shaking me down now."

"Yo, nigga, watch yo' motherfucking mouth, yo." He pointed a gun at me. "Now, give me the money and get the fuck outta my shit."

I hesitated, but then I peeped the desperation in his eyes. Those eyes were glossy and bloodshot. I knew he was a cold-blooded killer, and I didn't want to take any chances.

I threw the bag at him. "Nigga, fuck you. Lose my fucking number, or the next time we meet, I'ma show you how a *real* nigga gets down." I opened the truck door and jumped out. The nigga pulled off before I even closed his door.

"Fucking fool," I said out loud.

I sped to my car, looking around to see if any police cars were approaching me. The coast was clear, so I jumped into my car and burned rubber through the neighborhood. I swear, I hoped that was the last time that I'd ever have to cross paths with that nigga. I should've brought my own gun with me. I got it after Destiny's bitch-ass nigga threatened me. I needed to start carrying it around 'cause I was tired of niggas thinking I was a pussy.

I had a call from my divorce lawyer. I didn't like any of what dude was saying. This bitch Destiny was all up in my business, so she was asking for half of everything I made since the marriage. What the fuck? That's half of my shit. What possessed that bitch to think she was going to get half? I fucking busted my ass e'ery damn day to make sure I got where I am today. I really thought my money was fucking safe overseas, but this bitch got wind of that also. I swear to God, I wanted to take that gun I got and blow that bitch's head off. I punched the wall in my office, bruising my hand. I was going to teach that bitch a lesson—one that she would never forget.

My world was tumbling down. It didn't work out too well the other day with Imani, but I knew I had to humble myself and try again. My freedom depended on her dropping the charges. I took out the cell phone and scrolled to her name. Her phone rang until the voicemail came on. I hung up and decided to hit redial. Again, there was no answer, so I hung up and sent her a text.

Hey, babe, it's me. I'm sorry for everything I did to you. I really love you and hope you will find it in your heart to forgive me. I want to be the man for you. Please, just let me show you. Love you, Hassan.

I knew it was only a matter of time before she'd call me back. Imani was so predictable. No matter what I did to her, she would get mad and turn right back around and forgive me. We've been doing this so long that I could tell her pattern. This time was different for me, though. I was officially done with the bitch. There was no way I would ever fuck with a bitch that got me locked up. I was going to get her to drop the charges, and then I was going to break the news to her ass. I never wanted to see her or that little bastard—ever again.

Chapter Eleven

Destiny Clarke

Amaiya was in school, so I stopped by Mama's house. I had so much on my mind the last few days. I kept seeing Imani's dead body in my dreams. I tried to get it out of my head, but I just couldn't. I was happy the bitch was out of the picture because there was no way I was going to give that whore my husband or my money.

I just needed to see Mama's face. I had no idea how things were going to turn out for me, and I needed to let her know that no matter what happened, I was still her daughter. I wasn't a monster. I'm just a woman that loved the wrong fool and made a bad decision because I was fed up. I wanted to break down and tell Mama what I had done, but how could I? There was no way because if anything happened, I needed her to take care of my only child.

"Baby, something is worrying you. I can tell by the look on your face," she said as we sat outside on her steps, taking in the warm breeze.

"Mama, there is so much turmoil in my life. I just want it all to end, you know? I want my old life back. I miss the days when I laughed and had no worries in the world."

She put her hand on top of my knee. "Baby girl, you started the process, now give it a little time. It'll be over soon. God don't put on us more than we can bear. It's a test to see how strong you really are, and you're proving that you're built for the storm. Hold on a little while longer. That bastard will be gone out of your life for good, and you can be happy once again," she said as she rubbed my knee.

I tried not to cry, but it was too late. Tears started pouring down. I leaned my head on my mama's chest and let it all out.

"Baby, it's goin' be all right. I promise you, and you know yo' mama ain't goin' lie to you. Let it all out. Then get on your knees and give it to God. After that, you get up and push harder, you hear me? Push with all your might."

I sure wish I had the faith Mama had. She spoke with such conviction. A strong black woman she was.

"You know, Mama, I love you. You have always had my back since the first day I came into your life. Woman, thank you for being my strength through some of my darkest days."

"Hmmm, I guess we helped each other through some rough times. There were times when I felt like I couldn't go on, but I looked at you and knew right then that I *had* to go on because you needed me. You was the best thing that ever happened to me and still are, you and Amaiya."

Listening to those words gave me an instant rush of strength. She had no idea how she had helped me. I wiped my eyes with my shirt and squeezed her hand. No words were needed because we both understood.

"Well, Mama, I got to go. Amaiya will be home soon."

"Destiny, please be careful. Ever since you told me that bastard has a gun in the house, I worry every day for your safety."

"Love you, Mama." I smiled at her and walked away.

I got into my car and drove off as I cut the music up.

"I must admit I was set trippin', early on
So not myself, boy you had me completely gone
I lost my cool when I found out 'bout you . . ."

Ashanti's voice blared through my speaker. I sang right along with her because I was feeling every word that came out of her mouth.

I sang this song all the way to the house. I made sure that the words sank into my head. I was done, and I was ready to move on. I was ready to let Spencer know how I really felt about him. For the first time in years, I felt like I had control of my life.

I parked the car and walked toward the door when I saw the mailman pull up, so I turned back to retrieve the mail.

"Hello, there, Mrs. Clarke. How you doing today?"

"I'm well, and how are you?"

"Can't complain. I'm alive and kicking," the elderly gentleman said. "I need you to sign for this one."

"Oh, OK." I took the pen from him and signed the certified mail slip. Then I took my mail from him. "Thank you. Have a great day."

"Thank you, ma'am, and same to you."

I noticed there was a big manila envelope with my name on it. I immediately noticed it was from the Family Courts. My heart sank as I ripped open the envelope. It was a subpoena from the Family Courts. Hassan filed for full custody of Amaiya. I opened the door and walked into the house. I knew the bastard was there because his car was parked on the side.

I ran up the stairs and banged hard on his room door.

"Open this fucking door, you bastard. You think you're going to get my only fucking child?" I yelled.

"Oh, I see you got your mail. To be honest, bitch, I don't want custody of her fast little ass, but since you're going after my money and my company, I've decided to go after the one thing you treasure. How does it feel? It don't feel too good, does it?" He laughed in my face.

Without thinking, I stepped closer to him and spat in his face.

"Bitch, take a foot closer, and I will blow your fucking brains out all over this floor." He pointed his gun at my head.

"You're a fucking coward, Hassan. A fucking coward, you hear me? You will *not* get my child—I promise you that."

"We'll see. When I'm done with you, the courts will see how unfit you are. I'll prove to them that you are one unstable bitch. Now get the fuck of my face before I end your life, you worthless piece of shit. I told you not to fuck with me."

I looked at him, hiding behind that gun. Without the gun, he was a coward, and he knew it.

"You gonna get yours. I promise you that, Hassan Clarke." I winked at him and ran back down the stairs.

I hurried down the driveway and got into my car. I tried with all my might not to cry. I put the car in reverse, turned around, and drove down the street. I looked around for a phone booth. I needed to make a very important call. I finally found an old, dirty one, but I didn't care. I used a piece of napkin to hold it and dialed 911.

"This is the 911 operator. How may I help you?"

"Yes, I think sump'n bad happened to a lady ova at 2981 Barnes Avenue, Apt. C. Please send someone to check on har. Hurry, 2981 Barnes Avenue, Apt. C," I said in my best Jamaican accent that I practiced.

"Ma'am, please, can I get your name?"

I hung up and walked back to my car. By the time I returned home, Hassan was gone. I ran inside and locked the door. Then I grabbed a soda and sat in the living room, glued to the television.

The 11:00 p.m. news finally came on, and just like I figured, the whore made the news. I was kind of disappointed when they reported that the body had begun to decompose, and the police would have to wait on the coroner's office to determine the cause of death. They needed to hurry their ass up, I swore.

That night I barely slept. I was worried that Hassan might come back and do something crazy to me.

The next day, I dropped Amaiya off at Mama's house because I didn't want her around any drama. I could've stayed with Spencer, but I was kind of irritable and preferred to be by myself.

"Hey, babe," Spencer said when I answered the phone in the morning.

"Hey."

"Destiny, I tried calling you last night, but the phone kept going to voicemail. I almost popped up over there. You a'ight?"

"Sorry, I was tired, and I forgot to charge my phone," I lied.

"You sure? I mean, if anything is going on, you need to let me know."

"Spencer, I said I was tired. Now, drop it, please."

"You got it. A'ight, I'll be in the office all day. Call me when you feel better."

"All right."

I hate that I was taking my frustrations out on him. I needed all of this to go away fast. After I took a shower, I made me a cup of tea. Out of nowhere, I felt the urge to pray. I wasn't the most righteous female, but Mama taught me to get on my knees when everything else fails. I needed protection right now because I didn't want to go to prison.

"God, I know that I've done some wrong things, but I'm begging you for forgiveness. I promise, dear God, I will never kill another person if you just give me this one chance. I swear, God, I can't go to prison. I can't leave my baby girl alone. God, you know, I've been through too much already. I just can't," I cried.

"Standing ovation." Hassan's voice startled me as he clapped his hands.

I quickly jumped up off my knees and turned around to face this sick, deranged bastard standing there, grinning.

"I didn't know an evil bitch like you had it in you to pray to God. Well, bitch, you goin' need all your prayers to save you, 'cause you a dead bitch," he said and punched me in the face.

I stumbled back. I tried my best not to fall, but he stepped forward and punched me in my mouth again. Blood splattered everywhere. . . . I fell to the ground. Then I quickly curled up in a fetal position. He continued hitting and kicking me all over my body.

"No, stop, Hassan! Please stop," I cried out, pleading for my life. I knew he was going to kill me.

"You stupid bitch. I told you to leave shit alone, but, nah, you couldn't. Now you got to pay," he screamed as he continued kicking me.

Boom! Boom! Boom!

"What the fuck is that?" I heard him ask.

I was feeling dizzy and felt like my bones were broken from his severe beating.

"What the fuck the police doing here? You called the police on me, bitch? I'm not going back to jail," he yelled as he pointed his gun at my head.

I heard a bunch of commotion and people running up the stairs. . . .

"Police! Don't move! Put the weapon down and put your hands where I can see them," a voice hollered.

I barely opened my eyes. I saw it was the police—lots of them with guns drawn.

"Are you OK, ma'am?" a female officer asked.

I tried to talk, but I couldn't get the words out. Blood was spewing out of my mouth.

"Call an ambulance," was the last thing I heard.

Hassan Clarke

I was sick and tired of all the shit Destiny was doing to me. I had been good to that bitch regardless of what the fuck she told her stupid-ass mama. I kind of fell back and let her do her thing. She even disrespected me by bringing that fuck nigga into our home. The last straw was when this bitch lawyer demanded half of my fucking money. Over my dead body was I goin' give that ho a dime of what I busted my ass for. Shit, if you asked me, that ho should pay *me* for fucking that dry-ass pussy and putting up with her fucking bitching all these years.

Shit took a turn for the worse at the office. For two weeks, not one client came into the office. At first, I blew it off as nothing. Finally, I got up from my desk and walked into the receptionist area.

"Shari, this is strange. I haven't had any appointments in over a week. Are you sure the phones are working properly?"

"Yes, sir. They're working just fine. I don't know what's going on with that. It seems like that after Mr. Leon left, all the clients followed him. I'm going to put in my two weeks' notice also."

"What do you mean, after he left? He's not here anymore?"

"Uh-uh. . . . I thought you knew that he left. He cleaned out his office and told me to transfer his calls to his cell phone."

"Nah, I ain't know shit. And what you mean you giving notice?" I yelled.

"I'm sorry. I don't want to upset you. I just want to pursue other options."

I didn't say shit else to that bitch. I was too fucking pissed. That coward-ass nigga didn't even have the balls to let me know he was leaving. Fuck him and that bitch. I was Hassan Clarke. I didn't need no-fucking-body. I was born to stand out.

"Y'all hear me? I'm a fucking star. I don't need no-fucking-body," I yelled.

All this shit started because of this bitch, Destiny. My life was fine before I married that bad-luck bitch. First, I lost my son. Then my bitch. Now, I've lost my fucking clients. She was going to pay for all this shit—I swear she is. I grabbed my briefcase, locked the door behind me, and walked out of the office. I was going home to kill that bitch right now.

My phone started to ring. It was my mother. I didn't feel like talking, but I picked it up anyway.

"Hey, Mama." I tried not letting her know anything was wrong with me as I got into the car.

"Hey, baby. Are you by a television right now?"

"No, Mama. Why? What's going on?"

"They found a body in the Bronx, and they think it's Imani."

I gripped the steering wheel and steered it back toward the road again.

"Say what? Where you hear that from?"

"It was all over the news. That's why I called you. I 'ont fuck wit' her, but, damn, I 'ont wish death on anybody. What's goin' happen to that little boy?" Mama stated.

My head started to spin. All the words that Mama was saying were jumbled together, and I couldn't understand any longer.

"Mama, let me call you back." I didn't wait for a response. I hung up.

I made a U-turn and headed toward Imani's apartment. I hoped this shit was not true, because I would be the first person they looked at, even though I didn't have anything to do with it. The closer I got to the apartment, the more I started to feel sick. She couldn't be dead. She was the only bitch I ever loved. Who would kill her? As far as I knew, she didn't have any enemies.

My worst fear was confirmed when I pulled up at the apartment complex. Police tape was on her door, and all the neighbors were outside gossiping amongst themselves. A few police cars were still at the scene. I stopped where a group of people was standing.

"What happened out here?" I asked.

"The young lady Imani was found dead in her apartment," an older woman said.

"Thanks," I managed to get out before I pulled off.

I loosened my tie as I drove down the streets. A few tears fell from my eyes. What the fuck happened to her? I know I said I hated her, but deep down, I loved her. She was my bitch, and now she's gone.

This day couldn't get any worse than this, I thought as I drove.

"I hate you, bitch, I never thought I'd say.
Too many years, I done paid the price.
Why you gotta put all this drama in my life . . ."

Z-RO's lyrics blasted through my speakers. This was the perfect song for the way I was feeling. I played it all the way to the house.

I sneaked my way inside and tiptoed up the stairs to my room, where I grabbed my gun that was in my nightstand. Then I walked to her room, where I heard crying coming from. . . . I caught that bitch kneeling on the floor. Ha-ha, that wicked bitch was praying, which was fucking hilarious. I stood there, staring at her. Each word that that flowed from her lips angered me more by the second. My patience was running out and my temper was flaring. Rage boiled through my body. I barely had a chance to think of my actions. The only thought running through my head was getting her to shut up. I hated that bitch with everything in me, and it all had to end.

I pursed my lips and raised my hand back. I threw my fist forward as hard as I could, punching her in the face. The crack of skin smashing skin echoed off the walls. Vibrations of pain started in my palm and spread to my fingertips. My palm was bright red, the same red mark that matched the one on her face. She stared at me with her eyes wide as her hand slowly made it to her fire-red cheek. I should've felt some kind of remorse, but I didn't. Not one organ in my body could produce guilt for my actions.

A triumphant grin spread across my face as I tried to stomp a hole in that bitch's face with my brand-new pair of leather skin flats. The more that bitch screamed, the angrier I got. I pulled my gun out because I was going to shut her up for good.

Then I heard banging. *What could that be?* I thought.

I quickly dismissed the interruption and went back to focusing on this evil bitch. That's when the banging got louder, and I heard yelling loud and clear. It was the police—the fucking police. Did this bitch call the police? How? My mind started to race, and I got desperate. I raised the gun to shoot the bitch, and then I would turn the gun on myself. There was no way I was going back to jail.

"Put the gun down. Raise your hands!" one of the officers ordered.

"OK, Officer. Don't shoot!" I said.

I placed the gun on the carpet and put my hands in the air.

They quickly tackled me to the ground.

"Stay down! Stay down!" someone said as an officer placed cuffs on me.

"Hassan Clarke, you're under arrest for the murder of Imani Gibson and the attempted murder of this woman. You have the right to remain silent. Anything you say can and will be used against you in a court of law. You have the right to have an attorney present during questioning. If you cannot afford an attorney, one will be appointed for you."

"Murder? I ain't killed nobody. Y'all got the wrong man."

My pleas fell on deaf ears. They dragged me downstairs and into a police car. I saw all the neighbors outside peeping and whispering. I held my head down in shame as I saw the reporters pull up. I couldn't believe this shit, but I wasn't worried. I knew I'd be out in hours because I didn't kill Imani. As a matter of fact, I still loved her.

Chapter Twelve

Destiny Clarke

I woke up in the hospital with bandages all over my face. Mama and Spencer were sitting by my side. I couldn't remember what happened or how I got here.

"Hey, love. You're awake," Spencer said.

"Yes, I'm thirsty. Can you get me something to drink?"

He poured me a cup of the ice water that was in a pitcher by my bed.

"Hey, Mama."

"Hey, sugar. How you feeling?"

"A little sore, but this cough is killing me more."

"Did the doctor say anything about that?"

"Yes, he said I have pneumonia, but can't come up with the cause. I don't know . . . maybe the change of weather or something."

"Well, maybe. I'm praying you get some comfort soon. I'm ready for you to come home and get some real rest."

"I know. If all goes well, I should be home real soon." I smiled at her. I saw the worried look across her face.

They stayed with me, and we chatted for a little while. I couldn't control this terrible cough, and I was tired. I hated to see them go, but I had to get some rest. Besides the cough, I was exhausted and had difficulty breathing.

Hassan Clarke

I thought I was dreaming, but, nah, it was a cruel dose of reality. One minute I was about to kill that ho, Destiny, and the next minute, I was being arrested for the murder of Imani. My thoughts ran back to Corey but were soon interrupted when the arresting officer said, "You're under arrest for the murder of Imani Gibson." I stared at this fool like he had two heads. There was no way I killed Imani. Shit, regardless of what went down, I loved her ass. I might've beaten her ass, but that was only to scare her so that she would know I'm that nigga. I didn't want her dead.

I went in front of the judge who denied my bond. His excuse was that I was already out on bond with charges pertaining to the victim. I wanted to collapse when that cracker spoke those words. This shit was more serious than I thought. I was sure they didn't have any evidence, so how could they link me to her death, all because I was arrested for beating her up? Bullshit. They better find her killer. Shit, it might be her motherfucking son.

I was tight as fuck, I wanted to spaz out, but I kept my cool. I had to think fast. The first thing I needed was a lawyer. Maybe he could get a better understanding of what the fuck was going on.

Mama got the news that I was arrested. Of course, the entire city knew because they had it plastered all over the major TV stations. This was so fucking embarrassing. I could imagine all the whispers and gossip behind my back. I ain't goin' lie. . . . I wanted to crawl under a rock and stay there.

By the next afternoon, I heard the guard calling my name. "Clarke, Hassan Clarke, you have an attorney's visit. Step to the front."

I jumped off the top bunk, ran down to the bottom tier, and walked up to the door. He escorted me to the area where my attorney was sitting waiting. He stood up when I walked in.

"Hassan, my man." He gave me dap.

"Yo, please, tell me this is a mistake and you 'bout to get me up out of here." I sat across from him.

"Sorry, I wish I could. You are charged with the murder of Imani Gibson, and two new charges have been added: conspiracy to commit murder against Corey Griffin and the attempted murder of your wife. I spoke to the DA handling the case, and he informed me that they found the murder weapon in your house, and they also have you on tape confessing to the murder of that Corey fellow."

"What the fuck you mean?" I jumped up and flipped the table over. Rage filled my heart, and I was no longer thinking clearly.

The guard rushed in and looked at the attorney and said, "Is everything OK in here?"

"Yes, everything is under control."

I paced back and forth with my fists closed tightly. I couldn't believe what he was saying to me. *Murder weapon, confession . . . Bullshit,* I thought.

"Sit down. You need to control yourself while you're here. Honestly, the shit doesn't look too good for you, and I'ma need you to focus so we can sort through this."

I walked back to the table and sat down. "Man, what the fuck you talking about—murder weapon and confession? I don't know how to say this any clearer. I did *not* kill anyone, especially not Imani, and I did not confess anything to anyone. As far as Destiny, the bitch I'm married to, she's bitter because I don't want to be with her, and she attacked me. I was only defending myself," I yelled and pounded on the table.

"Well, I haven't seen the videotape as yet, but as far as I understand, you're on tape confessing, and the gun that was used to kill Miss Gibson is registered in your na—"

"Bullshit." I cut him off. "Ain't no motherfucking way that's possible. I own a 9 mm Glock, and I've never taken that shit out of my nightstand. Them motherfuckers tryin'a to frame me, Boss man. Get your own forensic team on my case, 'cause word to my mama, there's no way that can be possible. No way, bro."

"I'll be going down to the DA's office first thing in the morning, and I'm getting my whole team on the case. As far as a bond, I'm going to request one at your arraignment, but I doubt they're going to give it to you because you were already out on a previous one. I suggest you sit tight and let us figure out what's really going on. I need you to be straight with me. Don't hold anything back."

"Bro, I'm telling you, I didn't kill her, and it wasn't my gun. I'm innocent. The police might be trying to get back at me, 'cause I done got a lot of niggas off serious charges."

"Well, I'm going to go over to the house also to speak to your wife."

"Fuck that bitch. She not goin' help you."

"Maybe not, but I need to talk to her to understand her frame of mind."

"A'ight," I said reluctantly.

"Sit tight. I'll be in touch."

***

I didn't feel any better after talking to the lawyer. Shit was crazy. I didn't want shit to eat, even though I hadn't eaten in days. My appetite was gone. Maybe it's the fact that I saw my life spiraling downhill. I took a shower and decided to lie down on my bunk.

All kinds of thoughts invaded my mind. How the fuck I got in here on some bullshit-ass charges? I racked my brain, trying to figure out what the hell was going on. "*Confessed on tape.*" I kept trying to figure out what the hell they were talking about. . . . That's when it dawned on me that the only person that knew what went down was the nigga Big Dre. He had to be wearing a wire. "Fuck outta here, snitch bitch." I should've followed my gut not to trust that pussy nigga. My head was pounding, and I felt sick. *What the fuck have I gotten myself into?* I thought as a tear fell from my eye.

Chapter Thirteen

Destiny Clarke

After numerous tests, the doctors were still not sure what was causing that terrible cough I had. There was also a rash on my arm that would not leave. The nurse gave me a cream to put on it, but that didn't help. I was getting irritated because I didn't know what was wrong with me.

Out of the blue, something popped in my head. I remembered the doctor telling me that he did every test possible. . . . But did he? I pressed the button for the nurse.

"Yes, may I help you, Mrs. Clarke?"

"Can you come here for a second?"

"Give me a minute. I'll be in."

While I waited for the nurse to come, I was nervous about what I was about to ask her. I tried to calm my nerves down because I needed to know the answer. Being in the medical field for most of my life, I knew the importance of knowing your status.

"Yes, Mrs. Clarke, how may I help you?"

"I know Dr. Chezc said he did a lot of tests on me trying to find out what's going on with me. I want to know, did y'all do an HIV test on me?"

"Uhh . . . I'm not sure, but I can look in your files and let you know."

"OK, please do, and if he didn't, I want one done ASAP."

She shot me a strange look, then quickly smiled at me. "Sure, I'll get on it right away."

Waiting on an HIV test result was detrimental to my mind. I tried my best to block out all the "what-ifs." Even though I remained positive most of the time, I couldn't help but wonder. The symptoms of HIV were there, and even though I wasn't a whore or had niggas running all up in me, that didn't mean shit. Hassan was a ho, and God knows how many bitches he done fucked before he got with me.

People say, be careful of what you ask for. That statement was so true. One afternoon around 2:00 p.m., Dr. Chezc walked into my room.

"Good afternoon, Mrs. Clarke. How you feeling?"

"Not feeling too good. I stayed up last night, coughing, and this damn rash won't leave me alone."

"Well, your test is back from the lab and . . ." he paused.

"And what?" I asked as I sat up in the bed.

"You tested positive for HIV. . . ." His words trailed off.

I didn't say anything. I sat there, staring at the doctor. I wanted to curse him, to tell him to get out, but the words were not coming out.

"I'm sorry, Mrs. Clarke. I know it seems like the end of the world, but it's not. Some great medicines are on the market that can help treat the virus. I'll get the grief counselor in here to talk with you. Please take care of yourself."

I watched as he walked out of the room and closed the door behind him. Then I reached for my phone and dialed my mama's number.

"Mama, please come see me," was all I managed to say.

"Baby, what's going on? You all right?"

I hung up the phone without saying another word, then pulled the cover over my face. That's when the tears started flowing. A sharp pain ripped through my chest. *Lord, I hope it's not another heart attack,* I thought. What the hell. I was going to die anyway. My child, Amaiya. How do I tell my baby girl that her mama is going to die? Too many questions and not enough answers.

About an hour later, Mama showed up.

"Hey, baby. Amaiya wanted to come, but I told her that you'll see her tomorrow."

"Mama," I busted out crying.

She walked over to my bed and hugged me. "What's going on, baby?"

"Mama, I got HIV," I cried as loud as my voice allowed me to.

"You got *what?* No, they mixed up your test with some other person's test." She let me go and looked at me.

"Yes, I do. You know the cold, the rash? All that came from me having HIV." I broke down.

"When and how? Baby, who gave this shit to you?" she yelled.

"I-I don't know, Mama. I'm guessing it's from Hassan. He's the only man that I've been with for over fifteen years. And I've always taken the test, and I ain't no dirty bitch. I don't deserve this, Mama."

She hugged me tightly. "I know, baby, I know. You goin' get through it, baby. *We're* going get through it, you hear me? My God is a powerful God, and he has worked some mighty miracles."

God? All this faith and how God works—I was sick and tired of hearing it. If God's so wonderful, how did he allow me to get this shit? I'm not wicked, and I didn't abuse my body.

"Baby, I love you, and there is nothing—I mean nothing—that we can't get through. Your life is not over. You have a teenager relying on you."

I continued crying as Mama tried her best to restore my faith. I knew there was a God, but I didn't want to acknowledge him right now.

I was finally released from the hospital. Spencer was there by my side every day, taking care of me until I felt better. Each day that I was around him made it harder for me to tell him that I was HIV-positive. Numerous times, I tried, but he would say something nice, and I would forget about it. I was tired of hiding it and decided that today was the day.

It was right after dinner, and we were sitting at the table talking about our lives and our plans for our future. I pulled my chair closer to him and took his hand.

"Babe, I need to talk to you."

"Damn. Don't tell me you breaking up with me," he joked.

I wasn't in a joking mood. I had to stop myself from crying. "Babe, listen. You know how I had that bad cough and that rash, and I kept having difficulty breathing? Well . . . I-I have the virus."

"The virus? You mean the cold virus?" he stared at me for confirmation.

"Nah, babe. The HIV virus that causes AIDS."

"You serious? Don't play like that," he said while searching my face.

"I wish I were playing," I burst out crying.

He got up out of his chair and knelt in front of me. "Baby, please don't cry. I know that nigga gave you that shit. I'm going to fucking kill him, you hear me?" he yelled as he squeezed my hands.

"Ouch! You're hurting me." I pulled my hands away.

"Sorry, babe. Come here." He pulled me up from the chair.

I followed him into the living room, and we sat on the couch together.

"Listen to me, baby. I 'ont know too much about the AIDS virus, other than it can kill you. What I do know is that I love you, and there's nothing than can separate us but us. I love you, Destiny, and I'm not going anywhere. As a matter of fact, after the divorce is final, I want to marry you. You are the woman that I want to spend the rest of my life with, and we are going to fight this together."

I looked into his eyes. I wanted to say something, but the words wouldn't form. I lay my head on his chest and cried.

"The worst part is, I don't know how I'm going to tell Amaiya," I cried.

"Tell me what?" Amaiya said as she walked into the living room.

I sat there frozen. Now wasn't the time. I wasn't ready.

"Tell me what, Ma?" she asked again.

"Let me step out. I got a few runs to make. I'll call you later," Spencer said, and then he kissed me on the cheek and left.

"Sit down, baby."

Please, God, give me the strength, I thought.

"Listen, baby, while I was at the hospital, I found out that I was infected with the AIDS virus. I know you learned about that in school."

"What? I know you get that from sex. Did Daddy give it to you?"

"I don't know, baby. All I know is that I got it."

"I freaking hate him. You're a clean person. He was the one cheating. I hate him, Ma, I swear," she cried.

I grabbed my baby girl and squeezed her. "I love you, sugar. Don't you worry about yo' mama. I got this, you hear me?"

"Ma, I ain't going to college. I'm going to stay here and take care of you."

"Nonsense. You will go to medical school like you planned. Mama is stronger than you think." I tried my best not to break down in front of her.

We continued talking as I tried to convince her that her mama was fine. Deep down, I was screaming for help. I didn't know how I was going to make it. Depression was setting in, and my mental state was diminishing. I wanted it all to go away—fast.

Chapter Fourteen

Hassan Clarke

Six Months Later . . .

"I'm telling you, somebody set me the fuck up. I don't give a fuck what ballistics say, I did not kill Imani," I yelled.

"OK, say that is wrong. How do you explain the tape? You were on it confessing to getting Corey killed, and they found it in your room. The prosecutor's case is solid. I'm going in here to defend you, but how can I defend you against a tape that you're the star actor in? I can't. You're one of the best in the business. You know it don't look good."

"Man, I can't plead guilty to some shit that I didn't do. As far as the tape, I was drinking. That bitch might have slipped something in my drink. I know it sounds strange, but there's no other way to explain it, man. That bitch Destiny might be tied up in this. Shit, she knew about Imani. She must have taken my gun, shot her, and put it back to frame me."

He looked at me as if I were tripping. Shit, it was far-fetched 'cause that bitch was a coward, but there was no other explanation.

"Yea, we looked at that too, but there is no evidence that supports that claim. Your wife doesn't seem like the kind that could hurt a fly. I could be wrong, but I need evidence. Something that shows reasonable doubt."

"Yea, I know," I hung my head down.

I went back to my cell, wondering about everything. How did that gun leave my house and kill Imani and get back into my drawer? Did Destiny hate me that much, that she framed me for murder, and what about Imani? Why did she record our conversation and us having sex? My brain was hurting. I needed an outlet to let out all this aggravation.

The thought of not having Imani around was killing me softly. I swear to God, I loved that bitch, even though she pulled a fucked-up-ass move. Now her ass was dead, and I'm locked up for murdering her.

After another month of back and forth with the DA's office, my lawyer informed me that a trial date was set. I was adamant about going to trial to prove my case. There was no way in hell I was going to confess to some shit that I didn't do. Mama was heartbroken because she couldn't bear to see me in shackles. It broke my heart that she had to go through that. What was strange was Destiny. Her ass didn't bother to come see me. See, where I'm from, loyalty is everything. It don't matter if we fuss and fight each other. That ho should've been right beside me fighting these motherfuckers. I would've never done her like that, but if God helped my black ass, and I get out of this hellhole, that bitch would never speak to me—ever again. Mark my fucking words. That ho is dead to me.

***

A day before the trial started, I called my lawyer and told him I wanted to take a plea. In my heart, it was not the best move for me, but being an attorney, I knew if I went to trial, those crackers were going to burn my black ass. After talking to Mama, I decided to plea out. Maybe then, I would have a chance to see the streets again.

Just maybe, I thought.

Destiny Clarke

Hassan's lawyer came to the house a few times, fishing. He would ask me the same questions over and over. See, Mama didn't raise no fool, and I was married to an attorney. I knew he was trying to see if I was involved in anything. Hell nah, I ain't involved in no murder. Shit, if you checked, I didn't have as much as a speeding ticket. Oh, I'm happy that I used that Obama phone when I contacted Imani. I was ready to put Hassan and his whore out of my life for good. He tried calling my phone a few times, but I put a block on it after the third time.

It was a quiet day at home. I was feeling tired because I had a herpes breakout, and all my energy was drained. I realized after I was diagnosed with the virus that I started to have outbreaks more frequently. I cleaned up the house, then decided to lie on the couch.

The doorbell rang. I got up to see who the fuck came to my house without calling first. I put my eyes up to the peephole and noticed a woman standing out there holding a baby.

"Hello, how may I help you?" As soon as the words left my mouth, I realized it was the white bitch that was sucking my husband's cock in the living room.

"I-I'm looking for Hassan. I want him to take his son.

Help me out a little, you know?"

I looked down at the little white-colored monkey she was holding.

"Say what? Hassan does *not* live here anymore and do your homework the next time before you knock on my fucking door," I warned.

"Damn, you don't have to be rude. I'm going through a rough time. My parents are riding my ass, so I decided that I didn't want to be there."

"So, what I'm trying to understand is that you're saying this little bastard belongs to Hassan, and you're here because . . .?"

"I'm here because he needs his daddy. He is your husband, so if he's not here, you can watch him until he gets here."

I took a deep breath. This bitch had no idea how tempted I was to drag her little hundred-pound frame into the house and beat her to death, but I dismissed that idea fast. The bitch is white, so I know the police would be all over the place, causing havoc.

I took a step down onto the outside step. "Listen, you little cracker bitch. Hassan is not here and won't be here ever again. Now, take your little illegitimate mutt and get the fuck off my property before I drag your white ass across this lawn. Don't you *ever* ring my fucking doorbell again."

"Damn, you're a cold bitch. He's only a baby. He didn't ask to come in this world. He's innocent."

"Bitch, I don't give a fuck about you or that mutt. Now, go on before I lose it. And for the record, the next time you open your legs, make sure it's with a nigga that can take care of a child. Also, please, go get checked out for HIV. That nigga is spreading the virus."

Her face turned pink after I said that.

"Lady, you're sick. Stop making up things. I love Hassan, and that won't change." She turned around to walk off.

I watched as she strapped the bastard in, then got into her car and drove off. I looked around, stepped back inside, and closed the door. Jeez, what's up with these hoes, telling me that they're fucking that bum? I mean, at one point, I was gone over the cock. But those days were long gone. A bitch like me didn't give a damn anymore. Shit, you fucking him means I don't have to fuck him.

"Ha-ha," I chuckled to myself and locked the door. "These young bitches will never learn."

So, the mailman came, and I got a letter in the mail. I knew right then it was from Hassan. I thought about throwing it in the trash, but my nosy behind decided to rip it open. I was eager to see what that fool was talking about.

My Love, Destiny,

I'm sitting here in this cold cell, wondering what I have done to you for you to abandon me like this. I loved you from the first day I laid eyes on you, and up to today, I'm still in love with you. I know I have not been the best husband to you, but I tried my best. I never had any love when I was growing up. I didn't want to treat you the way my daddy treated my mama, because it was nothing short of hell.

I remember the way you used to smile at my silly little jokes, and when I touched you, the way your body shivered. I know I can't erase the past, but, please, know my soul yearns for you. If I ever make it out of here, I will make sure you get treated like a queen. I know you're

upset right now, but I'm begging for your forgiveness.
Those bitches didn't mean shit to me. I was only screwing
them. I only wanted you. I swear on my mama's life.

I know these folks saying all kinds of bad things about
me, but, please, don't believe any of it. You know the
real me. You know I ain't no murderer. I might talk that
shit, but I would never kill anyone. Anyway, it's chow
time, and I have to run. Please, kiss my daughter for me
and let her know her daddy loves her. Please, fill out
the visitation form so you can see me soon. I love you,
woman, with everything in me.

Hassan, your husband

I balled the paper up and threw it in the trash in the
kitchen. I wanted to laugh, but the shit was serious. This
bum almost killed me, and now he was professing his
love for me? That shit made me sick to my stomach. This
nigga just didn't know how much hate I had for him, but
he will know soon, though.

My lawyer called to let me know Hassan pled out.
Instead of going to trial and facing me, that bum pled
guilty. That was so him. He had all the balls to hurt a
woman, but in the end, he bitched up and took a plea.
I'm not going to lie. I was disappointed because I was
looking forward to my day in court when I would sit
there and face the coward that almost killed me.

Oh well, I will be there, sitting in the front row, when
it was time for him to get sentenced. I wanted him to see
my face for the last time because I will be permanently
closing that chapter of my life.

I felt bad for my child because even though she didn't
show it, I knew she loved him. After all, he has been

in her life since birth. I planned on getting her some counseling when it was all over.

The day of his sentencing came very quickly. I was one of his victims, so the DA asked me to speak. I gladly accepted. I got up early and got dressed in an all-black Vera Wang pantsuit. I had my hair pinned up so that my face would show. I used minimum makeup. I kept in mind I was going to court, not the club.

I dropped Amaiya at school and made it to the Grand Concourse. His sentencing would begin at 9:00 a.m., and I didn't want to get there late.

Traffic was bumper to bumper, and horns were honking everywhere. I remained cool and waited until it was my turn. I woke up in a great mood and didn't want anything to draw me out. I finally made it to the courthouse in enough time to park, put money in the meter, and run upstairs.

On the way in, I passed Hassan's mother, sister, and what looked like his whole damn family. His mama shot me a dirty look, and I stared back at the bitch, daring her to try it. I beat her ass once and wouldn't have an issue with doing it again. I continued walking toward the courtroom. I heard his sister scream something in the far distance. I turned around to answer her, but instead, shook my head. As a queen, I was tired of addressing these fucking hood buggers. All of them combined didn't have a pot to piss in. If I were in their shoes, I would be upset also because their money machine was broken and God knows . . . They're going to be a bunch of hungry bitches. Silently, I straightened my jacket and walked into the courtroom.

All eyes were set on me. I took a seat in the first row behind the prosecutor. I didn't like the police, but fuck it. We were on the same team right now. Team "Lock Up That Nigga."

A few minutes later, the bailiff brought Hassan in. Damn. What a sight he was. His cheeks were sunken in, and his body looked like he was malnourished. The clean cut he used to wear was long gone. I swear, if I passed him on the streets, I would not have known this was him. To say the nigga was looking bad would be an understatement. He stared at me before sitting down. I looked him dead in the eyes until he turned away.

After the judge came in, the lawyers and prosecutors went back and forth. Then the judge asked if anyone wanted to speak.

"Yes, Your Honor. Mrs. Clarke is the defendant's wife and also one of his victims."

I stood up and gracefully walked to the stand. I glanced around to see who was in the courtroom.

"Your Honor, my name is Destiny Clarke. I married the defendant over seventeen years ago, and ever since then, my life has been nothing but hell. This man has put me through so much pain, some of it, I can't mention because I'm too embarrassed.

"One night, while I was asleep, he attacked me. First, he tried to rape me, and when I fought back, he beat me down. I asked him to leave my house, but, instead, he stayed there to terrorize me. The last straw was when he beat me unconscious and pulled a gun on me. If it weren't for the help of the officers that night, I would not be here today.

"Your Honor, I'm scared for my life and also for my daughter's life. I beg you to sentence him to life, Your

Honor, because anything else would be unjust." I wiped the tears that were freely flowing. Quickly, I glanced over at his table and saw he had his head down.

"Thank you, Mrs. Clarke. You may step down now."

I walked hurriedly back to my seat. I was so nervous while I was on the stand. I hoped I did well enough.

"Does anyone else have anything to say?"

"Yes, Your Honor. Mr. Clarke's mother wants to address the court."

That bitch. What the fuck could she say? She raised him to be a bitch-ass nigga. I watched as her fat gorilla-looking ass walked toward the front.

"Hello, Your Honor and the Court. Hassan Clarke is my only son, and, Your Honor, my son is a gentle, caring man. I have never seen him raise his voice or hit anyone. Your Honor, he is not the wicked person they are painting him to be. He wouldn't hurt a fly, Your Honor. The real killer is out there because my son is innocent of all charges. Your Honor, as a mother, I'm begging you to sentence him to probation so he can come home to his family . . . his *real* family." She broke down crying.

I didn't know who that bitch was talking about, but it damn sure wasn't her son. She raised him like that. Now, she's trying to dress that shit up. *Bitch, that was a good performance, but I did not believe you.*

"Your Honor, the defendant pled guilty to a lesser charge, which is second-degree manslaughter and aggravated assault. We ask that you sentence him to twenty-five years in prison and five years' probation."

"Well, Mr. Clarke, please stand up. This case is difficult for me because I've worked with you before on a case. Like your mother, *that's* the man that I know, but we are not here because of the man that you used to be.

We are here for the inhumane acts you've committed. Based on the evidence, I hereby sentence you to twenty years in prison and five years' probation."

"Your Honor, I didn't do this shit," he screamed. "Please, believe me," he yelled some more.

"Fuck you, Destiny. You goin' get yours, bitch. I promise you will," he yelled.

"Counselor, please control your client, or he will be removed."

"Go ahead. I didn't do this. I'm going to sue all y'all."

"Bailiff, remove Mr. Clarke from the courtroom," the judge yelled.

Everybody gasped and started whispering to each other.

"If we're finished here, the court is adjourned."

I hung my head down in shame. I regretted knowing this fool. The big bulky Hassan was a little, scared-ass punk today. I got up and turned to leave. As soon as I got to the door, his bitch-ass sister blocked my path.

"You know that's fucked up how you get on that stand and lied like that. My brother has been nothing but good to you and your daughter. You turned on him when he needed you the most."

"Little bitch, listen up. Unless you was fucking and sucking your brother, you have no idea the piece of shit he really is. I lived with the bastard, so *I* know. Now, get the fuck out of my way before I move you my damn self like I did yo' ugly-ass mama."

"You know what, bitch? Karma is a motherfucker, and you goin' get yours."

"So, it must be safe to say that your brother got his." I shoved that bitch to the side and strolled down the stairs.

What a bunch of peasants. I hope I never have to see them people anymore. I stepped out into the sun, put on my glasses, and walked to my car. I felt like a burden was lifted off my shoulders.

Chapter Fifteen

Hassan Clarke

It took a lot to break a nigga like me. I barely ever shed a tear in my entire life. Only today was different . . . to sit and watch the State crucify me as if I were an animal, then rip my soul out, when the ho I gave my last name to took the stand and begged the judge to sentence me to life. All I ever did was cheat on her, and *this* was what she did to pay me back? I shook my head in disbelief. My mama was hurting, and so was I. I heard the pain in her voice as she begged the judge to send me home. A tear fell from my eye as Mama's words echoed in my mind. I wanted to hold her, let her know that I will always be her baby boy, and I wouldn't stop fighting until I got home to her. I looked at my pops, and as usual, he didn't wear an expression. I know he was also hurting. He just wasn't good at showing emotions.

After the judge sentenced me, I couldn't keep in my wrath anymore. I knew I took a plea deal, but never in a million years did I think the fucking cracker would give me all that time. I wanted to rip his fucking neck off. Then I glanced at that ho, and she was sitting there like she had no worries in the world. I exploded. I had nothing to lose at this point. I started yelling at that ho. I had to let her know this shit was not over—not by a long shot.

That night in my cell, I broke down. The words of the judge kept playing over and over in my head. This can't be real. I tried to convince myself it was all a dream—a nightmare. God, what was I going to do? I have a firm to run and clients to defend in court. I couldn't be locked up with all these sweaty-balls niggas. I needed pussy in my life. Ain't no way I was goin' beat dick for all them years. *The fuck, man,* I thought. This can't be life. This is not how it's supposed to be.

Right then, my cell door opened. I sat up to look. A Big Bertha-looking dude walked in.

"Clarke, this is your bunky, CeCe," the guard smiled.

"What the fuck!" *Oh, hell no. How the fuck they goin' put me in the cell with a faggot-ass nigga?* I thought.

Chapter Sixteen

Destiny Clarke

After Hassan got sentenced, I kept getting threatening phone calls. These bitches played on my phone all times of the night, but I didn't trip. I went to Sprint and got my phone number changed. I wasn't trying to address them lower-level hoes. As long as they didn't cross my path and put their hands on me, I was fine.

I woke up extra early and decided to take this trip to see Hassan. Yes, I know. I might look stupid, but it was very important to me. I wanted to look this nigga in the eyes and let him know how much I despised him and how much hurt he had bestowed on me. I decide to put on a nice dress and let my hair down. I made sure my curves were visible.

I parked my car and took the bus over to Rikers Island. I saw I was amongst the other baby mamas, side chicks, the whores, and the wives crew. Only difference was, my visit wasn't friendly. I waited until they called "visit for Clarke." I got up to walk to the desk, and that's when I noticed the little white bitch walking up in full stride. I turned back toward her.

"What the fuck do you think you're doing? Only one visitor, and that, my dear, would be me. The Mrs."

"I came over here so he could see his son."

"And what the fuck that got to do with me? I'm married to the bastard, so that means *I* will be the one that gets the time."

I turned away from that retarded-ass bitch, then walked up to the window where Hassan was standing on the other side. His facial expression changed when he noticed it was me.

"What the fuck you doing here? I told you I never wanted to see your ass, ever again."

"Relax, Hassan. I just wanted to see how my future ex-husband is living. By the looks of your appearance, I think life ain't too good for you up in here."

"Ha-ha, you know, Destiny, I should've finished you when I had the chance. You are a coldhearted bitch that deserves to die slowly."

"Cold? You made me this way. I just want to know when did you start hating me." I stared into his eyes.

"Hate you? Bitch, I *never* loved you. That dry-ass pussy was horrible, and your fucking mouth was annoying. I've always loved Imani. You was only our meal ticket to a better life," he coldly stated.

I almost fell for that shit. My emotions were starting to show. I swallowed hard and quickly regrouped.

"By the way, you need to get checked for HIV. Also, please know that while you're cooped up in here, I will be living my life, running your company, and spending your money. Who is the joke on now, baby?" I winked at him.

"I ain't got no HIV, so I'm good. That nigga you screwing must've given that shit to you. It doesn't matter because you are nothing but a whore. *That's* the reason why your daddy was fucking you and your mama at the same time. I know you missed him tearing up that young pussy," he chuckled.

"At one point, your words would've hurt me, but not anymore. And don't you worry about who was tearing me up. You make sure none of these faggots rip open your asshole. Anyway, I hope you enjoy every bit of your stay. I will *never* see you again, Hassan Clarke."

"Don't be so quick to write me off. I know you killed Imani. I just can't prove it. But please know, while I sit in this cell, I *will* be working on my appeal. You won't get away with this. I promise you *will* pay."

"You're delusional. You keep talking like that, and they goin' put your ass in the psyche ward."

"Destiny, I'm going to make you pay, bitch. I promise youuuu," he screamed.

I walked off before he could get another word in, went through the double doors, and out into the waiting area.

I walked up on his bitch, who was sitting down, looking disappointed. "He's all yours, honey." I put my shades on, buttoned my peacoat, and walked out into the brisk air.

Hassan Clarke

I couldn't believe this bitch had the nerve to show her face up in here after the performance she gave in court. I meant to take her off the visitation list, but it slipped my mind. I was excited when they called me for visitation because Tanya and my baby were on the way. Yes, you heard me right. Tanya had the baby, and I was a proud daddy. Hell, why not? Imani was gone, Destiny's bitch ass was history, and Tanya was the only one that stuck around. Even though she didn't have much, she made sure my books were straight, and I had visitation on the regular. So, it's only fair that I play daddy to the little bastard.

I walked hurriedly back to my cell. Something that Destiny said grabbed my attention. The bitch said I had HIV. I played it off in front of her, but I was shivering on the inside. At first, I thought the bitch was playing a cruel joke on me, so I searched her face. I saw no signs of deception. The minute I got back to the cell, all the emotions filled my soul. Was there any truth to what that bitch said? Only one way to find out. . . .

I wanted to die. The nurse confirmed I was HIV-positive. I wanted to break down in front of her, but I didn't want to come off like a bitch. The minute I got back to the cell, I collapsed. All I could think about is which one of these dirty bitches gave that shit to me? I knew I lived recklessly, but my dick stayed clean. *I know it was one of them,* I thought as I bawled out.

I was happy that I was in my cell by myself 'cause I had them move that faggot out after he made a move on me. They had to get me off his ass. I don't play that fuck-boy shit at all. Pussy was the only thing that had my interest.

I couldn't take the pain that I was feeling inside. I can't live like this, not with no HIV. The thought of having bumps, face sinking in, and me losing weight . . . I just can't.

"Sorry, Mama. I love you, but I just can't."

I grabbed the sheets off my bunk. If this is living, death, here I come.

Chapter Seventeen

Destiny Clarke

The doctor prescribed Atripla to treat my HIV infection. At first, I was nauseated, and often, I was dizzy and drowsy. But after my body got used to the drug, it worked fine. As far as my mental state, after crying for weeks, I decided to get some counseling because I couldn't handle it. My daughter and I had been through so much shit that we both needed professional help.

The divorce was final, and I got most of everything. I also went to juvenile court and got full custody of my baby. Later, I got a phone call from my lawyer, informing me that Hassan tried to kill himself. I wasn't surprised at all. Hassan was a coward by nature. He wasn't so big and bad, after all. I was mad that he didn't kill himself. I don't think I'll ever feel completely safe until that bastard was six feet deep.

Things were starting to get to normal. Did I say normal? What was normal anyway? Here I was, living with herpes and HIV. I knew what the end result could be, but I didn't focus on any of that. I tried to live day by day and just focus on the happy times with my daughter, Spencer, and Mama.

"What's on your mind, lady?" Spencer interrupted my thoughts.

"Nothing, just thinking. I need to pack up all this junk that I have in this house. I haven't moved in over twenty years."

"Well, you can always walk away from it all. Start over fresh, you know?"

"Yea, but . . ."

"But what?" He kissed me on the cheek and walked back into the house.

I never believed in fairy tales and still don't. However, I believed his love for me was real. He was so different. He was the regular kind of dude I usually dated. Don't get me wrong. He wasn't no punk either, and that's what made him more attractive. My life felt so good these days. There was no one calling me out of my name or asking me for money.

I can't remember the last time I spent a dollar on anything. Not that I didn't want to, but because my man made sure I didn't do it.

I looked up at the sky and smiled. I didn't know how long I had left on this earth, but I planned on enjoying every bit of it.

"Ma, Ma, it's a letter from Daddy. He said he's going back to court and is coming home soon." Amaiya yelled, waving a letter in her hand.

"Hell no," I said as I snatched the letter out of her hand.

This bastard just won't go away, I thought as I started reading the letter.

Chapter Eighteen

Josiah Clarke

A Year Ago . . .

I stood over my mama's casket, staring down at her. I touched her powdered face as a tear dropped from my eye. I quickly wiped it away, hoping that no one saw it. I stood in a church full of motherfuckers that never gave a fuck about my mama when she was alive. Not a phone call or a visit. Now that she was dead, they were all up in here crying and carrying on, like they were hurting and shit. I was too ready for the bullshit to be over so that I could get down to the *real* business.

I bent down and planted a long kiss on my mama's cheek. I then turned around, put my shades on, walked down the aisle, and out of the church. The pain I was feeling was so intense at that point that I felt like I couldn't breathe. As I stepped outside, I noticed that the rain was pouring down. I looked up to the sky, wondering if those were tears coming down from Mama.

I got into my li'l Toyota Civic that I'd copped a week ago from the money I had hustled. Quickly, I grabbed a blunt that I'd rolled earlier and lit it. I needed something to help ease the pain. I hadn't been able to sleep or eat since I got the call that she was gone. What was eating me up the most was the fact that she and I had not been talking. I was so fucking mad at her that I kept ignoring her calls. I never thought in a million years that the last time that we got into it would be the last time I laid eyes on her.

I didn't give a fuck how many times we fought or how many times I told her that I hated her. At the end of the day, she was my mama, and the only person I had in the world. See, I knew my mama was into some shit, lying to niggas and all that, but the shit didn't matter to me 'cause she always made sure we ate and had a roof over our heads. The shit started to bother me when she kept letting that fuck nigga beat on her, and then days later, she'd take him back. I used to sit in my room, listening to her crying over that nigga. I tried to tell her to leave his ass alone, but she didn't listen. She allowed that nigga to play her, which resulted in her death.

I took one last pull off the weed, then drove away. This was the day that my life changed. *On my dead mama's grave,* I vowed to seek revenge on everyone that caused her harm. Yes, I am Josiah, and I *am* my mama's keeper.

Chapter Nineteen

Hassan Clarke

Present Day . . .

I can't believe that I tried that weak-ass move, attempting to kill myself. After that fucking judge sentenced me to all of that time, I became sick. Nah, I wasn't physically sick, but mentally. I couldn't sleep, and the thoughts of being locked up broke me down.

I was grateful that somebody was watching over me and saw fit to keep a nigga alive. I had too much shit on this earth to do, but the most important thing was paying that bitch, Destiny, back in full. I knew in my gut that I didn't kill Imani, and from experience as a lawyer, I saw guilt written all over Destiny's face.

See, that wicked bitch had a lot of people fooled, but not me. I saw that bitch for the snake she really was, and the way that she performed in that courtroom only confirmed that her sole purpose was to get rid of Imani and place the blame on me. I didn't know how she had pulled it off, but I knew that she had something to do with it.

"Hey, babe," Tanya said as I walked into the visitation room.

"Hey, babe," I greeted her.

Over the past few months, Tanya and I had grown closer. After all was said and done, she was the only bitch that stuck around when the shit hit the fan. Although she and that little bastard annoyed me at times with all that whining and shit, I still had to keep her close. She was the only one that made sure I was straight. Mama had been up here to visit, but because I'm not out there, money was kind of tight with her. I tried to tell her that this shit would be over soon, and her baby boy would be home. The look she gave me kind of let me know that she felt like I was feeding her bullshit. The pain that I saw in my mama's eyes made me feel like a piece of shit. I knew that I had to get up out of here one way or another.

"Hey, babe, you all right?" Tanya interrupted my thoughts.

"Yeah, I'm good. So how you been doing at the new job?"

"Job? If that's what you call it. Did your lawyer get you your money yet?"

"Damn. You acting like it's *your* shit," I snapped.

I was getting sick and tired of that white bitch asking me about my damn money. She was behaving just like those money-hungry bitches, Imani and Destiny.

"Babe, I didn't mean to make you upset. Calm down. I just need a little something for Hassim and me. We've been struggling, you know." She started to cry.

This bitch must not know where the fuck I am. Shit, she selfish as hell. All she cares about is herself and that li'l monkey that I'm not even sure is mine, I thought.

"Babe, don't cry. I tell you over and over that I'm almost out of here. Shit, you might have to do what you have to do 'til I come home. I wouldn't look at you any less." I stared at her.

"What are you saying to me, Hassan?" She looked puzzled.

"You know you're a very attractive girl, and you need money. Shit, a little fucking and sucking here and there ain't goin' hurt nothing, as long as the nigga's paying."

"*Really?* You would want the mother of your child to go out and sell her pussy?"

"Ouch, you make that shit sound so bad. Tanya, a woman's got to do what she's got to do to feed her offspring. It ain't as bad as it sounds."

She looked at me and started crying more. I had no idea why she was acting like that. I mean, the bitch said she was broke, and I was only trying to help her ass out.

"Visitation is up," I heard the burly guard yell.

Without another word, Tanya walked away from me. I wanted to holler at her, but instead, I kept quiet. I knew her ass couldn't stay mad at me for long.

Destiny Clarke

God knows I didn't need any more drama in my life. The day the judge sentenced Hassan, I just knew it was over. Who was I fooling? Something that he said to me when I visited him kept coming back to me, and to make matters worse, Amaiya brought that letter from him to her. I couldn't say that I was a bit surprised that he was appealing his case. Hassan was a damn good lawyer that fought for others, so I knew he wasn't going to go down like that. Not without a fight.

"Babe, is something bothering you? It's damn near 2:00 a.m., and you're wide awake," Spencer said as I lay beside him thinking.

"I can't sleep again. Is there any chance of Hassan getting out of prison? I swear, Spencer, I can't go through this shit all over again."

"You want the truth? I'ma give it to you. He can be granted a new trial, and if he does, he may be given bond until his new court date."

"So, they would just let a criminal walk out of jail?" I felt tears welling up in my eyes as I thought of the possibilities.

"Destiny, listen to me, babe. I swear on my dead mama, if that nigga come anywhere close to you or even breathes on you, I'm going to dead that nigga. I promise you that." He stared into my eyes. I could tell that he was dead serious by his tone and the look in his eyes.

"Lord, I don't need this to get that far," I whispered a prayer in my heart.

I lay there as he squeezed my arm like he was trying to protect me. See, Spencer thought I needed protection from Hassan, but that weak-ass nigga wasn't my issue. *My biggest fear is going to prison. I knew damn well I had killed Imani and framed Hassan,* I thought.

Chapter Twenty

Josiah Clarke

"When I was young me and my mama had beef
Seventeen years old kicked out on the streets . . ."

I was definitely in my zone as I searched through my mama's things. I had my little CD player on repeat, playing Tupac's song "Mama." I tried not to break down 'cause a nigga wasn't weak, but the words of that song had me feeling some type of way. I picked up a picture of us from the coffee table when I was a little boy. Even though I had no memory of that day, the picture said it all. It was back in the day when she was happy and full of life. I looked at the way she hugged me. I knew she felt proud. I threw the picture into the bag and started bawling. It was the first time since her death that I was able to let out any kind of emotions.

"Mama, I am so sorry for the shit I said to you. I wish I could take it all back," I cried as I knelt on the ground.

I had so much anger and hatred in my heart toward that nigga, Hassan, the bitch he married, and the little slut they called their love child. See, my life was fucking good up until the point when that bitch walked into our lives. I didn't know the full story, but I knew enough to know that my mama's blood was on their hands.

I sat in my one-bedroom apartment on Gun Hill Road and watched my mama on a video that I found the day I was cleaning out her things a year ago. She had it stuffed in an old sock. I thought it was a sex tape at first, so I just threw it into a bag. God knows the last thing I needed was to see her butt-ass naked, screwing a nigga. However, something about it kept nudging at me, so I got it and slid it into a little camcorder I bought. It was my mama in the flesh.

"This message is for anyone that is watching this. I'm about to meet Destiny Clarke, Hassan Clarke's wife. I am making this video because I don't trust her. This bitch is jealous of my relationship with Hassan. He is about to leave her, and he and I are going to get married. I am scared for my life because this woman kidnapped me before and kept me hostage in her basement. She did let me go but threatened to kill my son and me if I went to the police. If anything happens to me, please don't let her get away with it. I hope I'm just paranoid, but my gut feeling tells me that my intuition is correct."

"Mama," I yelled out as the tape went blank, and her face disappeared from the screen.

I sat there for a minute as I tried to digest everything that I'd just heard. I'd never met the bitch that she mentioned, but I knew she had caused so much havoc in our lives. I wondered what Mama was meeting her for, and why was she so sure the bitch was going to hurt her.

I couldn't ask Mama because she was dead, so that left only one person—the bitch that had all of the answers.

Hassan Clarke

I had about a week before I was scheduled to get shipped. I wasn't sure where they were sending me yet. I guess I would just have to wait and see. I was tired of pumping weights all day. That was the only way I could pass the time. My arm was sore from the push-ups, so I took a hot shower and decided to lie back on the bunk and take a quick nap. I had to welcome sleep when it did show up because ever since I got sentenced, I could barely sleep at night.

I turned the music on and put my headphones in my ear. That punk, CeCe, wasn't in the cell, so I felt a little bit relaxed. I closed my eyes as that nigga Plies's song, "Tha Realest One," blared through the little radio that they sold in the commissary. I was in my zone, plotting on ways that I was going to kill that bitch when I made it out of this cell.

I thought I felt something touch me, but I brushed it off as just my nerves. That was . . . until I felt a weight on top of me.

"What the fuck you doing, nigga?" I opened my eyes and saw that it was CeCe's big cock diesel-looking ass on top of me with a hard-ass dick.

I yanked the earpiece out and threw that faggot-ass nigga off of me. Then I jumped on him and started pounding his face into the cement floor. The punk bitch started hollering in his feminine voice.

"Help, help me. Guard, please help me," he screamed.

The sound of his faggot-ass voice only sent me into a mad state of mind. I took his head and banged it onto the floor until blood started spewing out.

"Fight, fight!" another punk hollered.

"Clarke, get off him. Get the hell off him," one of the guards ordered.

I wasn't trying to hear that shit, so I continued putting the hurt on him.

Whap! Whap! Whap! The guard hit me on my back. I jumped up because I was about to attack his ass too. "Step the hell back before I use this on you." He raised the baton and aimed it at me.

"Nigga, fuck you. This motherfucker tried to rape me," I yelled.

"Lock down the unit. I repeat, lock down the unit," he commanded on his radio.

By then, three other guards rushed inside of the cell.

"Holy shit! What did you do, man?" The female guard looked down at CeCe and then back at me.

"Man, y'all deaf? This motherfucker tried to fucking rape me. I ain't no damn faggot. I told y'all niggas not to put him in the cell with me, but y'all ain't listen to me."

"Take him out of here, put him in solitary, and call medical down here, right now."

"Let's go. Yo' ass is in some big shit."

I didn't say shit because I was tired of repeating the same shit over and over. I was in pain from the guard hitting *me,* and I could barely walk straight.

"Yo, I need to go to medical."

"Nah, the only place you're going to is solitary. You know the nurse is coming through, so fill out a sick call form."

"Nigga, I'm hurting now from that damn hit."

He ignored me and just led my ass to solitary, but I was happy when I got there. I was still fuming from that fuck nigga trying me like that. I loved pussy, and I didn't give a fuck how long I was locked up. Another nigga could never hold my interest. That nigga straight violated me. He was a bold-ass punk coming at a straight nigga like that. I swear, they better keep me in isolation until I got shipped because if they don't, I was gonna finish that punk off.

Chapter Twenty-one

Destiny Clarke

I finally found a house in White Plains, which wasn't too far from Mama. I was excited because it was a bigger house, and it was in a much-nicer neighborhood. The house was in my name, but Spencer gave me half of the money. He had offered to pay all of the money, but being the type of woman I was, I decided to go half. There was no way that I was going to let myself fall for any kind of foolery anymore. I wanted to make sure that if anything happened to me, my baby was going to be secure. I was the only person she had that she could rely on. I kept Amaiya at her school because it was her last year, and I didn't want to pull her out. I would have to drive her back and forth every day.

Amaiya and I were bringing in a few things that were left in the car. Spencer had to be in the office that day and had left earlier, so it was only us girls.

"Hey, Mama, can I ask you something?"

"Yes, sure." I looked at her.

"How do you know when somebody is the right one?"

"The right one for what?" I put the box on the counter and turned to face her.

"The right boy."

I looked at her and then swallowed hard. I was very careful about how I answered her question.

"Well, baby, I mean, you'll know. You'll feel it in your gut, and when you see him, your stomach will be doing flips."

"Hmm. Interesting."

"Do you feel that way about someone?" I looked at her, afraid of the answer that I might get.

"Well, kind of. I don't know yet. I do feel the things you described. So, he may be the one."

"How long have you been seeing this boy, and who is he?"

"Ma, I've been talking to him for a little over a month, and he's from the Bronx. You don't know him. So, Ma, did you feel like that for Daddy?"

My stomach turned as soon as she mentioned that bastard. I swear, I blocked out everything about that nigga. I tried not to even think of his name. I was so over him and all of his bullshit.

She must've seen the look on my face. "Sorry, Ma. I know things are still painful for you."

"It's okay, baby." I squeezed her hand. "Baby, I know you're growing up and all, but you still have time to fall in love. Right now, you need to focus on finishing school and going away to college."

"Ma, I make straight A's, and I'm going to college, remember? I'm not doing anything to let you down."

I couldn't even say anything. She was right. She was doing great in school. Graduation was right around the corner, and she was going away to college in Buffalo in the fall. I should've been grateful that my only child was not pregnant or screwing every little boy out there. As far as I knew, she was still a virgin.

"Amaiya, are you still a virgin?"

"Ma, why would you ask me that? I think that's private."

"I'm your mother. Ain't no privacy. Baby, if you're having sex, can you please let me know so I can put you on birth control?"

"Mother, I'm not having sex, and, yes, if I decide to, I *will* let you know," she replied sarcastically and walked off.

I stood there thinking, *She doesn't know how lucky she is. I wish I had the opportunity to choose who I wanted to sleep with. Instead, that old bastard took away my innocence and scarred me for life. I'm going to make sure my baby doesn't have to go through that shit. As long as I'm breathing, I will make sure that a nigga never takes anything from my daughter that she doesn't agree to.*

Spencer called and asked me to get dressed. I learned never to question where we were going. All I knew was the man was full of surprises. I looked in my closet and realized that it was time to do some shopping. I was going to get rid of all of my old clothes and buy some younger, sexier clothes to show off the little weight that I had lost.

By the time I finished dressing, I heard a horn blowing. I was dressed in a skintight dress and some sandals to complement it. Quickly, I grabbed my Dooney & Bourke clutch purse and my keys.

"Amaiya, I'm stepping out for a little while. Lock up these doors and call me if you need me."

"A'ight, Ma," she yelled back.

I doubted that child heard a word that I said. She was still giggling on the telephone. Whatever that boy was saying must've been hitting the spot. I laughed to myself, set the alarm, and sashayed out the door.

I smiled as I spotted my sexy lover standing outside of the car, waiting for me. I walked up to him and fell into his arms.

"Hey, love. Hmm, you smell good. Maybe we need to stay in tonight."

I poked him and burst out laughing. "You're so damn nasty."

"But, you love you some me." He hugged me tightly. "Let's go, lady." He walked to my side and opened the door.

I got in the car, and then, he got behind the wheel and pulled off.

"So, where are we off to, Mr. Mysterious?"

"Relax, babe. I got you."

I smiled and closed my eyes as I lowered my seat. I loved how I was feeling. I wanted that forever, but somehow, I thought it might not last. I hoped it was just my mind playing tricks on me.

The smooth rhythm of Luther Vandross's voice came through the speaker, definitely putting me in a serene mood. I felt peaceful as he reached over and took my hand in his. This was definitely the kind of love that you only saw in the movies. This was our fairy-tale life, and I didn't want it ever to end.

He pulled up to Benjamin Steakhouse. It was an upscale restaurant that celebrities frequented. I knew the man had some connections, but this was definitely a different kind of scenery. Once we were seated at our table, I ordered the seafood platter while he ordered a steak meal. I also ordered red wine to go along with my meal. After we finished eating, Spencer scooted closer to me. I knew he wasn't trying to get any pussy at the table, so that seemed strange.

"Woman, you know I'm in love with you, right?"

"Yup, and I'm in love with you too, babe."

He got up from the seat and knelt in front of me. I looked around, feeling kind of embarrassed that he was kneeling in front of me like that.

"Spencer, get up. Everybody's looking at us." I grabbed his arm and tried to pull him up.

"Always and forever
Each moment with you
Is just like a dream to me . . . "

Luther Vandross's song blasted loudly over our heads.

"Baby, Destiny, you're my life and the person that I want to spend the rest of my life with. Will you be mine forever?"

He reached into his blazer pocket and pulled out a ring box. My throat got dry instantly, and tears welled up in my eyes. I couldn't believe that the moment was real. I blinked to prevent the tears from falling. I looked around and saw that the other patrons were gathered around, smiling and clapping. I looked down at him still holding the ring in his hand.

"Spencer, yes. You know I want to marry you." I started to cry.

He took the ring and placed it on my finger. The ladies in the crowd started yelling and clapping. He got up and hugged me, and we started kissing.

"You're one lucky woman. Hold on to him, honey," an older woman yelled.

"Can I have this dance?"

Spencer took my hand, and we danced to the sultry voice of Luther. I was an emotional wreck as I held on tightly to my future husband. I'd been down that road before, but this time, it felt different. I felt the strong hold that Spencer had on my heart.

I was floating on cloud nine because I knew that he loved me, and I loved him. However, I had no idea that he wanted to marry me. After all, I was damaged goods. On the way home, we were both silent. I guess we were caught up in our thoughts. I closed my eyes and imagined what our life would be like as husband and wife.

Chapter Twenty-two

Hassan Clarke

I finally got shipped to Clinton Correction Facility in Upstate, New York. I didn't belong there because they housed some of the country's most notorious criminals. It was funny because I frequented that very prison when I was an attorney.

I wasted no time once I hit the compound. I immediately flocked to the law library. I spent countless hours researching cases that were similar to mine. I used my expertise and knowledge of the law to aid me. I was determined to fight my case. I knew that they didn't have any evidence on me because the truth was, I was nowhere near Imani when she got killed. There was no way that I was going to lie in there and take the blame for that.

I lay in my cube and wondered what the fuck Destiny was doing. I wondered if she were still fucking that nigga she dissed me for. It was fucked up that every letter I sent that bitch was returned. The bitch even went as far as turning my daughter against me. I would bet you any money that bitch had my daughter calling that other nigga, "Daddy." The thought of that stirred up hatred in my heart. *I have to get out of here,* I thought before I jumped up and grabbed the papers that I had printed from the law library.

"You straight, partner?" My bunk mate, Junior, asked in his thick, Jamaican accent.

"Nah, son. I've got to get outta here. I won't rest 'til I get outta here."

"Well, dats sometin' we all want. Hopin' is not bad at all."

"Fuck hoping. I didn't do that shit. That bitch set me up."

"Who, your wife?"

"Yes, that bitch killed my whore and blamed me."

"Bloodclaat, you is serious, boss man. Di gyal set yuh up. Yo, some lick that gyal want inna har bomboclaat face."

I tried my best to comprehend, but I couldn't understand shit except for the fact that he was angry. I just looked at him and lay back on my bunk, burying my head deep into my thoughts.

Josiah Clarke

I was in a deep sleep when the buzzing of my phone interrupted me. I tried to ignore it, but I couldn't. Damn, I had pulled an all-nighter and just lay down. I reached and picked up the phone from the nightstand.

"Yo," I answered, still half-asleep.

"Hey, babe." Her sexy voice woke me up.

"Hey, boo," I responded.

"Boy, you know what time it is?"

"Nah, B, but you already know I was grindin' all night, so a nigga is tired."

"Yeah, I guess so. I was tryin'a see you today," she whined.

"Lemme get a few hours of shut-eye. Then we can chill. Did yo' mom say it was cool?"

"I ain't ask her. I told her I was going to the mall with Trish."

"That'll work. A'ight, babe." I hung the phone up and put it back on the table.

"Ha-ha," I chuckled to myself. I rolled back over and thought back on the day that I met her.

After watching the video that Mama left, I knew I had to act fast. It was easy for me to find the address. I spent many days scoping out the scene while trying to figure out how I was going to get my revenge. I watched as Amaiya, yes, that was the little bitch, got in her car and left for school. I followed them and watched as she hopped out of the car and walked into Truman High School. The rest was easy.

Truman was like my old stomping ground, and I had a few homies who also attended that school. It wasn't as easy as I thought. It took me almost three weeks before she even gave me any play. At first, she pretended like she wasn't interested, but I could spot a freak a mile away, and her little ass was ready to fuck. That was then, and this is now. Amaiya Clarke was now officially my bitch. That bitch was looking for love, but for me, it was personal. Fucking her was an added bonus. What I really wanted was to fuck that little bitch while her mama watched. *Be easy. Patience,* I thought as I dozed off.

It was a little after 3:00 p.m. when I finally woke up. I felt good because that little nap really gave me life. I took a quick shower and rolled me a blunt of that Loud. I had to get my mind right before I met up with ole girl. I took a few pulls and then took a sip of some Peach Cîroc. The mixture of weed and alcohol had me feeling tipsy. I picked up my phone and dialed my bitch's number. She didn't pick up, so I hung up. That wasn't like her. Normally, she would pick up on the first ring. I called right back.

"Hello," she answered with an attitude.

"Yo, what's good? You a'ight?"

"I'm mad as hell. Trish is on punishment, so she can't go to the mall, and my mama trippin', talking 'bout she got to meet you first."

"So, what's the problem? I think it's time I meet my future mother-in-law. Don't you think?"

"I guess. It's just that I don't know if I'm ready for you to meet her. My mom's kind of crazy."

"Chill out. I promise I'll be on my best behavior."

"Aargh," she growled.

"Babe, listen, I plan on being with you forever. I know we young and shit, but I can't imagine my life without you in it."

The phone got silent for a while, and then she spoke. "Aww, bae, don't make me blush."

"Man, I'm on my grown-man shit. You my bitch, for real."

"Boy, what did I tell you about that word? I ain't no female dog. I'm a *queen*."

"Man, you know what the hell I was trying to say. Girl, you're mine. Straight up."

"All right. Do you want to meet her in an hour?"

"That's cool with me. I'll be there."

"Okay, I'll see you in a little while."

"Bet." I hung up the phone.

Shit, I spent days, probably weeks, trying to figure out how I was gonna make it up in that house, and come to find out, I didn't even have to try hard. I jumped up off the couch, grabbed my car keys, and headed out of the door.

Chapter Twenty-three

Destiny Clarke

Amaiya was definitely feeling herself because her ass tried to pull a fast one on me. She wanted to hang with her friend, but as usual, I made the phone call to make sure that she was going with whomever she said that she was going with. Come to find out, her friend was on punishment and was not going anywhere.

"Why did you lie?"

"Ma, what you talkin' 'bout now?"

"Amaiya, I just spoke to Trish's mother. She's grounded and is not going to the mall with you," I said.

"Why did you go behind me? I am *not* a little girl anymore," she yelled.

I looked at her like she had lost her goddamn mind. "Lower your effing voice before I do it for you. I don't know how your friends talk to *their* mamas, but in here, you *will* respect me. You hear me, little girl? Now, let's try this again. Where are you going and with whom?"

"I wanted to go to the mall with José, but I knew that if I told you that, you would trip out."

"So your ass was just goin' lie to me? When did you start lying to me? I taught you better than that. I thought we had a bond where you could come to me. I don't have an issue with this boy, but before you start going anywhere with him, I need to meet him. It's too dangerous out in these streets."

"Ma, c'mon," she whined.

"I'm so serious, Amaiya. If you want to continue seeing this boy, I need to meet him and possibly his parents."

She looked at me like I was talking in a foreign language. I was done saying what I had to say. I turned around and walked out of her room.

I wasn't feeling that lying shit, especially over simple shit. If she didn't know, her ass would learn fast that I was *not* one to play with.

Josiah Clarke

I turned the music up loud. "Kept It Too Real" by Plies blasted through the speakers. I was a street nigga who believed in an eye for an eye. I was gonna get my revenge at any cost necessary. I chilled with my niggas on the corner of 225th and White Plains Road for a minute. Finally, I checked the time and realized that it was ten to five. I gave them daps and bounced.

"Text me your address," I told Amaiya before I clicked *end* on the phone.

I glanced at the address and then pulled off. I noticed that she lived in the country. It wasn't no biggie. Thirty-five minutes later, I pulled up in front of a mini-mansion.

A rush of jealousy came over me. I shook the feeling real fast and put Visine in my eyes to hide the fact that I was high. Then I put on a dab of oil to mask the smell of weed. Finally, I got out of the car and walked toward the door. The door opened slowly. I thought that Amaiya would be at the door, but instead, it was an older woman who looked like her twin. I stood there, frozen for a second. I tried to find the words to say "Hello," but it was like my tongue was tied up.

"Hello. You must be José?" I almost asked who the fuck José was, but then I quickly remembered that José was the name I had given Amaiya.

"Yes, that's me. You must be Mrs. Clarke."

"Well, I'm divorced, so you can call me Destiny. Come on in."

I followed that bitch inside, and she locked the door behind us.

"Hey," Amaiya said.

"Hey." I smiled at her.

"Come on in and sit down. Dinner is almost ready."

I followed both those bitches into the dining room and noticed that Amaiya was acting nervous. I figured that was because she was around her mother. The truth is, I wasn't really hungry, but I had to play the role. Besides, I didn't want to raise any suspicions. I sat beside Amaiya and across from the bitch that had caused my mother's death, and as I stared into her eyes, I plotted out ways to kill her. I glanced at the knife that was beside the roast beef and thought about sticking it in her throat. Nah, I quickly changed my mind. I didn't want a bloody situation, plus the timing wasn't right. *The hardest part was getting in here. From this point on, it should be a piece of cake,* I thought as I took a big piece of the roast beef.

I had a feeling that the bitch wasn't feeling me. She thought I didn't pay attention to the way she screwed her face up when she thought I wasn't looking. I was happy when dinner was finally over. For a minute, I thought I was gonna snap on that bitch, but I kept it cool.

"It was nice meeting you, José. Let me ask you a question. Are you from around here?"

"Nah, we're from Queens. We moved to the Bronx a few months ago."

"You and your family?"

"No, ma'am, just my mom and me."

"I see. Maybe next time, we can invite your mom over for dinner."

"That's very thoughtful of you, ma'am, but my mom passed last year."

"Oh, I'm sorry to hear that."

Chapter Twenty-four

Destiny Clarke

There was something about this José boy that I didn't like. From the minute he stepped foot in my house, I smelled trouble. I dismissed it at first, but that feeling stayed with me the entire time he was here. I sensed that he was bad news. I didn't say much because I didn't want to anger my daughter. The way that she looked at him made me aware that she was falling fast and deep.

After dinner, Amaiya and José left for the mall. I really didn't like the idea, but I had to trust my daughter's judgment. Spencer was in the room lying down when I walked in.

"Hey, babe. I need to find out something."

"What you talkin' about?"

"I need you to run somebody's fingerprints, and I need the full rundown on him." He glanced at me.

"Don't look at me like that," I frowned.

"I didn't say anything. So, who is the culprit?"

"Here's the glass. His fingerprints should be on it." I passed him a glass that this José person had drunk out of. I had been careful to pick it up with a napkin and put it in a Ziploc bag.

"You sure you want to do this?"

I shot him an evil look, which indicated my response. "Got you."

Amaiya was my only child, and I needed to know if that boy was who he said he was. I didn't feel bad because Mama knows best.

Hassan Clarke

That bitch-ass nigga that I called my lawyer kept playing with me. Every motion that I suggested he file, he found some damn reason to tell me why it wasn't going to work. See, this bitch-ass nigga didn't know what the fuck he was talking about because I had gotten many niggas freed on some of those same motions.

I waited in line to call him. I was paying this nigga, and the last time I checked, *he* was working for *me*. I went to see my counselor so I could get an attorney-client phone call. Those calls were supposed to be private, but I didn't trust those motherfuckers. Ain't shit private up in the joint.

"Hello, Hass, my man. I was expecting your call."

"Listen up, bro. I sent you some mail, and you ain't responded to me. I want to know what the hell is going on. Why you ain't tryin'a take the case back in front of the judge?" I yelled into the phone.

"First, you need to calm down. We're not going to get anywhere with you yelling like that."

"Fuck that. This is *my* fucking life we're talkin' 'bout. The only place I'm tryin'a go is out of these mother-fuckin' walls."

"Hassan, you're making it hard for me to represent you."

"Nigga, listen up. You sat back and watched those crackers sentence me to some shit I told you I had nothing to do with. If you fucking ask me, I think that bitch, Destiny, fucked you real good, and in return, you sold me out."

"You are very delusional, my man. You need to get it together. If you don't, you won't be walking out of those doors anytime soon."

"Nah, nigga. Fuck you. You're fired. Now, watch *me* work. I've got this shit. Your punk ass wasn't a good lawyer any-motherfucking-way."

I slammed the phone down in that pussy-nigga's ear. I was mad as fuck. That nigga wasn't trying to help me.

On my way back to my unit, a tear fell from my eye. I was hurting deep inside. I couldn't believe that prison was where I ended up fucking with the wrong bitch.

I was up early. I wanted to be one of the first ones in the law library. Starting today, I was my own fucking lawyer. I was gonna file my appeals and get my black ass out of this hellhole.

As soon as they opened the door, I pranced inside and jumped on the law library computer. I was gonna file the motion that was related to my charges. The most difficult charge was the attempted murder on that bitch. The other two, I knew they didn't have any evidence on me. I also knew that I pled out, so it was gonna be a struggle to get out of those charges. Nonetheless, it wasn't impossible. When I was in the free world practicing law, I had seen plenty of niggas make it home after being sentenced to life. Shit, I was determined to be one of those niggas.

I logged on and then put my skills to work. After all, I was Hassan Clarke, the attorney that can make the impossible possible.

Josiah Clarke

Instead of taking Amaiya to the mall like I told that bitch I would, I decided to take her to the crib.

"Where we going?" she asked when I turned off of White Plains Road.

"I thought you wanted to come chill wit' yo' nigga for a little while?"

"Uh . . . I do, but my mom thinks we're going to the mall."

"Listen, babe, your mother doesn't have to know what we're doing. I'm your man, and I will take good care of you." I reached over and rubbed her hand.

"What if she calls me? What do I tell her?"

She was starting to piss me off with all of that little girl shit. "Listen, if you don't want to be my bitch, just let me know so I can drop your ass off back at your house, and you can be that little girl your mama wants you to be," I snapped.

"Don't talk to me like that. I ain't no little girl. I just didn't want to get grounded."

"You're right, and I'm sorry. I just got a little upset because I want to spend some time with you. I want to hold you and let you know how much I love you." I rubbed her hand, trying to get her to relax a little.

"So, do you want to go to the mall, or do you want to come chill with me for a little while? I'll get you home before it gets late."

"No, we can go to your house."

I let out a long sigh. I had no idea how much longer I was going to be able to play the role of the doting boyfriend.

I sensed her uneasiness once we got to my door.

"You ain't got nothing to be scared of. I ain't goin' hurt you." I put my arm around her as I pushed the door open.

I then closed the door behind us. "Sit down, babe. I've got to piss real quick."

I glanced back at her as she sat down on the sofa. That little bitch had no idea what I had in store for her and her mother. *Easy, not just yet,* I reminded myself.

"Do you want anything to drink?"

"Yes, some juice."

"Juice? Ha-ha. I only have liquor. Come on, just a sip. I promise you'll feel relaxed."

I handed her a small glass of the drink I made her while I was in the kitchen.

"If you say so. Don't you try anything, boy." She laughed and poked me.

"Girl, you're tripping." I smiled at her.

I watched as she took the first sip and made an ugly face.

"You wuss, drink some more," I teased her.

She took a few more gulps, and soon, the glass was empty. I took the glass out of her hand and walked back into my small kitchen.

I watched as she seductively looked at me. That was my cue to go in for the kill. I started kissing her, and she started kissing me back. I wasted no time and started rubbing on her breasts.

"Bae, stop. No, I don't think . . ."

"Shhh. Relax. Daddy's got you." I stripped off her clothes and started sucking on her breasts.

"Oh, bae. I can't," she moaned. I continued kissing her passionately. I decided not to waste any more time. I pulled out a condom, put it on my erect dick, parted her legs, and slid inside of her moist pussy.

"*Aargh,*" I yelled out as I ripped through her young, tight pussy.

"Stop it. It hurts," she barely managed to say.

I paid her no mind. Instead, I continued to hit those walls. I won't lie. The pussy was so tight that it sent chills through my body. I held her close to me while I tore that pussy up. The enjoyment didn't last long, though. Images of my dead mother invaded my mind. I started to grind harder and harder. I couldn't control myself. I wanted to hurt that little bitch the same way I was hurting inside.

"Stop! You are hurting me. Noooo!" Her cries interrupted my actions. I looked at her and saw the look of desperation on her face. I snapped out of it fast. Now wasn't the right time. The police would be all over me if anything happened to her right now.

"I'm sorry, boo. I don't know what happened. I'm so sorry." I held her tightly as she sobbed. I used all my might and mustered up some tears also.

"Babe, I'm so sorry. I love you so much. I just got carried away," I bawled.

"Oh my God. What time is it? My mom's gonna kill me." I could tell that the drink was wearing off. "What did you do? Did you put something in my drink?"

"What the fuck you mean? What kind of dude do you think I am? You think I have to drug you to fuck you? Man, you have no idea how many bitches try to throw pussy at me daily. I turn that shit down because I love you." I was visibly upset.

"I'm so sorry. I can't believe we had sex. I just wasn't ready."

"There you go again, acting like a little girl. You have a man now, and fucking is normal between couples. The bottom line is, if you ain't fucking me, someone else will. Get dressed so we can go."

"Oh my God. I'm bleeding," she yelled, showing me the blood on her fingers.

"Maybe it's because you were a virgin. You can wash up in my bathroom." I wasn't trying to be mean, but, shit, the bitch was acting like it was the end of the world.

I was ready to get this bitch out of my place. I had some planning to do, but I had to be careful not to get caught. Prison wasn't on my to-do list. At least not now anyway.

Destiny Clarke

It was getting dark, and Amaiya still hadn't walked her behind through the door. I called her phone a few times, and it just went to the voicemail. My nerves were on edge, although I kept trying to tell myself that I was overreacting. She was no longer a little girl, and in another few months, she would be eighteen and off to college.

I walked downstairs and poured myself a glass of wine to relax my nerves. Then I began to pace back and forth. This was her first time out of the house after dark without me. I heard my phone ringing upstairs. I dashed up there, hoping that it was her ass calling me. I was disappointed when I looked at the caller ID and realized that it was Mama.

"Hello," I answered with a little more attitude than I'd intended.

"Well, damn, you all right?"

"No, not really. I'm worried about Amaiya."

"What you mean? Did something happen?"

"She went on a date with her boyfriend, and she was supposed to be back, but she isn't. I've been calling her phone and no answer."

"Des, you need to calm down. You've had that poor child locked up in the house all these years, and she just got a little bit of freedom. Amaiya is a good girl, and you need to ease up a little on her."

"Are you serious? Not the sergeant that made sure I was in the house by seven *every* night. She's my baby, and I don't want anything to happen to her."

"Times have changed. Amaiya is a lot smarter than you give her credit for. Now, stop worrying about her before you get sick. You know how that sickness is. You start worrying, and you start breaking out," she warned.

"You're right, Mama . . ." Before I could finish my sentence, I heard the door opening. I hung the phone up without saying bye and dashed down the stairs.

Amaiya walked through the door. I waited for her to lock it, and then I spoke.

"Where in the hell have you been? I've been worried sick about you all damn evening."

"Damn, Ma, we were at the mall. I lost track of time. I'm sorry."

"Sorry, my ass. Have you been drinking? You smell like alcohol."

"No, I wasn't drinking. Ma, you're trippin'."

I looked into her eyes and sensed that something wasn't right. I took a step toward her and grabbed her arm.

"What the hell were you doing then? You look tired like you were sleeping."

"Ma, you're hurting me. Let go. You need to stop acting so overprotective. I'm not a little girl anymore, so stop treating me like one," she said with an attitude.

"You listen to me, little girl. Don't you raise your voice at me ever again in my house. Just because you're smelling yourself, it doesn't give you the right to talk to me like that. Let this be your first and last warning," I snapped.

"Why are you acting like this? Ever since you and Dad broke up, you've been nothing but angry. It's like you blame me for what he did to you," she cried.

"I'm not going to allow you to turn this around on me. This is *not* about your father. This is about *you*, little girl. You're not going to disrespect me, and you damn sure ain't gonna run up in here all hours of the night. So I suggest that you let that little boyfriend of yours know that."

"I'm not you, and José is nothing like Daddy. He doesn't call me names or disrespect me with other chicks."

I walked away from her and headed into the kitchen. I wasn't no fool. She *had* been drinking, and even though I didn't have any proof, I had a feeling she was out fooling around with that boy. I knew from the minute I laid eyes on him that he was bad news. I needed Spencer to hurry up and let me know what he had found out, if anything.

***

That night, I couldn't fall asleep for anything. The situation between Amaiya and me rested heavily on my mind. I loved my child, and I wanted her to be happy, but I wasn't going to sit back and watch her get caught up with a street dude. He didn't look like he had a job or even a high school diploma. If he thought that he was going to knock up my baby with his old bum ass, he needed to rethink that because it wasn't gonna happen. Not over my dead body.

"Babe, you good? You were tossing and turning all night long."

I sat up and faced him. "Spencer, Amaiya didn't come in 'til late last night, and when she did, I smelled alcohol on her breath. I don't trust that boy with her."

"Babe, you're worrying yourself too much. You have to trust her, you know?"

"I trust her. It's *him* I don't trust. I know how these little niggas are."

"I'll go ahead and run his prints as soon as I go to the office, and I'll talk to my partner down at the station to see if he has any history of breaking the law. That should put your worries to rest."

"Thank you." I rubbed his hand.

"While you're up, we have a wedding to plan, lady." He poked me in the side.

"I know we do. I plan to get a wedding planner this week," I sighed. "I can't believe I'm trying to walk down the aisle for a second time. I had sworn that I wasn't doing that shit anymore."

"Well, I'm happy you decided to give a nigga a chance. I love you, woman, and I will protect you until I take my last breath."

I loved it when he spoke to me like that, and 90 percent of me believed him. However, that 10 percent kept reminding me that he was a man, and they could not be trusted. I didn't say anything because I vowed not to let my doubts and insecurities fuck up my relationship with him. I was willing to give him a chance, but at the first sign of trouble, I swear, I was going to get rid of his ass.

Chapter Twenty-five

Hassan Clarke

I filed an ineffective assistance of counsel appeal. The basis of that motion was that my attorney was so incompetent that he essentially denied my Sixth-Amendment right to a fair trial. This occurs almost exclusively in criminal defense cases, and the standard for the appeal is very high—courts are extremely deferential to the competency of attorneys and maintain a strong presumption that the lawyer's assistance was within professional limits. But that doesn't apply to me because that fuck nigga was bullshit. As I thought about it, I thought he just decided to defend me so he could help bring me down. Now that I was out of the way, his law firm was doing great.

Also, they didn't have any evidence against me. I knew for a fact that I was nowhere near Imani's apartment when she was killed. I remembered where I was when she was killed. I was determined to prove to the court that Destiny had set me up. This was my only chance to get out of prison. Now, on that statement about Corey, shit, I was drunk when they said I confessed. They would have to prove that my desperate ex-girlfriend drugged me. I intended to show the court that either Destiny had set me up by herself, or they both were in cahoots, and Destiny double-crossed Imani.

***

Man, I was mad as hell. It was my day to do commissary, and that bitch, Tanya, still hadn't put money on my book. I should've followed my mind and not given that bitch my money to hold on to. I should've given it all to my mama. I tried to call that ho last night, and she just answered the phone and hung up without accepting the call. I was furious. That shit had never happened before, and that had me thinking that the ho had another nigga at her house. That white bitch knew better than to play with me. I was giving her ass another hour, and I swear that money better be on my damn account.

It was minutes to three, and my account still was on empty. I walked into the phone booth and dialed that ho's number with the last few dollars that I had left on the phone account.

"Hello," she answered.

"Yo, where the fuck you been? I've been tryin'a reach you. You know today is Wednesday, and I need to go shopping."

"I was busy, and why didn't you go shopping then?" she replied sarcastically.

"Bitch, with what money? Did you forget that you have my damn money, so you can pay my lawyer and put money on my books?" I yelled.

"That money is gone. I paid your lawyer and used the rest to take care of your fucking child. You remember him, *don't* you?"

"Over fifty grand is gone? Bitch, what the fuck you mean? I swear, you better have my damn money. I swear."

"What you goin' do, honey? I just told you that money is gone. As a matter of fact, you need to get one of those prison jobs in the kitchen or something. I'm gonna need child support soon."

"Tanya, bitch, stop trying me. You better bring yo' ass up here Saturday, and that money better be on my books this evening before count time." I slammed the phone in that ho's ear.

I couldn't believe what I just heard. See, that bitch knew that if I were out there, she wouldn't be talking to me in that manner. Then the bitch's gonna tell me that she used my money to take care of that little bastard? Truthfully, I don't give a damn if that motherfucker ate or not. Shit, that bitch wanted him, so she better find a way to feed him. I was so aggravated that my head started to hurt. I walked out of the phone booth, feeling lost as I got back to my cube and jumped in my bed.

I was feeling weak and nauseated. I knew I hadn't been taking my damn pills, and I needed to. I couldn't risk losing my life before I got out and paid those bitches back.

Josiah Clarke

I was tired of playing that "in love" shit with that little bitch. What made me angrier was when she told me that her bitch-ass mother didn't want her to hang out. I knew then that the bitch wasn't really digging me, and it was a front when she acted like she liked me when I was there for dinner that day.

A lot of shit has been bugging me lately. That nigga, Hassan, had been on my mind heavily too. Last I heard, that nigga was somewhere upstate. I tried to ask Amaiya 'bout her pops, but she barely even talked about him. I realized that if I needed to get to that dude, I was going to have to do it on my own. I knew that my ex-grandma and auntie would know exactly where he was. I didn't fuck with them after I found out that nigga wasn't my daddy, but I saw his mama the other day. That old bitch still referred to me as her grandbaby, so I knew she wouldn't hesitate to give me info on that nigga.

I got the info I needed to reach out to that nigga, so I drove to the store and bought me a notepad, a pen, envelope, and a stamp. I needed to write this fuck nigga a letter.

After writing each other for over a month, he finally agreed to put me on his visitation list. I was feeling all kinds of emotions when I got on the highway. My final destination was Clinton Correctional Facility, which was a five-hour drive. I smoked a blunt before I left the house. I was trying to ease the anxiety that I felt because I knew I couldn't act a fool up in these people's shit.

I parked and emptied my pockets. I had to make sure I didn't have any illegal shit up in them. Then I straightened up my clothes and walked into the gates of one of the biggest prisons in New York State.

I felt violated when the fucking officer asked to pat me down. Shit, I thought about leaving, but I'd waited too long, and the visit needed to be done. Finally, I was cleared and told to go into the waiting area, where I took a seat.

I held my head down for a minute, trying to get my emotions under control. I didn't see it when he approached me. "Hey, man. What's good?" His voice startled me.

I stood up and gave that nigga dap. I knew that if I wanted to get anywhere, I'd have to act at least cordially toward the fuck nigga.

"I'm good. How are you?"

"Living, I guess," he chuckled.

"Well, shit, you're looking sick and shit, like you ain't eating."

"Man, that's what I try to tell these people. The fucking food they feed us ain't shit to get us full at all."

"Anyway, you know that I wanted to see you face-to-face 'cause I felt like it's because of you that my moms is dead." I choked up, saying those words.

"Damn, Josiah, I thought you just wanted to see how your old man was doing?"

"My old man . . . I'm confused. The last time we spoke, I called you dad, and you went off on me, telling me that nigga, Corey, was my dad and not you. So, how you goin' even say that shit? You ain't my pops. You just the nigga that was fuckin' my moms."

"Josiah, I was hurting, and I didn't know how to deal with that shit. Your entire life, I thought you were mine. You were my little nigga, and then, out of the blue, some nigga that was my right hand was claiming he was your father. I was devastated. Put yourself in my shoes. How would *you* feel?"

"I ain't got no feelings about the shit. The only feeling I have is for my mom, who is dead and buried in some cold-ass grave. You, that bitch, and her fucking daughter are all alive."

"Son, like I told you in my letters, I'm sorry about the death of your mother. I loved her, and I'm also hurting."

"You never loved her. I used to hear you calling her all kinds of names. I saw the bruises. She loved you, and you dogged her out. You're not a man. You're a straight-up pussy nigga."

"Yo, she's dead. Get over that shit. You say you want us to move forward. Now, let's drop the past and move forward, son."

I moved over closer to him so no one else would hear what I was saying. "Bro, you not hearing me. There is *no* moving on until you, that bitch, and her daughter are all six feet deep. Only then will I be able to move on."

"You threatening me, little nigga? 'Cause I 'ont do well with threats. I'm telling you now, don't you ever threaten my life again unless you're ready to join your dead mama and daddy."

"Ha-ha. Make sure you read the papers daily." I winked at the nigga and got up to leave. He also got up and hurriedly walked up behind me.

"We *will* meet again, little nigga. I promise you that," he yelled.

I didn't respond. I kept walking until I heard the door slam behind me. His empty threats didn't faze me. He was always screaming "little nigga," but he had no idea that *this* little nigga had nothing but bloody murder in his heart.

Chapter Twenty-six

Destiny Clarke

The wedding was only three months away, and although I was one of the happiest women walking these streets, deep down, I was going through some shit. For one, that bitch's death kept tugging at my soul. Sometimes, at night, I would jump up out of my sleep because I kept seeing her before me. That bitch kept laughing at me like shit was funny. I wished I could kill that bitch again so she would leave me the hell alone. I wished there was someone that I could talk to about it, but I was no fool. I would never—and I mean never—confess to no shit like that, not even to my mama, and I knew she wouldn't turn on me.

I was up bright and early. I had a doctor's appointment. Lately, I'd been feeling weaker and weaker. I tried to eat well and exercise, but I still felt bad. I called my doctor the other day, and he did some blood work on me. Going into his office made me nervous. I knew I already had HIV and herpes, but I was praying that with the help of God and my medication, I wouldn't have full-blown AIDS.

As I walked into the doctor's office, I felt a tear drop down my face. I quickly wiped it away and walked up to the receptionist's desk.

"Good morning, Miss Clarke. How are you this morning?"

I wanted to say, "Bitch, how the fuck do you think I'm doing?" but I didn't. Instead, I smiled and said, "I'm good."

"Great. Doctor Chezc will be right with you. Go ahead and sign in for me, and then, take a seat in the waiting area, please."

"Thanks."

I sat there in silence, and for the first time, my mind was blank. I pushed all thoughts out of my mind. I didn't want to worry about things that I knew I had no control over.

"Miss Clarke, Doctor Chezc is ready to see you."

I nodded at her, walked into the doctor's office, and immediately took a seat.

"Good morning. Let's start by you telling me how you are feeling today."

"Well, it's the same old, same old. Nausea and fatigue."

"Have you been taking your medication daily?"

"Faithfully. Doc, let's skip all the bullshit. I know my tests are back. So, please, let me know if I need to worry."

"Well, Miss Clarke, you are correct. Your tests *are* back." He sat down and grabbed a folder. "It seems as if your immune system is badly damaged, and you have become vulnerable to infections and infection-related cancers called opportunistic infections. The number of your CD4 cells fell below 200 cells per cubic millimeter of blood. In other words, the herpes and pneumonia that kept attacking you are opportunistic infections, which resulted in your body breaking down, and the HIV has now progressed to AIDS."

"Noooo! I thought you told me that the medications were working, and I was doing okay," I yelled out in between my cries.

Doc ran over to me and hugged me tightly. "I'm so sorry. I was hoping that your T-cells would go up, but instead, they kept going down while the virus level kept going up."

I didn't say a word. Fuck that. I couldn't utter a word. I just sat there with my head on his shoulder, crying my soul out. He held me as he tried his best to comfort me. My body was there, but my mind was off in the distance. It was on that bastard who destroyed my life.

After what seemed like an eternity, I finally got myself under control. I used my shirt and wiped away the tears. Doc took my hands and then spoke. "It's not the end of the world. You are going to fight. I'm going to provide the best possible treatment available, and you're going to fight this. Do you hear me?"

I wanted to respond, but I had too much anger and hatred in me to answer him civilly. I just nodded at him as he fed me the shit that they taught him in medical school.

"Okay, let's get down to business. The goal is to get you healthy. You can still benefit from starting antiretroviral therapy. Our goal is to get you some better treatments and prevention of opportunistic infections. I've had patients that live a healthy life although they have AIDS."

I was ready to go. Just a month ago, that nigga told me that I was doing well under the circumstances. Now he was telling me that I had full-blown AIDS. I was a nurse. I knew what the fuck that meant, no matter how the fuck he dressed it up. The bottom line was that my days on this earth were numbered.

After he sat there trying to counsel me, I decided that it was time for me to go. He wrote me some prescriptions, and I walked out of his office with a heavy heart. I jumped in my car and pulled off, letting the tires squeak. I just wanted to get home and crawl in my bed.

God, why is life so unfair? I know people who lived with HIV for many years without getting AIDS, so why the fuck did my shit have to move along so quickly? I swear I don't understand that shit at all.

I entered the house, and a delicious smell hit my nose. As I walked toward the kitchen, I realized that it was Spencer cooking. I cleared my throat so he would know I was there.

"Hey, there, beautiful. I was trying to surprise you by making lunch."

"I see. What are you cooking? Whatever it is smells really good."

"I put a roast in this morning after you left. I also have some Jasmine rice on the stove cooking."

"Oh, you shouldn't have." I tried my best to smile.

"What do you mean? You're always cooking and making sure we're well taken care of. It's only fair for me to return the gesture every once in a while."

I was feeling weak, so I sat on the chair. I used everything in me not to break down. I stared at the man who wanted to give me the world but couldn't give me the only thing that I needed. Life. I trembled inside as I thought about what I was about to lose.

"Is Amaiya up?"

"I haven't seen her."

"Oh, okay. She might be sleeping in late."

"Are you gonna eat something?"

"Nah, I'm not really hungry," I sulked.

"Babe, talk to me. What's been going on with you lately? Is it the wedding? 'Cause you know we can wait."

"Why would you say that? You don't think I want to marry you?"

"Destiny, slow your roll. That's not what I'm implying. I've noticed you've been under a lot of stress lately," he said, sounding annoyed.

I wanted to yell at his ass because, shit, nobody had an idea about the hell I was going through. I was tired of people pacifying me and telling me that it was gonna be okay. Hell no, it was *not* gonna be all right. My life was falling apart right in front of me.

"I mean, I'm HIV-positive—better yet, scratch that. I just found out I have full-blown AIDS. So, am I supposed to walk around here all happy and shit? I try my best every damn day to please everybody in my life. There are fucking days when I am too weak to get out of bed, but I pop these damn pills, swallow my fucking pride, and get up, wash, cook, clean, and do my duties as a woman and a mother without complaining," I cried out.

"Babe, come here." He rushed to my side of the table.

"Don't touch me. Don't sit here and pretend like you know what the hell I'm going through."

He put his hands up in the air. "You know what? You're right. I have no idea what you're going through, but I've told you numerous times that you don't have to take this walk alone. You need to stop trying to be this superwoman and let me help you. Ha-ha. I swear I know what you're doing. You're trying to push me away, woman, but I tell you what. I ain't going no-damn-where.

I'm here to stay, whether or not you like it. So you need to figure out a way to deal with it."

He threw the dishcloth down on the counter and rushed out of the kitchen. I sat there with a dumb-ass look on my face. I wanted to get up and run after him, but I was feeling too weak, and furthermore, I needed some time to myself. Spencer definitely wasn't the kind of nigga that I wanted to go off on.

I continued sitting at the table with my head on the counter and let the tears flow freely. The pain was so deep that I felt like it was a sharp knife slicing me inside.

I dozed off, sitting in that same position. The slamming of the front door awakened me. I jumped up and walked out of the kitchen and noticed Amaiya walking in.

"Where are you coming from? I thought you were in your room."

"Damn, Ma, do I have to tell you every time I come and go? I'm not a baby anymore, so please stop treating me like I'm two or something." She tried to walk past me.

"I'm going to tell you this for the last goddamn time. This is *my* shit, and you *will* respect my rules while you're still living here. As a matter of fact, give me my damn house keys."

"Here you go." She handed the keys to me. "You know you can't lock me down forever, right? Whatever issues you have, you need to deal with them and stop taking it out on me."

"Little girl, go to your room and stay there." I walked off on her ass. I was not playing with her ass, but my body wouldn't physically let me address her the right way. There was no way her ass was going to keep talking to me like she was crazy. I needed to nip that shit in the bud before that heifer felt like she could address me any old way.

Josiah Clarke

I stood by my bed, staring at my mama's picture. Her face was the last thing I looked at when I went to bed at night, and the first one I looked at when I woke up. It was about that time to visit her graveside again.

I took a quick shower, smoked a blunt, then left and was on my way to see my mama. She was buried at Woodlawn Cemetery in the Bronx. This was only my second time going to visit her. It wasn't because I didn't want to. It was just too fucking painful for me.

I parked and got out of the car with the rest of the blunt in my hand. I searched through the graves until I reached hers. Then I sat on the ground and just stared off into space.

"Mama, guess who this is. Your baby boy," I laughed. I remained quiet for a few. In my crazy mind, I was waiting to hear her respond to me or run one of her whack-ass jokes. That didn't happen, and it only angered me. I started sniffling, trying my damnedest not to shed a tear, but I wasn't strong enough. Before I knew it, I was lying on top of the grave, hugging it and bawling my eyes out.

"Mama, I'm so sorry I didn't treat you like the queen that you were. I'm sorry, Mama." My voice cracked. I took out my lighter and lit the blunt again, took a few drags, and then continued bawling. "Mama, your baby boy has some good news, though. I plan on paying back all those motherfuckas that did you wrong. I know that bitch killed you over that nigga. That's cool, though 'cause I got her and that little bitch. I promise I'ma make you proud. I promise." I bawled some more because I wanted my mama. I had nobody in this world. I held my head as a sharp pain ripped through my brain. "I can't live without you, Mama. I can't. I swear, I need to be with you." I continued talking to her. I just needed her to say something back.

Finally, I was all cried out, and all of my weed was gone. I knelt so I could rub my hand across her name on the stone. Then I kissed the grave. "I love you, Mama. I fucking love you." I got up and walked off, still shedding tears for my mama.

I walked back to my car and jumped in. I was careful not to speed out of there because the Bronx River Parkway always parked the Bronx police. Today wasn't the fucking day because I was riding dirty. I had crack and my burner on me. I won't lie. I was on a mission, and nobody, including NYPD, was going to stand in my way.

I picked up the phone and dialed Amaiya's number.

"Hey, bae." Her sexy voice filled my ear.

"Whaddup, ma? What you doing?"

"Nothing. My mama's trippin' again. She done took my damn house key, and now I'm grounded."

"Damn, that's fucked up. I'm sorry that you have to go through such drama, love. What happened to your dad? Can't you stay with him for a while?"

"Um, no. That nigga is in prison for some shit. I think he was cheating on my mama, then turned around and killed the woman."

"Damn, bae. I'm so sorry. You've had such a rough life. I promise you, I'm gonna get you out of all this shit."

"I don't know how much more of this I can bear anymore. I can't wait to graduate from school so that I can get the hell out of her house. Ugh, I'm about to lose my mind," she yelled into the phone.

"Baby, calm down. I told you, I got you. Just humble yourself. I'm about to get you out of this shit."

"Okay, you better hurry up, though, 'cause I feel like running away."

"Listen, boo, ain't nothing or nobody that can stop me from seeing you. Believe that. Now, dry them motherfucking tears. The only time you need to be crying is when I'm pumping this dick inside of you."

"Shut up, boy," she laughed.

"That's more like it, baby girl. Now, lemme hit you back later. Got some shit to handle in these streets."

"Love you."

"Love you too, baby girl."

It was not even funny how dumb that little bitch was. In another life, I could've easily made her my bitch. I quickly blocked her out of my mind and went back to plotting. The time had come for me to implement my next move.

Hassan Clarke

Who said that God wasn't looking out for a black-ass nigga like me? I got a letter from the court, notifying me that my petition was granted for an appeal. I wasn't the most religious-ass nigga, but fuck that. I got down on my knees and prayed to the big man. I knew it didn't mean that I was going home, but, shit, it damn sure meant that I had a chance.

I immediately jumped on the phone to call Tanya.

"Hello." She answered the phone as if she were tired.

"Damn, why every time I call you, you sound so freaking depressed? Fuck, you acting like *you* the one that's in prison."

"Hassan, you ever thought that it was because you called that I'm depressed?"

"What the fuck you mean, baby?"

"Hassan, I'm so tired of pretending like shit is cool between us. You're locked the fuck up, so that means you can't fuck me. Your ass is broke, so that means you can't support me. So, please tell me why you think that I'm going to stick around? Is it because I'm a white bitch, and you think I'm stupid? Because I've got news for you. I am *far* from stupid. I loved you when you were out here, but you didn't want me. You wanted those black, nappyheaded bitches. Well, guess what? Those bitches are not worried about your ass right now. Shit, that wife of yours might be fucking and sucking that nigga I saw her with one day when I drove past the house. Yes, sorry to inform you, but she has another nigga living up in your shit—"

"Bitch, shut up talking stupid. I know that you're hurting because I'm not there to take care of you and my little man. Don't you worry, though. I called to let you know that I—"

"Hello, hello, Tanya, you still there, bae?" I was tripping because the bitch was gone. All I heard was a dial tone in my ear. I knew that my time wasn't up, and she did that bullshit. I looked at the other nigga on the phone. He was a nigga that I didn't fuck with. He looked at me, smiling.

"Nigga, what the fuck you looking at?"

"Hold on, bae. Lemme holla at this fuck nigga real quick. Nigga, you mad 'cause yo' bitch hung up on you.

Shit, that other nigga must be breaking her back right now, and she couldn't take the pressure, so she hung up," he laughed.

I balled my fists up and then stepped toward him. Something held me back, though. I still had the letter in my hand. There was no way that I was going to risk my freedom behind that fuck nigga who had no chance of ever seeing the streets again. Instead, I smiled at him. "You got that, my nigga." I turned and walked out of the phone booth.

I got in my bed tight at the way that bitch had just carried me on the phone. I grabbed my notepad to write that white bitch a letter, but my mind drew a blank. Angry, I threw the notepad down and jumped back out of bed. Quickly, I grabbed my radio and jetted out of the unit. The only way to get rid of some of that frustration was to run the track.

Destiny Clarke

I wasn't feeling too good, but today was the day that Mama and I chose to get my wedding dress. Time was flying by, and I needed to get things in order. I pulled up at my mama's address and honked the horn. Knowing her, I knew she was ready. That woman was always on time and would fuss at someone if they were not.

I watched as she locked the garage and walked toward my car. I smiled every time I saw that lady. The way she walked with elegance was admirable. She could be going through the worst storm in her life, but you would never see her frowning, and she always walked with her shoulders straight.

"For the first time in life, my child is on time," she joked.

"Whatever, lady. Put your seat belt on," I laughed.

"How you feeling today, baby?"

"Same old, same old, but you know I have to keep on pushing through."

"I always tell you, God ain't goin' give you more than you can bear."

I rolled my eyes. *I hope this day ain't goin' be spent on her preaching to me,* I thought.

"Have you thought about getting baptized? I think it would be a great idea to have a church that you go to regularly and have the support of the sisters in the church."

"Mama, I told you that I'm not ready for that, and, please, can you drop it right now? I'm not feeling too good."

"All right, I hope you not goin' be ready when it's too late."

I breathed a sigh of relief. *Lady, shut the hell up already.* The rest of the ride to the bridal shop on White Plains Road was in silence. I glanced over at her, and she had her eyes closed. I hated to be so hard on her, especially when I knew that she meant well. I just wasn't in the mood to have anyone preaching to me. One day I'd get there, and I'd have a relationship with God, but just not right now.

I was surprised that I found the perfect Vera Wang dress. The minute I laid eyes on it, I knew that was the dress I wanted to walk down the aisle in. I got my measurements done, and we left.

"A'ight, Mama. Now that we have that out of the way, how about I treat you to lunch?"

"But, of course. Let's go." She burst out laughing.

We decided to grab some food from this nice Chinese restaurant on Gun Hill Road. *I sure miss living down this way,* I thought.

"Baby, you're looking thinner than the last time I saw you. You sure you're eating?"

"Yes, Mama. I'm eating and taking my medicine."

"When was the last time you went to the doctor?"

"Matter of fact, I just went to the doctor a few days ago." I hung my head down.

"And what they say?" She reached over to touch my hand.

"I was . . ." I paused. "I was waiting to tell you. Mama, the doctor said that I have full-blown AIDS now." I fought the tears.

She tightened her grip on my hand. The silence between us was killing me.

"Baby, you've been a fighter since the day you came out of the womb. I wasn't there, but the social worker told me how you were treated as a baby, so I know that fighting is normal for you. This time is no different. You're goin' fight—*we're* goin' fight. I don't care what man says. God has the final say over this. You may not pray, but trust me, your mama prays enough for both of us, and I promise you, you goin' to make it. . . ." Her voice cracked.

I took a tissue out of my pocketbook and used it to dab at my eyes. I tried not to cry because my face was dolled up, and I didn't want to smear my makeup.

"Here you go, ladies." The waitress interrupted us.

That was great because I was seconds away from crying a river in that restaurant. I looked at Mama and noticed that she'd been crying. Her wrinkles were now visible. Since I told her the news, it seemed like she had aged about twenty years. I ordered some chowder soup while she ordered rice and pepper steak. I tried to drink a few spoons of the soup, but I swear, I had no appetite. I didn't want to force myself because I knew that I would throw it back up.

After lunch, I dropped Mama off at her house. Before she got out of the car, she looked at me and smiled. All of the wrinkles I'd seen before had disappeared. "You know, you're all I've got. I can't lose you, baby girl. I just can't. Fight with everything in you. Fight." Those were the last words she said before she exited the car. I watched as she let up her garage door and walked in. Then I pulled off.

I felt tired and drained and just wanted to go home and crawl in bed. I couldn't, though, because I had a few stops to make. My phone started ringing. I looked at the screen, and I noticed that it was Spencer. *Lord, that man stays checking up on me,* I thought. I smiled and said, "Hello."

"Hey, love. Where are you? I thought you were at the house, but you're not."

"You must've forgotten. I told you that Mama and I were going gown shopping today."

"Shit, yeah. I forgot."

"You home early today? You all right?"

"Yeah, everything's cool. I'll see you when you get here."

"A'ight, babe. See you in a little while."

There was something about the sound of his voice. I wondered what was wrong. I hoped that nigga wasn't getting cold feet on me. I shook the feeling off and continued driving.

Macy's wasn't crowded, which was a great thing. I went straight to the MAC counter to get some makeup. I was a fool for good makeup and lipstick. Even though I didn't feel my best most days, I still tried to look my best on the outside. I'd been lucky not to have bumps and dry skin because of the virus. Instead, my skin was clear, and my hair was growing so fast. I remembered the doctors saying that when HIV patients took their medicine regularly, their skin was flawless to the point where you would not know they had the virus.

I paid for my items and left the mall.

I pulled into the driveway, thinking that all I needed was a hot shower, some ginger tea, and my bed. I parked, checked the mailbox, grabbed the mail, and walked into the house. I thought it was all trash, so I was about to throw the papers away when I noticed a letter from Hassan. I ripped it open, wondering how the fuck he got my new address.

My Dearest Destiny,

I hope this letter finds you in the best of health. How is my baby girl doing? Let her know her daddy loves her and would love to see her. I won't be long. I just want you to know that not a day goes by that I'm not thinking of you and the bond that we shared. I loved you from the first day I laid eyes on you, and I will continue loving you for the rest of my love. Anyway, love, I won't take up anymore of your time. I love you.

Your man forever,

Hassan

"Amaiya!" I ran upstairs, hollering.

"Amaiya!" I didn't bother to knock. I just pushed the door open.

"What are you yelling for?"

"Have you talked to yo' daddy lately?"

"Noooo, why?"

"How did he get my new address? I just got this letter in the mail." I waved the letter in the air.

"I 'ont know. Like I said, I ain't talked to him. What he saying, though?"

I gave her ass a stare down, and then I turned away and walked down the hallway. I swear that nigga just wouldn't go away. I walked into the room where Spencer was and flopped down on the bed beside him.

"What's going on? Why were you yelling?"

"This." I waved the letter at him.

"Who is that from?"

"Who do you think? That bastard won't leave me the fuck alone. And how the fuck is mail coming here from him? I never gave out my address."

"Remember, you asked the post office to transfer your mail. So, they did just that. Babe, listen to me. He's just tryin'a get under your skin. That nigga ain't got nothin' but time on his hands, so he's using that to torture you. Monday morning, you need to contact the prison and let them know that you're one of his victims, and he keeps writing to you."

"I want it all to end—this virus, the pain, him— everything. I want it all to end."

He took my hand and used his other hand to lift my chin. "Babe, I hate that you're hurting like this. If that nigga was out here, I would've buried him already, and he wouldn't be around to terrorize you. But he's in there, and I can't reach him. That angers my soul."

"I know, babe. I know." I leaned my head on his shoulder.

"Anyway, so why were you so agitated earlier when you called me?"

He looked at me. "Listen, you're already having a rough day, so that can wait."

"'That' what? What are you talking about, Spencer?"

"Well, you know you asked me to run that boy's fingerprints—"

"Yes, so what happened? Who is he?" I cut him off.

"Well, his name is not José. He had a run-in with the law last year and was fingerprinted. His name is Josiah Clarke."

"Josiah Clarke . . . Why would he lie about his name? And who is this boy?"

"I talked to my buddy down by the precinct, and he assured me that was the only run-in he had with the law."

I sat there quiet for a minute. I was buried deep in my thoughts. Why would he say his name was José when it was really Josiah? Those thoughts wouldn't leave me alone.

"Hold on a sec," I said to Spencer as I got up and exited the room.

I pushed open Amaiya's door. She was wearing her earphones, so I walked over to her and snatched them off her head.

"What are you doing?" she yelled.

"Lower your voice and shut up."

"What is it now, Ma?" She folded her arms across her chest and stared at me.

"What is José's real name?"

"Ha-ha. What do you mean by his *real* name?"

"His name is not José; it's Josiah." I threw the mug shot at her. "And since you're fooling around with him, I figured you needed to know."

She snatched up the paper and stared at it. "Where did you get this?"

"Don't worry about where I got it. The question should be, why did he lie about his name, and did you know?"

"Ma, why are you doing this? I know you 'ont want me to be with him, but to make up some stuff just to break us up is crazy."

"His name is Josiah Clarke. He has the same last name as you."

"So what? Plenty of people go wit' each other, and they have the same last name. And his name is *not* Josiah. Trust me. I would have known. The police must've messed up."

"*Really?* What do you know about him other than what he told you? Have you met his family? Little girl, stop thinking with your heart and use your brain. Do you even *know* where he lives?"

"Yes, I know where he lives," she blurted out.

"All I'm saying is, there's a reason why he's lying about who he really is, and I'm going to find out why. You are *not* allowed to see him anymore."

"You can't do that. I love him, and it doesn't matter if his name is José or Josiah. His last name is Clarke, but my daddy ain't got no other kids, so I know he ain't my brother. It's pure coincidence."

I froze when those words left her mouth.

"Ma, you a'ight? You looking at me like you just saw a ghost."

I didn't respond. I just looked at her, turned around, and walked away, slamming the door behind me.

I didn't feel like dealing with Spencer, so I walked downstairs to the kitchen. I knew I was not supposed to be drinking, but the urge was overwhelming. I opened the cabinet, grabbed a bottle of red wine, and poured myself a glass. I didn't hesitate before I gulped it down. Then I put the bottle back in the cabinet, walked into the living room, and lay down on the sofa to think.

Chapter Twenty-seven

Josiah Clarke

I was on the block doing what I did best . . . grinding.
I had to step up my game after my momma passed. I
looked around at my surroundings, but there wasn't shit
in the Bronx to do. I was planning to go out to VA with
my big cuz after all of this revenge shit was over with. I
heard there was some major paper out there. I was ready
to show those down South niggas how to get money.
Maybe I could find me one of those Southern bitches. I
heard they had a big thing for up-top niggas.

My phone started to go off. I looked at the caller ID
and saw that it was Amaiya. I pressed *ignore* and went
back to doing what I was doing. She didn't ease up,
though. She kept calling back-to-back.

"Hey, boo. I told you I was goin' be out on the block
today," I answered with an attitude.

"Man, I need to talk to you."

"Can't it wait 'til later? You know I don't like to be
distracted while I'm out here. Plus, today, them pigs are
out in full force."

"Boy, you not listening to me. My mama talkin' 'bout
José is not your real name."

"What the fuck you talkin' 'bout?" She damn sure had
my full attention now.

"I was in my room, listening to music when she came in here wit' your pic on a mug shot and talking 'bout your real name is Josiah Clarke."

"Why would she do that? Your mom's checking up on me now?" I was pissed the fuck off.

"I 'ont know what she doing. All I want to know is . . . What's your name?"

"So you feeding into that bullshit. You can't see that she's just trying to separate us? Babe, my name is José. Why would I lie to you? I love you. You my motherfucking heartbeat."

"I know that she's just trying to break us up, but why, though? You never did anything to hurt her or me."

"Babe, no disrespect to your moms, but sometimes mothers get jealous of their daughters because their love life ain't going good, or maybe your mom just wishes she had a good man like me in her life."

"Man, this is too much. I love my mom, but she needs to quit already."

"Listen, babe. Lemme get this sale real quick, and I'll call you back. I love you, yo." I quickly hung up the phone.

"Yo, my G, I'ma be out for a li'l while. Hit my phone if you need me." I gave dap to my nigga, Trey.

"A'ight, be easy, my nigga."

I walked around the corner to my car and jumped in. That bitch had upset my nerves with that bullshit news she just gave me. I wanted to know what her bitch mother was up to and what she was doing with my mug shot pic. I knew that bitch was up to something, but what it was, I had no idea.

I decided to head home. I had no more time to waste. I was ready to make my move. I only hoped that Amaiya would agree to what I was about to ask her.

Hassan Clarke

I couldn't sleep at all. Instead, I tossed and turned all night. I glanced at the clock, and it was only a quarter after three. I was leaving in the morning to go to court, so I prepared mentally to provide the best case of my life. I fucked up the first time, but that time around, I was a different person. The once cocky and arrogant Hassan Clarke was gone. I was a lot older and smarter now.

A few days ago, I had to swallow my pride and contact my old partner from the law firm. I begged him to help gather some information that I needed. I guess he felt sorry for me because he decided to help without charging me. One of the best pieces of evidence that I had was my cell phone records. At the time of Imani's death, I was nowhere near the Bronx. I wasn't there until that evening when my mother called me to tell me about her death. There was no forensic evidence that linked me to her death, nor were there any witnesses against me. As a matter of fact, the PI that we had on the case found two women who saw a woman entering Imani's apartment on the day of the murder. They couldn't remember what the woman looked like, but that was enough to put a dent in the prosecutor's case.

My goal was to get released so that I could get all of the evidence I needed against that bitch, Destiny. I promised that her ass would rot in prison for the rest of her life. I smiled to myself because I was a step closer to getting my revenge on that bitch.

***

I got to the courtroom extra early, and as usual, a bunch of niggas was crowded in the holding cell, trading stories, and most of them were just lies. Prison was definitely the place where people could pretend to be a big shot when, in reality, they were nobodies. After being in prison, I was tired of hearing the same old stories. I closed my eyes and leaned back against the wall. I started daydreaming about my freedom and the first thing I was going to do when I walked out of there.

"Clarke, let's go," the bailiff hollered and opened the cell.

I jumped up and eagerly walked out of the cell. *God, please help me in the courtroom. I promise, God, I am a changed man,* I silently prayed. The courtroom was kind of empty, but I immediately spotted mom-dukes. That was my first time seeing her in over a year. She waved at me and blew me a kiss. I smiled back at my queen. No matter what, she was always there to provide support.

Leon was already sitting down. I sat beside him. "Whaddup, man?"

"Ain't nothing. I've got everything ready to present to the court. You ready, partna?"

"Hell yeah. I've been waiting on this day for a long time now."

"All rise. The court of the Criminal Division is now in session. The Honorable Judge Morales is presiding."

"Be seated," Judge Morales commanded.

I almost pissed in my pants when I heard the judge's name. I looked up and realized that she was one of my old flings. We didn't end on good terms, so I had no idea how things were going to play out.

"Your Honor, this is first on the docket. Docket number 67721-63. The State of New York vs. Hassan Clarke."

My lawyer got up, and, boy, that nigga showed out. It was nothing like my first trial. That nigga was on point. He provided reasons why I couldn't have killed Imani and also told the court that my ex-wife, Destiny, had set me up so she could get rid of the woman that I was cheating with. In the process, she also got rid of me so that she could get my money. He provided witness statements, phone records, and he emphasized that there was no DNA evidence to link me to the crime.

On the second charge of conspiracy to commit murder, a charge that they claimed I confessed to on tape, my lawyer dug right into it by saying that I was drugged by a woman that was out to get me, and I was coaxed by her trying to frame me.

"How did I do?" he asked when he sat down.

"Man, you did damn good."

The overzealous DA interrupted my seconds of happiness. I felt like that bitch had it out for me because although the evidence was given to her office, she still persisted in trying to keep a nigga locked up. I swear, that bitch just wanted this dick.

"Your Honor, I know that Attorney Smith just gave us a whole speech on why the defendant could not have committed those murders, but the defendant tried to kill the victim a few weeks before her death. He was arrested and charged for that crime. He was angry that Miss Gibson did not want to drop the charges that would definitely cause him to lose his law license. He was also having an affair with the victim, and he was scared that she was going to tell his wife, which would have resulted in his wife leaving him and taking their daughter.

"Another reason why the defendant should not be granted a new trial is that he tried to kill his now ex-

wife. The police officer and his ex-wife both testified
to that in the previous trial. His best friend is dead, and
he was caught on tape testifying that he ordered the hit.
Your Honor, this man is a menace to society, and if you
let him out, God knows who he is going to hurt next. He
deserves to stay behind bars for the remainder of his sentence."

"Thank you, DA Martin.

"This case is not an easy one, but as a judge, I can't
get my personal feelings involved. I have to hear both
sides of the story and make a decision based on evidence.
When I walked in here today, I was ready to make a
ruling, but as I listened to both sides, I realized that I
needed more time to review the new evidence that was
presented in these motions today. I will make my ruling
in fourteen days, which is the twenty-eighth, at 9:00 a.m.
If there is nothing else, this court is adjourned."

I looked at Leon, and he had the same puzzled look
on his face. I turned around and saw the sad look on my
mama's face. I wished I could walk over and hug her, but
that was impossible. I mouthed, "I love you." Then the
bailiff cuffed me and walked me to the back.

I waited until I was in the holding cell to let everything
register. *What the fuck just happened?* I thought. I
quickly put on my lawyer hat. It wasn't bad news. I think
the judge actually believed what my lawyer was saying.
Two weeks was too fucking long, though, to wait on
those fucking crackers, but there wasn't shit that I could
really do about it.

Stress is a motherfucker that I didn't need. Those
motherfuckas knew that I had the fucking bug, and stress
wasn't good for me mentally or physically.

"All rise. The Honorable Judge Morales is presiding."

"Please be seated. Will the defendant and his attorney remain standing? I said two weeks ago that this was not an easy case. I've reviewed the evidence that the State presented in the original case. I've also thoroughly reviewed the new evidence presented to me two weeks ago. I've heard the passionate pleas of the district attorney, and I've heard the argument presented by the defense attorney on behalf of the defendant. After going through the evidence thoroughly, I am very disgusted by the way that the previous defense attorney handled this case. He didn't provide proper counsel to his client. That's my first issue with this case. Second, there is proof that Mr. Clarke was nowhere near the victim's house when the victim was murdered."

"But, Your Honor," the DA interrupted.

"No, ma'am. There are no interruptions during my ruling."

"Mr. Clarke, I'm hereby throwing out your convictions on the murder of Imani Gibson and the conspiracy to commit murder against Corey Griffin. I am also granting you a new trial on the attempted murder of Destiny Clarke. I am setting your bond at one hundred grand."

"Thank you, Your Honor," I blurted out without thinking.

"Please remain quiet, or the bailiff will remove you from the court."

"Yes, ma'am," I mumbled under my breath.

"While you're out on bond, you're not allowed to go within one hundred feet of the victim, Destiny Clarke, or her residence. You're not to break the law while you're out on bond, and if you do, your bond will be revoked immediately. Do you understand these terms, Mr. Clarke?"

"Yes, Your Honor."

"That's it. If there's nothing else, the court is now adjourned."

"Thank you, man." I hugged my attorney.

"Don't mention it, man. I'm just happy it worked out for you."

I walked out of the courtroom, feeling like new money. I was so geeked up that I totally forgot that I was a broke-ass nigga who didn't have any money to pay my bond. *The bitch said my bond was a hundred grand. Where the fuck am I gonna come up with that kind of paper?* I thought. Mama had some money that she was holding for me, but it was nowhere close to that amount. Since I got locked up, that bitch, Tanya, spent all of my damn money, and the niggas that I knew with that kind of money stopped rocking with me a long time ago. My happiness was dimmed by sadness as I realized that I might not be able to make bond.

Three days later, I was still in Rikers, waiting to get shipped back to prison. There was no way that I could come up with that kind of money. I tried to call Tanya, but the bitch didn't pick up.

The next morning, I was up early. I was ready to get away from those fuck niggas. Jail niggas behaved differently than prison niggas. In jail, they were loud and spent all day running their mouths. In prison, niggas had real time to worry about, and most niggas had jobs, so the unit wasn't noisy during work hours.

I decided to do a few push-ups to occupy my mind. That was one of the days when I didn't feel drained from all of these damn pills.

"Clarke, Hassan, grab your things. You've made bond."

I thought that I was tripping, so I continued doing my push-ups and counting. I was finished and decided to take a quick shower.

"Hassan Clarke, gather your things, and let's go," the CO yelled over the intercom.

Oh shit. I stopped in my tracks. I wasn't tripping. I heard him correctly the first time.

"Who the hell posted my bond?" I asked the CO as we walked up the ramp.

"I have no idea. You'll have to ask at the front desk."

As I walked beside him, I prayed that it wasn't a joke, and my bond was really posted.

Chapter Twenty-eight

Destiny Clarke

Josiah Clarke. That name just kept playing over and over in my head like a broken record. Amaiya was so wrong, and Hassan did have a little bastard with Imani's ass. See, Amaiya didn't know about it because I tried to shield her from all of the drama that was going down. I wondered what happened to him after his mother died. I'd never seen him or knew what he looked like.

"Ha-ha, you're trippin'. That monkey may be somebody's foster child or is up in somebody's jail." A little voice interrupted my seconds of craziness. I wished for once that I could ask Hassan what the boy's name was, but I would die first before I spoke to that bastard ever again.

Speaking of Hassan, I remembered him telling Amaiya that he was appealing his case. I wondered how that worked out for him. His ass was too cocky and thought that he could con his way out of every situation. Not that time, buddy. His ass wouldn't see the streets until he was as old as dirt.

"Amaiya, you need to get fitted for your dress. Tomorrow is Thursday so that we can do it then."

"Why do I have to wear a special dress?" She frowned up her face at me.

"Because it's my wedding, and you're one of my bridesmaids. The color is fuchsia."

"If I tell you that I don't want to go, would you be upset?"

I turned around to face her. *Did I hear her ass right?*

"What did you just say to me?" I was ready to slap the shit out of her ass.

"See, I knew you were going to be upset. That's why I kept quiet."

"You know what? That might be the best thing for you to do. You'll be there, whether or not you like it." I walked out of the room in a hurry.

I rushed to my room and got under the covers. Where in the hell did I go wrong? Amaiya and I used to be so close, but all she did now was give me an attitude. I loved my daughter and just wanted the best for her, but it seemed like all I was doing was driving a wedge between us. I didn't want that, especially now that I have full-blown AIDS. I had no idea how long I would be here. I needed my only child to know that her mama loved her. I burst out crying as I thought about losing her.

"Baby girl, you have no idea how much your mama loves you. Please, let's make this right before it's too late," I mumbled before I dozed off.

Josiah Clarke

It was 8.30 p.m., so I picked up the phone and dialed my bitch's number. I hoped she picked up the phone because everything that I was about to do relied on her love for me.

"Hello." She answered like she was asleep.

"Hey, babe. Whatchu doin'?"

"Just lying here, thinking about you."

"Shit, I'm on the same shit. I need to see you."

"I told you that her ass put me on punishment, and I can't leave the house."

"Baby, listen. I can come and see you."

"Boy, you trippin'. You know she'll go the hell off if you come to the house."

"Listen to me. She ain't got to know. We can wait 'til she's asleep, and then I can sneak in."

"I 'ont know, José. My stepfather is working late tonight, and I don't want him to come home and see your car in the driveway."

"Baby, stop and listen to me. I won't park in the driveway. I can park on the other side of the street. I can call or text you, and you can let me in. Trust me. She won't know. I just really want to see you, babe," I pleaded.

"Okay. Just text me when you get up here, and, please, be careful."

"I love you, babe. See you in a little while."

I hung up the phone and jumped in the shower. My adrenaline was rushing as I washed my body. I had waited for this day, and I was ready to make my mama proud of her only baby boy.

Twenty minutes later, I was on the road to White Plains. I popped a few of my Xanax and swallowed them with a bottle of water. Then I turned the music up loud as Plies's "Runnin' My Momma Crazy" blasted through the old speakers.

"Shit killin' me to know I'm runnin' my momma crazy.
Goon to the streets but to my momma I'm still her baby . . ."

I cut the music down once I got on the street where they lived. I also cut my lights off as I cruised toward the house. Silently, I pulled up and parked across the street in front of the neighbor's house. After I grabbed my gun, I stuck it in my waist and also grabbed my ski mask just in case I needed it.

I'm here. I'll be at your door in five seconds.

I got out of the car, looked around, and walked toward the door. It was a quiet area, so everyone was inside their homes. As soon as I got to her door, she opened it. I stepped inside as she took her time silently closing the door behind us. She was careful not to alarm her mother that the door had been opened.

She motioned for me to follow her up the stairs. I quickly took my shoes off and tiptoed behind her up the stairs and into her room. I wasted no time. As soon as I got into the room, I started kissing her. The Xanax had me horny as fuck, and I needed some pussy right away. More than anything, I needed her to get comfortable with me.

I pulled off her little nightshirt and started sucking on her nipple aggressively. She started groaning. "Shh," I whispered in her ear. The last thing I needed was her mother walking in on me fucking her daughter.

"Babe, you know what? I ain't come over here for this. I want to lie here and hold you."

"But I want you, bae. I want to feel you inside of me," she pleaded as she rubbed on my dick.

"Chill out, babe. We have plenty of time for that. I came out here 'cause I miss you, so let's just hold each other," I said in a stern voice.

"Okay, then," she said with an attitude.

We got under the covers. She put her head on my chest while I wrapped my arms around her. I knew that she felt my heart beating fast, but the sad thing about it was baby girl had no idea why.

I held her close and kept rubbing her head. She slowly dozed off and then finally fell soundly asleep. I continued lying there until I was sure that she was out cold. I took my time and eased my arm from around her. I put her pillow close by her so I could ease out without alarming her.

Then I put my shoes back on, grabbed her cell phone that was on the dresser, and walked lightly out of the room. Standing in the hallway, I tried to make out which room I needed to go into. I didn't see the nigga's car parked outside, so I was banking on him not being there.

I saw the TV light coming from the room directly in front of me. I walked to the door and slightly pushed it open. Bingo. The bitch was lying in bed, out cold. I took my gun out of my waist and stood over her for a while. I touched her shoulder slightly to wake her up.

"Spencer, is that you? I'm not feeling too good."

"No, honey. It's not Spencer," I said.

"What?" She jumped up as if she weren't sleeping.

"Who are you, and what are you doing in my house?"

I walked over to the light and cut it on. "Hello, Destiny. That is no way to greet your future son-in-law."

I could see the shock written all across her face when she realized that it was me.

"Ha-ha. Are you surprised, bitch? Ain't no need to be. I heard you've been doing a little bit of snooping around."

"Where is my daughter? Amaiya!" she yelled.

I took a few steps back, closing the door behind me.

"What the hell do you want? You're not going to get away with this."

Blap. Blap. I slapped her ass in the face with my gun.

That bitch grabbed her face as blood spilled out from the corner of her mouth.

"You have no idea who I am, do you? Well, lemme introduce myself to the bitch of the house. You're right. My name is not José. It's Josiah Clarke. See, we carry the same last name because my mama was screwing your husband, and I'm the bastard that came from that. Now that you know who I am, you can put two and two together."

"What are you doing, José?" Amaiya's voice startled me.

"Step in, bitch, and join the party." I pulled her inside the room and locked the door behind us.

Destiny Clarke

Spencer was working late tonight, and I wasn't feeling too good, so I took some pills and went to sleep. Any other night, I would've set the alarm, but I totally forgot, and that could've cost me my life.

I was barely dozing off when I heard someone enter the room. I just knew that it was Spencer because he was the only one who would come into my room late at night. It wasn't until I said something that the bastard that was standing in my room replied. I only spoke to him once, but I never forgot how he sounded. I knew right then that I was in trouble.

I turned around to face the nigga that my child brought into our lives. He was standing in front of me with a gun pointed directly at me. I swallowed hard and looked around, but I didn't see an escape in sight. I didn't have to ask who he was, because that coward introduced himself.

I sat there, staring at him. I saw that he was jittery and possibly on some drugs. That made my fear level rise even more. I started praying to God in my mind as he slapped me with the gun. The pain shook my body so hard that I saw flashes of light in front of me. I grabbed my face. Blood spilled out of the corner of my mouth. I also felt a tooth loosen, but losing a tooth was the least of my worries. My child was on my mind. What did he do to my daughter, and where was she? It wasn't long before my questions were answered.

Amaiya entered the room. I could tell that she was just as shocked as I was.

"What are you doing, José?"

"Sit yo' ass down, bitch. My name is Josiah. I know you're probably in the dark about this, but yo' mama killed my mother because she was fucking your daddy."

"Mama, what is he talking about? José, what's going on? What are you doing with a gun?" Amaiya started to cry. I could tell that she was scared.

"Baby, don't listen to him. His name is Josiah, and he's the son of the woman your daddy was sleeping with." I tried to comfort her.

"So . . . He's my brother? I slept with him. You knew this?" She turned to him.

"Bitch, shut your whining ass up. Now, take off your clothes."

"Why are you doing this? Amaiya ain't got nothing to do with this." I started to cry.

"Bitch, shut up and take off your fucking clothes too."

"José, Josiah—whatever your name is. This is me—Amaiya. You love me, and I love you." Her eyes pleaded with him.

"I never loved you. The only woman that I ever loved is gone because of this bitch. Now get over here and suck this dick."

"I'll do it." I got up and stepped closer to him.

"Step back, bitch, before I splatter your brains all over this floor."

I couldn't breathe. My chest was tightening up on me. I couldn't watch my daughter do that.

"Please don't do this. What do you want? Money? I can get you lots of it," I begged.

"Bitch, you think I want money? What I'm going to do is fuck this bitch in front of you. Then, I'm going to fuck you, and after that, I'm gonna kill both of you bitches. I want your lives just like you took my mother's life away.

"Now suck this dick, bitch." He forced his dick into Amaiya's mouth.

I couldn't look, but I had to make sure that my daughter didn't feel alone. I started throwing up the food that I ate earlier. I felt so sick inside, and then I started to shiver. I wanted to die as I watched him work my daughter's mouth. He then got up and turned her around and started raping her.

"Noooo! Please, stop. Please, I love you," Amaiya pleaded with that beast.

I put my hands over my ears as I started bawling. I leaped toward him and started clawing at his face. He used his elbow and knocked me to the ground.

I didn't stay down, though. I was angry, determined to get him out of my daughter.

"This pussy's so fucking good. Too bad I can't get it on the regular anymore," that sick bastard said as he rammed in and out of my child.

"Mommy, please help me," she pleaded and kept trying to get up from under him.

"God, please help us," I said out loud.

I jumped on his back and wrapped my hands around his neck. He still didn't get off of my daughter. I squeezed his neck with all of my might.

"Bitch, get off of me before I blow her brains out," he said in a cold tone.

"Step the fuck away from her." Spencer burst into the room with his 9 mm pointed at Josiah's head.

I guess he was so into raping my daughter that he was caught off guard.

"Pussy nigga, I ain't doing shit."

"I'm not asking you—I'm telling you. Ease up off of her and drop the fucking gun."

Without any more words, Spencer jumped at him and grabbed him away from Amaiya before throwing him against the wall. A fight transpired between them.

Pop! Pop! Pop! Gunshots rang out.

"Noooo!" Amaiya screamed as she got up and ran toward me. I didn't know who was shot. I just grabbed my baby and used my body to shield her.

I saw Josiah drop to the ground, and the gun fell from his hand. Spencer grabbed the gun from the floor.

"Help me. Please. I don't want to die," I heard a faint voice say.

"Nigga, ain't nobody goin' help you but God."

Pop! I heard a single gunshot.

"I'm scared, Mommy," Amaiya said as she held me tightly.

"Babe, you all right?" Spencer asked. "That nigga is dead. I'm about to call 911. Get Amaiya, and y'all go downstairs."

Amaiya let go of me and ran over to Josiah. She knelt over him and screamed.

"No. Oh my God," she bawled.

I walked over to her and snatched her up. "Come on. We've got to go."

"I can't leave him, Mama. He needs me." She tried to go back to the body.

Slap! Slap!

"Wake up, little girl. We need to go." I pulled her out of the room as Spencer dialed the police.

I helped her down the stairs and onto the couch after we dressed. She couldn't stop crying. I started to cry as I held her. I wasn't crying because that bastard was shot, though. I was crying because of what my baby was going through. That nigga had just raped her, and then she saw him dying on my floor.

"Why did he have to kill him, Mama? He could've just scared him."

I let her go and then looked her dead in the eyes as she cried. "You listen to me, and you listen good. That bastard was goin' to kill us both if Spencer hadn't come in when he did. You need to come to your senses fast because the police are on their way."

"The police are pulling up now," Spencer said as he rushed to the door to open it.

I was still trembling from everything that went down. I heard Spencer talking to the police and EMT, and then they rushed up the stairs. I had a strong feeling that he was dead, so the EMT wasn't necessary.

One officer stepped into the living room. "Ladies, I need to get a statement from both of you."

"Okay, Officer," I said as I wiped the tears away.

I watched as they wheeled the dead body out of the house as I held Amaiya while she cried uncontrollably. It was so terrible, and the officer couldn't get a statement from her because she was still in shock.

"Do you need us to take her to the hospital for a checkup for the rape? Can she talk to a grief counselor?"

"You know what? I'll drive her to the emergency room. She really needs me right now."

"Sure. I can't imagine what either of you ladies is going through."

I didn't respond. I just smiled at the officer.

"Amaiya, come on. I need to get you to the hospital so you can get checked out."

Spencer was still talking with the officers outside. I needed him now more than ever. I was so grateful to have him because only God knew what that nigga's intentions were. I knew that it wasn't good, and my daughter's and my lives had been in danger.

"Spencer, I've got to go. I'm taking Amaiya to the ER to get checked out."

"You sure you 'ont want me to drive you?"

"Nah, I've got it. Stay here and make sure that things are handled."

I walked Amaiya to the car and got her into the passenger side. Then I got in and pulled off.

"Are you okay? Do you need anything?"

"No," she barely answered.

Maybe I was too harsh on her earlier, but I didn't understand. How could a person feel any kind of way toward a nigga who'd just raped her and almost killed both of us? Maybe I didn't get how her mind worked, and honestly, I didn't give a damn about that nigga. Now his dead ass could join his fucking mama.

I kept glancing over at her while I drove to the hospital. Then I picked up the phone and dialed Mama's number.

"Hello. What's wrong? Why are you up at this time of night?"

"Mama, I know it's late, but something happened at the house tonight. I need you to meet me at White Plains Hospital. I'll fill you in when you get there."

"I'm on my way."

"God, please give me the strength right now because I am so weak," I mumbled as I pulled into the parking lot.

Chapter Twenty-nine

Hassan Clarke

I stepped out into the muggy air. The sun was beaming down on the pavement as I stood there for a second to take in the scenery. I pinched myself to see if I were dreaming. Hell nah, I wasn't dreaming. This nigga was free, even if it was for a little while.

Honk! Honk! Honk!

A car horn interrupted my thoughts. I looked up and realized that the car had stopped in front of me. I didn't recognize the driver, so I just stood there.

"Get in."

I hesitated, but then I thought, *What the fuck? I need a ride to get to my destination.*

"Yo, my man, do I know you?"

"No, but I'm following orders to pick you up."

"Orders from whom?" I inquired.

I was starting to feel nervous. I hoped this wasn't a setup. I knew I had a few enemies out there, but I doubted if those niggas were that bold to pull off some shit like this.

"Man, tell me who sent you, or you can pull the fuck over and let me out now," I said in a loud, deep voice.

"I'm only taking orders from the lady. You'll see her once we get there."

"What lady?"

He didn't respond. Instead, he turned the music up so loud that it irritated the hell out of me. I thought about jumping out of the car, but I knew I would hurt myself because he was speeding down the highway. All I could do was close my eyes and ask God to protect me.

About an hour later, I felt the car slowing down. I opened my eyes and saw that we were going through a gated community. I didn't let it show, but I was shivering in my pants.

"Well, we're here. You can get out now."

I jumped out of the car and looked around. There was a big-ass house, but I didn't know anybody that lived there.

"Mr. Clarke, welcome to mi casa," a sexy voice said.

I turned around to face the beautiful Judge Morales. Yes, you heard me right. It was the same judge that presided over my case and gave me a bond. See, when I filed my appeal, I had no idea that my case would be in front of the judge that I used to fuck every once in a while when I was going to law school. I had not seen her since she left school two years before I graduated. How could I forget the cute, phat-ass judge who used to ride this dick in the back of my car because she was married, and so was I?

"Judge Morales, is that you? But—"

"Shhh, let's go inside in, Mr. Clarke," she cut me off.

I followed the woman in the house, although I was kind of confused about why I was there.

"Thank you, Stewart." She winked at the driver.

"You do know that this is kidnapping, right?"

"Who's the victim? The great Hassan Clarke?" she chuckled.

There was always something about the way she carried herself. She was never afraid to go after what she wanted.

"So, I take it that you signed my bond?"

"You know I could never do such a thing. Let's just say a Good Samaritan paid cash for you to be bonded out."

"Well, in that case, please tell this special person that I said thank you," I said sarcastically.

I was caught off guard when she pushed me into the corner and started kissing me. I didn't have a choice but to return the favor. I picked her up and tried to take her to the edge of the stairs, but she stopped me. "Not so fast. You need to take a shower and wash those sweaty balls of yours. You know I'm a lady. I don't do musty nuts."

"Yes, sure." I then followed her up the stairs and into the bathroom.

"I already ran your bathwater. A washcloth and towel are sitting by the side of the tub."

It felt real good to be taking a proper bath. That hard-ass water that they had in prison was rough on a nigga's skin. As I washed, I took a long exhale as I thought about the pussy I was about to punish. It had been a minute since I've been close to a woman, let alone fucked one.

I hurried and washed off. After I dried off, I walked out of the bathroom with my dick hanging low. I stopped in my tracks when I noticed that she was naked in the bed, lying on her back, playing with her pussy.

"What are you looking at? Come taste this pussy," she teased and then took her finger out and licked it off.

That shit fucked up my head. I dove onto the bed, and without hesitation, I took her legs and spread them apart.

I hungrily slid my tongue inside of her already moist pussy.

"Aah, aah," she moaned as I latched on to her clit. Her moans made me suck harder, as if her pussy was my last meal.

"Baby, please fuck me," she pleaded.

She didn't have to say it twice. I jumped up and slid my rock-hard dick into her pussy.

I knew by the way she was behaving that she wasn't aware that I had the bug. Which was a good thing because that pussy was looking good, and there was no way I was going to wear a damn condom. I wanted to feel that pussy gripping my dick. Shit, that's her problem. She should've been more careful.

"Damn, lady. Your pussy's still tight," I mumbled as I pushed farther in.

"Oh, Hassan. Oh, I love your dick," she whispered in my ear.

I continued pounding her walls. The pussy felt so damn good to be in. Saying it felt like heaven would be an understatement. It didn't take me long to bust. I fell back on the bed, feeling drained. Either I was getting old, or her pussy was that good. I finally got up and washed off. She followed suit.

"Are you hungry?"

"You have no idea. A nigga is starving." She left the room, and twenty minutes later, returned with a plate fit only for a king. Steak, shrimp, mashed potatoes, and broccoli with a glass of lemonade. This is the bitch that I should've married. If only I'd met her before her husband. I wondered what happened to that old fool anyway. From what I remembered her telling me, he was a wealthy, controlling fool.

"So, are you going to tell me how I ended up in your courtroom?"

"To be honest, it was pure coincidence. I was assigned the case, and when I saw your name, I remembered hearing some rumors about you going to prison. I looked through the files, and there was your mug shot."

"I guess it was my lucky day, huh?"

"I wouldn't say it was luck. I think it's that you are blessed with that big ole dick."

"Ha-ha. You ain't changed a bit. Lemme ask you, whatever happened with your husband? Y'all divorced?"

"Yeah, I divorced that old fool. The bastard's dick couldn't get hard. He even tried using Viagra and still couldn't satisfy me. I had to get the hell on. I love to fuck, and any man that I marry has got to be able to satisfy this pussy."

"I hear you, Miss Judge. So, how is it looking for me?"

"Well, I think that with a good attorney, you can beat these charges. I won't be your trial judge, so your fate will be in the hands of someone else. I went through the evidence, and honestly, there's a lot that your lawyer can bring up in your new trial."

"Yeah, I'ma be working on my retrial."

"Don't be a fool, Hassan. I know a lawyer. He's one of the best in the business, and he's a close friend of mine."

"I'm dead-ass broke. I can't afford to pay no lawyer."

"Don't worry about paying him. He'll be doing a favor that he owed me. You better keep your mouth shut about all of this. If this gets out, I could lose my job and face criminal charges. Trust, a prison uniform won't look good on me."

"I know that. Trust me. I appreciate everything you're doing for me. When this is all over with, I promise I will repay you."

"Hmm. I do have one question, though. Did you kill that woman?"

"Nah, I ain't killed that bitch. I swear to you, right hand on the Bible. My ex set me up."

"Really? What would she gain by doing that?"

"Her rival was dead. I was in prison. She got the money from the firm and half of everything I earned. That bitch is money hungry and crazy."

"Wow! Well, you know that you can't go anywhere near her, or I will be forced to revoke your bond." I wanted to tell that bitch fuck her when she said that, but I was no fool. That bitch was beneficial to me at that point.

"You're right. I ain't stuttin' that bitch. I got a trial to get ready for."

Destiny Clarke

The police investigated Josiah's death. They took all of our statements and decided that the shooting was justifiable. After the shooting, I put Amaiya in counseling. She spent most days in her room without eating or showering. While I had compassion for what she was going through, I was mad as hell at her. I later found out that she let that boy in the house while I slept. I wasn't going to lie. I felt betrayed and hurt. As much as I did for my child, and she would betray my trust like that over a nigga that almost killed us. . . .

We spent a few days at a hotel, and then I called a professional cleaning crew to clean my room. I also had the carpet replaced. I thought about moving, but that would be too much strain since the wedding was coming up. Besides, I didn't have any attachment to the little bastard, so it was like it never happened.

Spencer wanted to put the wedding off after Josiah got killed in the house, but I disagreed. I reasoned that we had been through so much already, but we needed to get it over with. Every time that I thought things were going good and I could live a little, something popped and rained on my parade.

It was two weeks before my wedding, and my stomach was doing flips. My best friend, Amiya, was at the house. It felt so good to have her back in my life. I loved her ass so much. She was who I named Amaiya after. I just changed the spelling a little. When I was with Hassan, I distanced myself from her. That was a big mistake because she was the only one, other than my mama, that I could confide in.

"So, how are you feeling?" she asked as we sat in the living room.

"Girl . . . What can I say? Your girl is still standing. I've been to hell and back, but I'm still here. The doctor said I now have AIDS."

"No! I thought you were doing better."

"I thought so too, girl. You know, never in a million years would I think I would be sitting here talking about I have AIDS. That nigga fucked up my life, Amiya."

"Girl, I can't imagine going through what you're going through now, and I know it's not easy for you. I admire your strength. You are one strong, black woman." She reached over and rubbed my hand. I squeezed her hand in return. Tears welled up in my eyes. I saw the tears rolling down her face.

"We had so many plans. Retirement, traveling. Lying on the beach in Jamaica, drinking red wine. This nigga deserves to die," she cried. I got up and sat closer to her.

"You're my friend, and no matter what, please know that I love you. I hope I am here 'til we are old and gray, but the reality is, God has the final say. All I can do is take my medicines, eat healthily, and pray. I just need you to promise me that if anything happens to me, you will help my mama raise my baby girl." I looked into her eyes.

"Des, stop talking like that. You ain't going nowhere."

"I'm serious, Amiya. Promise me."

"I promise you. I will be there for my godchild. I love you, chica," she managed to say in between sobs.

"Good. 'Cause I love your crazy ass too. Now, dry them tears, and let's order some food. I'm starved."

After waiting for our food, we ate, laughed, and cried some more. It was definitely a mini-break from all of the drama that was unfolding in my life lately.

Hassan Clarke

Everything was cool for the next few days. I ate good, shitted, and fucked whenever I wanted to. That shit wasn't what I wanted, though. The bitch wanted to cuff my ass. She had the right idea for the wrong nigga. The only thing on my mind was to get the fuck on. I had some important business to handle, and lying up all damn day wasn't gonna get me anywhere.

I waited until she was up, getting ready for work. I sat up in the bed and tried to come up with the perfect lie. I didn't want to crush her feelings because that bitch had done a lot for a nigga.

"Aye, love, I'ma go to the city today. Want to go visit my mama and the rest of the fam, you know."

"Oh." She turned around to face me. "What time you coming back? I told you, you need to lie low because we can't risk anyone finding out about our relationship."

"I understand all that, but I've been locked up in this house for days. It ain't like my mama can come here to visit. I really want to see my family."

"Okay, then. Stewart can take you wherever you need to be. He can sit and wait so that he can bring you back here. There's a cell phone on the dresser. It's pre-paid, and here are a few dollars for you to spend."

I was gonna respond, but instead, I cracked a fake-ass smile.

"All right, babe. I've got to go. See you later."

"See you," I said sarcastically.

I sat on the bed until I heard the garage door going up. Then I got up and walked over to the window. I watched as her 2015 Lexus ES pulled out and drove away.

I jumped in the shower and did a quick wash off, then got dressed in no time and grabbed the envelope that had all of my letters that I'd received while I was incarcerated. I flipped through the letters until I found one with the address that I was searching for. Before I left, I went into the good judge's drawers and grabbed the gun that I saw in there a few days ago. *I will definitely need this,* I thought as I walked down the stairs.

"Aye, Stew. Did the lady of the house tell you that I need you to take me to the city?"

"She mentioned it."

"Good, so let's go, nigga."

He looked at me like I disrespected him or something.

"Nigga, I said, let's go. I got things to do."

He didn't respond. Instead, he just got up and snatched his keys up off the table. I walked out the door with him in pursuit, humming some old bullshit.

"Where in the city are we heading?"

I looked down at the envelope and gave him the address, then looked out the window and took in the scenery. It was funny how I hadn't been gone that long, but it seemed like it had been forever. The streets of the Bronx seemed the same. Niggas were still lined up on the blocks, either selling dope or gambling. I sure missed my home on some real shit.

He stopped in front of an apartment building. "Here you go, sir. The lady told me that I needed to sit and wait for you. So, I'm goin' park over on the other side."

"Yo, I don't care what she told you. Get yo' old ass outta here. I'm a grown-ass nigga. I 'ont need no babysitter." I stepped out of the car and slammed the door.

I heard him pull off, and then he yelled some shit, but I was too far gone to understand him.

A few niggas were hanging on the side of the building. I nodded my head at them as I walked past them with my head hung down. Luckily for me, a boy ran out the door, and I ran in before the door closed. I took the stairs instead of the elevator to apartment 4G. My blood pressure was rising the closer I got to the last steps. My steps were slowing down as if something were holding me back.

I used the doorknocker to bang on the door.

As I waited, I heard voices coming from inside. I knocked again.

"Who the hell is banging on my door like that?" Tanya popped the door open.

She stared at me like she'd seen a ghost. Her eyes seemed like they would pop out of her head.

"Don't just stand there and stare. You not goin' welcome your nigga home?"

"I-I-when did you get out, and what are you doing here?" She stepped outside and closed the door behind her.

"What the hell you doing? Let's go inside," I said as I pushed her to the side and stepped in the door.

"You can't go in there."

"Why not? My motherfucking son and my bitch live here, so that means I can. Why are you acting funny?"

"Nigga, you heard what the lady said. Get the fuck outta her shit."

I looked at that fuck nigga and sized him up real quickly. His eyes seemed glossy, and he kept on scratching like he had bugs.

"Fuck, nigga. Who the fuck are you?" I inched closer to him.

"Hassan, you have no right coming up in here like this."

Blap! Blap! Blap!

I openhanded slapped that bitch over and over until she fell to the ground, screaming.

"What the fuck you do that for?" that nigga said and lunged toward me.

I two-pieced that old, frail nigga, knocking his ass into the wall. Then I walked over and snatched up that bitch. "Where is my motherfucking son, bitch?"

"Get off me. He's *not* your motherfucking son. He's Randy's son."

Lights flicked in front of me as I had flashbacks at what Imani once told my ass years ago.

"What the fuck did you say to me, bitch? He's *my* motherfucking son. Now, where the fuck is he?" I was spitting fire.

"Say what the hell you want to say. My son only knows Randy as his daddy. He don't fucking know you. Now, you can get the fuck out of my life for good. I thought yo' ass would've got the memo. I don't fucking want yo' ass anymore. See, you thought I was stupid because I'm fucking white, but, boo, I'm far from stupid. Actually, your black bitches were the stupid ones. They were fighting over yo' HIV-infested ass. Ha-ha. You didn't think I knew about that, huh? Well, boo, I've been HIV-positive for over twenty years, and, yes, I fucked and sucked you every day. I bet you, your black bitches' pussies are on fire now. See, y'all thought, y'all had me fooled. Hell nah, I had y'all fooled," she smirked.

I blacked out, pulling out the gun that I had taken from the judge's drawer earlier and fired three shots in that bitch's head. Her brains splattered all over the dingy-ass carpet they had on the floor.

"Noooo! Noooo!" That nigga finally came to and ran over to her.

I turned to him and fired two shots in his chest. He fell on top of the dead bitch.

I tucked the gun in my waist and was about to leave, but I heard someone moving around in the back. I snatched the gun out and tiptoed toward the sound. I leaned against the wall and then peeped my head in the room. I saw the little bastard stooping down between loads of clothing.

"Ha-ha. Little man, it's your daddy. Come here."

My first instinct was to kill the bastard. After all, I didn't want to leave a witness behind. He walked over to me, and I held his hand. I raised the gun and pointed it at his little head, but I couldn't pull the trigger. Instead, I grabbed him up and ran to the door. Quickly, I peeped out. Nobody was outside of the door. I ran out, closing the door behind me.

I snuck out of the apartment building, through the back door, without incident, then walked away in the opposite direction of the building. I wasn't sure if anyone had heard the gunshots. The boy started crying. I threw him over my shoulder and kept patting his back so he would shut the fuck up. I was tempted to turn around and leave his ass on the steps, but truthfully, I felt like he was my seed. Shit, I thought he looked like me when I was younger. I had a hundred dollars that the judge had put on the table for me earlier, so I decided to walk farther up the block and then look for a cab.

I finally got to 214th and White Plains Road. I jumped in a cab and gave the driver the address. I was going home. I paid the driver and got out of the cab.

I walked to the door and rang the doorbell. This little nigga had fallen asleep and was weighing down on my shoulder.

"Who the hell is it, ringing my damn bell like that?" My mama yelled, as usual.

"It's me, Mama. Open the door."

Damn, that lady hadn't changed a bit. She'd been yelling like that since I was a kid. She opened the door. When she saw that it was me, she quickly opened the screen door.

"Boy, what the hell you doing here? Did they finally come to their senses and let my baby come home? And who the hell is this little boy?"

"Damn, Ma. You're killing me already. Gimme a chance to sit down and tell you."

"All right, all right. You know yo' mama just happy to see her baby boy. You hungry?"

"Nah, I ain't hungry, Ma. Yeah, they granted me an appeal and ordered a new trial. So, yeah, I'm free for now, and this is your grandson."

"Grandson? Where in the hell did this little mother-fucka come from? The last time you brought one of these little strays around here, it turned out that you weren't the father. Boy, stop letting these bitches put these babies on you 'cause they know you're a good catch. How you the daddy, and he looks like a mutt?"

"His mama's white, and it wasn't my fault that Imani lied."

"Yeah, that's why that wicked bitch is dead. I'm just mad that you got pinned down for her murder. By the way, that son of hers got killed by your ex-wife's man."

I looked at her, hoping that I didn't hear her right.

"Don't look at me like that. I was shocked too. It was all over the news. I recognized that child and that evil bitch. You know the news ain't goin' tell everything, but they saying he went up in the house and tried to kill them."

See, Mama thought I was shocked because the nigga was dead. Hell nah. I was shocked because she said that Destiny had a man. So that bitch *had* moved on. The mention of her name stirred up anger inside of me. I tried my best not to let it show, but I wasn't that lucky. I also remembered what Josiah had said when he visited me.

"Boy, you a'ight? I know you were close to that boy. I'm sorry I had to break the news to you like that. It's sad that he and his mama both died a violent death like that.

But when you do wrong, trust me, you *will* get what's coming to you. I'm happy you're home. You need to get on the case soon and find out how that bitch Destiny framed you. She needs to be locked up and rot in prison. That bitch done got away with too damn much."

"I agree, Ma. Anyway, where's everybody?"

"Your daddy's at the track, as usual, and Charmaine should be here any minute now. She'll be happy to see you."

"Mama, you know I don't deal with her like that."

"Y'all need to stop that foolishness. She was there with you every step of the way. She really loves you, Hassan."

"I love her too, Ma, but certain shit you just don't do. Period. Anyway, Mama, I need a favor."

"You just got here. What's the favor?"

"I need to get some things together. Do you have the money that I told you not to touch, no matter what?"

"Yes, I put the package under my mattress. I did use a few hundred dollars to pay for my medicine. I had to hide it from your daddy 'cause he'd gamble away every cent."

She walked off into her room. I sat there with my mind racing a mile a minute. I swear, killing that bitch was the last thing on my mind, but how could she stand there, telling me that she gave me this shit? All along, I thought I got the shit from Imani, but it was from this dirty white bitch who had told me she was a virgin when I met her. How could I have been so fucking stupid to believe that I was the only nigga she was fucking?

"Here you go, son." She handed me a big manila envelope.

I took it and ripped it open. It was five stacks, minus the few hundred she used. I put the money to my nose and smelled it. Then I rubbed my hand over it. It felt so good to be able to hold money in my hands once again.

"Where am I? Where's my mama?"

I turned around to face the boy. I wish his ass had remained asleep.

"Yes, Hassan, where is this little boy's mama?"

"Mama, I have no idea. I went by the house, and he was there alone. I snatched him up and came directly over here."

"So, why the hell didn't you call the police? Yo' ass ain't learned. What if that bitch claims you kidnapped the boy? What you goin' do then?"

"He goin' do what he always do . . . get his ass into some shit." My loud ass-mouthed sister walked into the living room.

"Go ahead on, Charmaine, wit' that bullshit."

"Damn, brother. No hello or hug for the bitch that was at every court date and ready to beat bitches up over you?" She gave me a dirty look.

"Damn, B. I done said thanks a million times already. I mean, what the hell you want from me—blood?"

"Whatever, and whose dirty-ass white baby is this?"

"Watch yo' mouth, Charmaine. Don't be talkin' like that 'round that child. That's your brother's child."

"Mama, don't tell me you're falling for this bullshit again. The last two children he claimed he found out one wasn't his, and the other one, he still don't know. You can buy this foolishness, but I'm not. This nigga love claiming people's children as his own."

Soon as those words left her mouth, I was standing there, wishing she wasn't my sister. I wanted to choke the life out of her ass. Ever since we were young, she never knew how to keep her mouth shut.

"Enough, you two. Charmaine, go upstairs while I talk to your brother. He's been through enough as it is. Don't let him feel like a stranger. We're all he's got."

"Okay, okay. I'm gone. But that's the problem. You're always babying his behind." She then walked off, pouting.

"Don't mind your sister. She's going through a rough time. She and that boy broke up, and she's taking it really hard."

I looked at my mama and almost said, "I don't give a fuck," but instead, I just walked into the kitchen. Mama followed closely behind me.

I turned around to face her. "Listen, Mama, I need you to watch li'l man 'til his mama comes for him," I lied.

"Hell no. I ain't been feeling too well lately."

I peeled off two grand and shoved it into her hand. Mama never ceased to amaze me. She'd always been money hungry.

"How long am I supposed to be keeping him?"

"Until his mama comes for him. She should be here in a few days."

"All right. So where you off to?"

"'Bout to find somewhere to stay, and then I got some business to handle."

"Be careful out there, baby." She hugged me tightly, and it lasted for a good two minutes. I was happy to see my mama, but I was also in my feelings because it might be the last time I saw her.

"I love you, woman. Tell Daddy I love him too."

I grabbed the plastic bag off the kitchen table and put the money inside. Then I walked out of the kitchen and back into the living room. I took one last look at li'l man and then walked out the door. I had no intention of ever seeing him again.

Chapter Thirty

Destiny Clarke

"Hey, babe. You asleep?" Spencer entered the room and asked me.

"Nah, just lying down."

"Turn around, babe," he demanded.

I obeyed his demand and turned around to face him. He handed me a gift bag.

"What's this?" I quizzed.

"Open it up, lady," he smiled.

I opened the bag . . . and it was the prettiest gun I'd ever laid eyes on. I took it completely out of the wrapper and examined it. It was purple, but I had no idea what kind it was. I just knew that it was pretty as hell. I rubbed my hand all over it.

"Is this mine?"

"Of course. After what happened with Josiah, I need you to have this. Especially those nights when I'm working late, or when I'm out of town."

"Thank you, babe. She's pretty too."

"That's a Ruger SR22-PG LADY Lilac 22. I knew you'd love it."

"Well, you're a man who knows what his woman wants." I winked at him.

"I sure do." He bent down and gave me a big, wet kiss on my cheek.

"Well, lemme jump in this shower. My damn back is killing me from sitting at the desk all day."

"I can imagine. Go ahead and take your shower. I'll give you a massage when you're finished."

"Shit, lemme go then. You know how much I love your massages."

I heard the shower running, and Spencer with his good ass singing. Boy, the sound of that man's voice did something crazy to my soul. My eyes started to gather water at thoughts of me not being able to enjoy my man fully. Yes, we had sex, but we had careful sex. I yearned for closeness. I wanted to feel my man's cock all up against my walls. But the reality was, we couldn't do that. Shit, I missed getting my pussy sucked on too.

The water was no longer running, so I knew that he was finished. I quickly wiped away my tears and placed my new gun in the drawer by my bed. He walked out of the bathroom buck-ass naked. I looked at him seductively as he walked toward the bed.

"Lie down on your stomach."

I got up from the bed and grabbed my Victoria's Secret Weightless Oil. Then I leaned over him, poured a little bit of oil on his back, and started working it in.

"Damn, babe. You got a nigga feeling good and shit. Them hands, though . . ."

"Hmmm . . ." I continued massaging him.

My pussy started to throb. I tried to ignore it at first, but the throbbing only got worse. I wanted to fuck, not make love. I wanted some hard-core, beat-those-walls-up kind of fucking.

"Turn around, babe."

"Huh?"

"You heard me. Turn around."

I wasn't surprised that his cock was already rock hard. I didn't waste any time. I quickly took it into my warm mouth while I massaged his balls with the oil. His moans and groans encouraged me to suck harder.

Before we knew it, his veins started getting bigger, and he exploded in my mouth. I quickly swallowed all of his come, and he was flipping me over and entering my pulsating pussy. Needless to say, that man never disappointed. I got exactly what my pussy wanted—a good old-fashioned pussy whipping. After what I saw as a marathon, he finally burst into the condom.

"*Aargh,* babe. Have I ever told you that you've got that shit that can kill a nigga?"

"No, but if it's like that, you need to be careful," I laughed at his crazy behind.

I kind of felt what he was saying because I was so damn tired, and my pussy was sore. I barely managed to get up out of bed to walk to Amaiya's room. It was late, and I was about to go to bed. I knocked on her door.

"Yes, Mama?"

"I don't want anything. Just saying good night."

"Good night. Love you."

"Love you back." I kissed her on the cheek and walked out, closing her door behind me.

Things were not back straight with her, but she was getting there. The counseling, along with me not really pressuring her, was working. I was happy that our relationship was finally back on track.

When I got back into the room, I heard the shower running, so I knew that Spencer was washing off. I thought about joining him but quickly decided not to. Instead, I got in bed, pulled the cover over me, and fell asleep.

It was a week before I was to walk down the aisle with the wonderful Mr. Spencer. I welcomed the name change, and I also looked forward to our honeymoon. We were going on a cruise through some Caribbean countries. That should be beautiful. Plus, I would get to spend that time with my new husband without him working or anything else in the way.

My mother was handling the catering and the decoration of the hall. At times, she seemed more excited than I was. When I married Hassan, it wasn't anything big, but this time around, Mama wanted to pay for the hall and the catering. Boy, when I tell you that lady was not holding back, she was *not* holding back.

I planned on spending the day going through some paperwork. I needed to make a will. Don't be alarmed. I don't plan on checking out any time soon. I just wanted to make sure that if anything happened to me, my baby girl and my mama were straight for life.

I heard my cell phone going off, and I wondered who the hell was calling like they were desperate. I finally got up from the carpet where I was sitting, going over my papers. I noticed it was my attorney that I had hired when Hassan's case was going on. I kept him on the payroll, just in case Hassan or his lawyers ever started some shit. Every now and then, he'd call just to see how I was doing.

"I'll call him later," I mumbled, and I went back to what I was doing. As soon as I sat back down, the phone started ringing again.

"Uuugh." I jumped up and grabbed my cell from the bed.

"Hello."

"Mrs. Clarke, how are you? This is Attorney Wallock."

"I'm fine. How are you?"

"Have you heard anything from the courts about your ex-husband being released from prison?"

A big lump formed in my throat. I took a few seconds to gather my thoughts.

"What the fuck do you mean, 'released from prison,' and why the fuck didn't somebody call me to tell me that shit?" I yelled into the phone.

Tears instantly started to flow. I was crying because I was mad as fuck.

"I'm not sure. The courts should've notified you of this. One of my friends, down at the DA's office, was talking to me, and he informed me that Mr. Clarke was granted bond on one charge and granted new trials on the other two. I am going to call the DA to file a complaint. There's no way this man should've been out without your know-ing."

"You don't have to file shit. I'm about to get dressed and go down there right now. They're going to fucking explain to me how this shit was even possible in the first place. Listen, I've got to go."

I didn't wait for a response. I just hung up the phone.

"Fuck you, Hassan. Why couldn't you just keep yo' ass in prison?" I yelled out.

"Mama, what's going on?" Amaiya rushed into the room.

"I just found out that your damn daddy is out of prison and running around here like a free man."

"What? Are you sure?"

"Yes, I'm sure. My lawyer just called to tell me."

She stood there looking like she was in a trance. I didn't have time to waste. Somebody had some explaining to do.

I jumped in the shower, washed off real fast, and then got dressed. I pulled my hair back into a ponytail and threw on my NY Yankee-fitted hat.

"Amaiya, I'm gone. Don't answer the door for anyone," I hollered as I made my way down the stairs.

I jumped in my car and backed out of the driveway. I was on my way to the city, but I wasn't worried about getting pulled over or anything else. My mind was racing. I was not feeling my ex-husband being free. That was definitely *not* good. I was moving on with my life, and only God knew what dirt that nigga was going to dig up.

Hassan Clarke

I got me a room in a rooming house since I didn't need anything flashy or big. I didn't plan on being there too long. First things first, I took the bus to Fordham Road, where I grabbed a few outfits and drawers. No matter what, a nigga gotta stay fresh. Plus, I planned on getting some pussy.

Speaking of pussy, I hadn't spoken to the judge since the day I left her house. Knowing her, she probably thought that I was on some shit. The truth was, I was not going back to her house. I really appreciated what she did for me, but I felt like I already repaid her with that good dick of mine.

***

I totally forgot that I had the phone that the judge gave me until it started to ring. Instantly, I knew it was her. I thought about not answering it, but I did anyway.

"Hey there, lady. I meant to call you, but I got caught up in handling some things."

"Hassan Clarke, where the hell is the gun that I had in my drawer? I went looking for it earlier, and it's gone. Are you out of your fucking mind? That gun is registered to me. If it gets into the wrong hands, my ass is gonna be in serious shit."

"You need to calm down and quit yelling at me. I'm not a child. The bottom line is, you need to report your gun stolen ASAP. Shit, make up something, 'cause like you said, your ass will be in serious shit," I chuckled.

"No. How 'bout I revoke your damn bond and get your ass arrested? I put myself out on a limb to help, and this is how you repay me? You're one ungrateful-ass bastard." She started crying.

"Listen to me, you stupid bitch. I'm calling your bluff. For one, your ass does *not* want the world to know that yo' lonely ass gave me a bond because you wanted to get fucked. See, it would bring too much shame on you and the entire judiciary system, and your ass would go to prison. Don't you fucking threaten me again. You must not know I'm Hassan Clarke. Now, you better get off the phone and figure out a way to report your gun stolen. If not, yo' ass got a whole lot of explaining to do. Also, yo' ass better go get checked for the virus," I chuckled.

I hung up the phone. I was pissed off that that bitch tried to threaten me like that. I looked down at the phone, turned it off, and then used my shirt to wipe it off good. I then waited until I reached a trash can and threw it inside. Now, that bitch could kiss my ass. Calling herself checking up on me. I wasn't a fucking child. I was a grown-ass man.

I spent the next couple of days working on my plan. I didn't know how I was going to find that bitch because I heard she had moved. I was tripping because I knew that I could find my daughter easily since I knew where she went to school.

I needed a car, though, so I went to my old car dealer that I knew in the Bronx. See, that nigga was as crooked as they come. You didn't need a license or anything. As long as you had money, you could get a car. I took the #2 train to Allerton Avenue and to Jacob Car Dealership.

As soon as I walked through the door, I spotted him. Shit, he hadn't changed much. He still had that old, groggy look. I walked up to him.

"Is this who I think it is? Hassan, my man, is that you?"

"In the flesh, Jacob."

"When the hell you touch down? Last time I heard, you were upstate."

"I just got out. That shit was bogus, but it just took a little time to clear it up."

"Hell yeah. Shit, you one of the best lawyers around here, so I knew you was goin' beat that shit. So anyway, what brought you my way?"

"I need a favor."

"Anything. You know I got you."

"I need a car for cash, but I need you to fix up the paperwork. I don't want it in my name."

"Shit, say no more. Let's take a walk out on the lot."

An hour later, I was driving off the lot with a used Charger. It wasn't anything fancy, but it was just right. I didn't want anything flashy to draw attention to me in any way.

Whew, what a day, I thought as I lay back on the full bed that came with the furnished room. I was tired of ripping and running, and it wasn't over. Tomorrow, I planned on finding a new gun. I needed something big and powerful that was gonna cause some serious damage. I still had the judge's gun, but I needed to get rid of it soon. As I rested, something that Mama said to me rang in my head. She said that the media was all over the case after Josiah got killed at Destiny's house. I knew that if they were all over it, her information and where the crime happened should also be public knowledge. I didn't have a computer but planned on doing some research tomorrow. I smiled to myself as I imagined what that bitch's face would look like when I confronted her.

"Destiny, my love, I am going to pay you back in full," I said as I dozed off.

Destiny Clarke

I walked into the Bronx District Attorney's Office. I wanted answers and was not leaving until I got them. I saw the receptionist and walked up to her.

"My name is Destiny Clarke, and I need to see the DA."

"Do you have an appointment?"

"Listen, lady, no, I don't have one, but I need to talk to someone right now."

"Please lower your voice, or I'll call in security to escort you out."

This bitch has no idea that I don't give a fuck about her or no goddamn security. They'll need an ambulance if that bitch keeps on playing with me.

"Lady, I asked you nicely to tell the DA that I'm here to see him. He already knows who I am. If you insist on not letting him know, I will go to your supervisor, his boss, and everybody else who will listen to me."

She must've sensed the seriousness because she told me to hold on while she walked toward the back. When she returned, she was more pleasant. "Sorry about that, Miss Clarke. DA Abrams will be with you shortly. Please have a seat."

I didn't respond to that two-dollar ho. Instead, I shot her a dirty look and walked away. I sat anxiously, waiting for that nigga to come from behind his fancy desk.

A few minutes later, I heard the door open. It was the DA.

"Miss Clarke, sorry for the wait. Come on in to my office, please."

I got up and followed him to his office.

"How are you doing today, and what brought you in?"

"What brought me in is that my ex-husband almost killed me and was convicted of that crime. However, I just learned that he was released from prison on bond and was also granted a new trial. So, I want to know why I wasn't informed of this. Do you know my daughter's and my lives are at risk?" I yelled.

"I could've sworn that we sent out a letter informing you of his release. Our office tried our best to present to the court reasons why he should not be released. However, the defense provided new evidence that created some doubt. The judge bought it and sided with the defense."

"So, you're telling me that some bitch just let this nigga walk out of prison. He tried to kill me. He killed another woman, and y'all let him walk out a free man? God help y'all if he kills again."

"Miss Clarke, I apologize from the bottom of my heart. We gave it our best shot, and we will be preparing to go to court for the new trial and present all of the evidence we have. I'm pretty confident that we will win the case, and he will be back behind bars where he belongs. I can get a unit to sit in front of your house, just in case he shows up there. I'll also get the word out to all precincts to keep an eye open for anything suspicious."

"You know what? You and your office can kiss my black ass. I don't need no bodyguards. If y'all did y'all fucking jobs, that bastard wouldn't be walking around here like shit is sweet. If anything happens to my family or me, all y'all will be held responsible, from you to the bitch who set him free. It might be that judge he was fucking. You better get off your ass and look into it."

I sashayed out of his office and slammed the door behind me. My blood pressure was rising, and I was feeling tired. An anxiety attack was about to come on. I pressed the elevator button as I breathed slowly. I started to count in my head, trying my best to escape an attack.

On my way home, I dialed Spencer's number, but he wasn't answering. Instead, his voicemail came on. I was getting a little irritated with him. I wanted to let him know that Hassan was out of prison. I threw the phone on the seat and continued driving. Since I was in the city, I decided to stop by Mama's house. I swear, I needed her right about now.

I parked and rang her doorbell. Surprisingly, she didn't take forever to answer it.

"Who is it?"

"Me, Mama," I yelled.

"Child, what in God's world are you doing down here? I thought you were home resting. Your big day is coming up, and you need all of the rest you can."

"Let's go inside."

"You okay? You look upset. Oh Lord, is everything all right?"

"Mama, that bastard is out of prison," I blurted out.

"Say what? What bastard? I know you ain't talkin' 'bout who I think you talkin' 'bout."

"Yes, that's exactly who I'm talkin' about."

"Are you fucking serious? Please, excuse my French."

Mama rarely cussed, and when she did, it just didn't sound proper.

"Mama, I am so pissed off right now. I just came back from the DA's office. Their asses didn't tell me that he was out. I was lucky that my lawyer found out. Mama, I thought this shit was over, but here goes something else. Is it meant for me not to be happy? I mean, every time something good is about to happen, this old stupid-ass nigga always pops up."

"I was just over here thinking, 'Why can't that bastard just die?' He's caused enough shit as it is. Somebody needs to put his ass out of his misery."

"Mama, I swear to you, if he comes anywhere near Amaiya or me, I'm going to kill him. I can't go through anymore of his shit," I said in a serious tone.

"I hope he has enough sense to leave y'all alone. He needs just to move on. Baby girl, listen. Please be careful. Watch your surroundings at all times and make sure you lock the doors at night. If you want, you know y'all can come down here and stay with me."

"Mama, I'm not leaving my house. I am not scared of that weak-ass nigga. This ain't the Destiny that used to cry over that nigga. I've grown up, and I *will* show that fuck nigga. He's got the right bitch this time." I didn't want to cuss in front of my mama, but I was too mad, and it was not the time for me to be worried about manners.

"Well, you know I love you, and I just want you safe."

"I know, Mama, and you know I love you too."

"So, how are you feeling?"

"I'm feeling a little better this week. I'm excited and nervous at the same time. I just want everything to go the way we planned with this wedding."

"Stop worrying. Everything is going to be perfect. You're the perfect bride, and Mr. Spencer is the perfect groom. Y'all are perfect for each other. You know I'll tell you when a man is full of shit. When I look at Spencer, I see how he admires you, how much he loves you. Just remember, what God put together, can't no man separate."

I smiled at Mama, and for a split second, I forgot how mad I was. I sat there, soaking up every word that she spoke. Old people be spitting some real shit.

We talked for a little while longer, and then I left. I needed to get home to check on my child.

Chapter Thirty-one

Hassan Clarke

When I first got locked up, I vowed to get out and build a case against Destiny so she would spend the rest of her life in prison, but all that shit changed. That wicked bitch deserved to die slowly. I wanted to watch her take her last breath and for her to know that *I* was the one who took her life.

Someone behind me honked the horn, interrupting my thoughts. I was so caught up with my thoughts that I didn't see the light had changed. I was on my way to Mount Vernon. I knew a nigga out there who I had defended a few times, and he knew how to get guns. I wasn't sure if he was in the same spot, but I had to try. I finally made it to Fifth Avenue and pulled up at the building that dude used to operate out of. I could see that the building was abandoned now. I was disappointed because he was the one I was counting on. I drove off feeling defeated.

I woke up bright and early the next morning. I needed a computer and a cell phone, so I decided to go to Fordham Road, where they always had discounted shit. I didn't need an expensive computer. Shit, I only needed to use it once, so the quality didn't matter as long as I could connect to the internet.

I copped the computer and also bought a prepaid phone out of Metro PCS. It's crazy how easy it was to get things nowadays. Then I jumped in my car and looked for a McDonald's so I could use their free Wi-Fi.

I finally found one and pulled into the parking lot. I logged on the computer and started to Google news stories. Nothing came up, but then I pulled up the news websites and typed in the info that my mama had given me.

There it was in black and white. I clicked on the link and started to read. The main thing that I was looking for was the address where that incident had taken place. And there it was. . . . That bitch had moved to White Plains. So much for hiding from me.

The story was very detailed and even named her live-in boyfriend. So, that dumb bitch had my daughter living with another nigga. I bet you she had her calling that nigga daddy too. I cringed at the thought of that happening. I was pissed all over again. I stored the address in my phone's notes, logged off the computer, and walked off.

"Sir, you're leaving your computer," the lady that was sitting next to me yelled out.

"You can have that shit," I yelled back. I continued walking, thinking about the shit I had just read about.

I decided to grab a bottle from the liquor store. I was pissed and needed something strong. Hennessy Black was my drink of choice. I was pulling off from the liquor store when this young, pretty, black chick walked up to the car.

"Looking for some company, baby?"

"Yup, get in."

She jumped into the car, and I pulled off.

"What you trying to do, baby?" she asked seductively.

"Everything. I've got money, so you're good."

I liked her because she wasn't nosy. She didn't ask me a million and one questions. She was a trick that knew what she wanted, and I just wanted to fuck and suck for a few hours. I pulled up at the rooming house, and we got out. She followed me inside, and I locked the door behind us.

Without wasting any time, shorty undressed, showing her curvy body. She had a phat ass on her, which made my dick hard. I was ready to run up in her and let out all the frustration I was feeling.

Shorty took my dick into her mouth and gobbled it up. She sucked it with passion, like she was making love to it. It wasn't even ten good minutes before I exploded in her mouth. I quickly got on top of her and let the beast go. I placed both of her legs on my shoulders and went in hard. I showed no mercy on that phat-ass pussy. I could tell that she was a pro because she didn't make a sound. She just threw that pussy on me while holding me tightly. She busted a few times all over my dick, which only made me pound that pussy harder. Eventually, I nutted all up in her pussy.

"Shorty, you got some good pussy," I said as I got up off her.

I peeled off three hundred, even though she didn't give me a price. That pussy was worth every last dime. I watched as she got dressed and smiled at me.

"See you around, baby. Do you want my number?"

"Nah, that ain't necessary."

"A'ight. See you around." She smiled and left.

As soon as she left, I locked the front door. Then I went back to my room, gathered my things, and went to the shower. As I bathed, a picture of Destiny popped up in my head. I would never forget the last time I saw that bitch . . . the way she belittled me and talked down on me like I wasn't worth shit. That bitch just knew that she had the upper hand. Let's see how much power that old dumb ho has when she meets her creator.

Destiny Clarke

I pulled into the driveway and parked my car. It had definitely been a rough day for me. I sat in the car for a few minutes, just trying to digest it all. I was worried about that nigga walking around, free as a bird, but my real problem was the fact that I knew he was going to find a way to drag me into a murder investigation. I swear, he was like a sore that never healed. Why couldn't he just take one for the team?

Flashbacks of the day when I killed that bitch ran through my mind. I remembered that I didn't go there to kill her. It wasn't until I saw that smile on her face that I decided that grimy bitch had to go. I was terrified that her ass would take the money, and as soon as she spent it, she'd be back for more. There was no way I was going to be blackmailed by that bitch. In that split second, I became a killer.

"God, please help me. I swear, I need you. I can't go to prison," I cried. I rested my head on the steering wheel and poured out all of my worries to the man above. I was so caught up in my pleas that I didn't see when Spencer pulled up behind me.

Knock. Knock. Knock.

I jumped as he knocked on my car window. I quickly tried to wipe away my tears, but it was too late.

"Open the door. Why are you sitting in the car crying? What the hell is going on?"

I unlocked the door and opened it. I looked at him and saw that he was waiting for an answer.

"Spencer, Hassan is out of prison. I got the call from my attorney this morning," I managed to say in between sobs.

"You're fucking joking, right?" He looked at me for confirmation.

"Nah, some stupid-ass judge overthrew his convictions, and now he's free."

He knelt in front of me on the hard concrete and took my hands into his.

"I know that's your baby daddy and all, but if that pussy-ass nigga comes anywhere near my family, I'm gonna body his ass. I'm about sick of this shit. This fucking system is flawed, and that's why niggas be acting like the judge and jury," he yelled.

I rested my head on his shoulder and continued to sob. He let my hands go and then wrapped his arms around me. I continued crying as he held me.

"Babe, listen to me. I've got you. On my dead mama, I swear, I got you. If that nigga so much as breathes on you, I'm gonna kill him and his motherfucking family, and I don't give a fuck about no jail time. I will gladly lay it down, as long as I know my queen is straight."

I knew that he was serious as hell. Spencer was one of those dudes who walked the walk and talked the talk, and he wasn't into playing games.

"Let's go in the house. Wipe those tears away. That nigga ain't worth it."

He held my hand as he led me into the house. I felt so much better now that he was home.

I woke up to the aroma of coffee. As I opened my eyes, I noticed Spencer was standing in front of me, holding a tray with breakfast. I smiled at him as I sat up.

"You were up early cooking, huh?"

"I wanted to do something special for my queen. I know you had a rough night. You tossed and turned all night long."

"Yes, I wasn't feeling good."

I took a sip of the fresh Folgers coffee.

"Spencer, would you still marry me if you found out that I did something bad?"

"As long as you didn't cheat, there's nothing that can make me not want to marry you. Now, tell me, what are you talking about?"

I looked in his eyes and tried to read him, but I couldn't. If he was feeling something, he was good at holding it back.

"Sit down." I patted the bed.

I started the story of how Imani showed up on my doorstep and how things went down after that. I didn't leave out anything. I even told him about the day that I decided enough was enough. By the time I was finished cleansing my soul, I was bawling like a child who was being whooped by a parent.

"Wow! That's some deep shit you just spit out."

"Spencer, I understand if you don't want to get married. I deserve that."

"Man, shut up, woman. You think I'm one of those weak-ass niggas out here. I'm irritated that you didn't trust me enough to tell me this before now. I mean, we're about to get married. Where's the trust?" He looked at me with intensity.

"I trust you, Spencer, but how do I come out and tell you that I killed a woman, and I'm scared I might be going to jail? I didn't know how."

"The same way you just told me. Destiny, please understand that I love you with everything in me, but from this day on, we have to be truthful with each other. Do you understand me?"

"Yes, I do."

I felt like shit because I knew I had betrayed him and our trust. I swear it wasn't intentional, but it was a secret that I had planned on taking to my grave. Well, that was until Hassan got released. Although that bastard and I were divorced, he still continued to cause havoc in my life.

"Listen, I'm about to leave for the office. I want you to keep your gun with you at all times. Even when you take a shower. Best believe, that nigga is no fool, and if he wants to get to you, he *will* find a way to. There's also a fully loaded 9 mm downstairs under the couch, closest to the TV. If you have to, reach for it and shoot without asking questions. Always remember, it's either him or you, and I prefer it to be him. Press the trigger, and don't stop till the motherfucker is dead. If anything happens, call me first before you call the police."

I sat there, taking in everything that he was spitting to me. Like a good student, I was making mental notes.

Hassan Clarke

What a nice neighborhood, I thought as I drove down the street, searching for the address that I put in my phone's GPS. It was definitely an upgrade from the house we used to live in.

"Your destination is on the right. Your destination is on the right. You're now at your destination."

I pulled up on the other side of the street and parked in front of the neighbor's house. I didn't want to bring any kind of attention to myself. It wasn't dark yet, and I could see a car parked in the driveway.

I sat there, just staring directly at the house and drinking a beer. I noticed a car pull in and scooted down in my seat. The car was parked, but no one got out, which was weird. I continued sitting there.

About twenty minutes later, another car pulled up, and that time, a man got out. I couldn't see his face as he walked up to the car that was parked. Whatever the fuck was going on, I wished I was closer so that I could see it. Minutes later, they walked hand in hand into the house. I knew that the bitch was Destiny, although I didn't see her face. I could tell by the way that bitch was shaped and how she walked.

I sat there for a few more minutes, and then I pulled off. "Gotcha," I said as I turned the radio on.

The sound of the alarm on my phone woke me up. It was only six o clock, but I wanted to be back in front of the house before anyone left so that I could get an idea of their comings and goings. I stopped at the Dunkin' Donuts on North Broad Street before I headed to their house.

The block was still quiet and seemed like those people didn't have jobs. I guess that's how the rich people lived. That thought only angered me. All of the money that bitch took from me, I saw where the fuck it went. That bitch even had a new fucking car. So, while I was eating fucking noodles every day, she and that nigga were spending my hard earned dollars.

As soon as the thought left my mind, I noticed that nigga walking out the door. That time, he was facing me, so I got a better look at his face. "Ain't this a bitch," I yelled out as I hit my steering wheel. I never forgot a face that I'd seen before. That was none other than the fuck nigga that was at the house the day I walked in on them. So that bitch was with the nigga that she was cheating on me with?

I opened the car door but quickly closed it. After taking a couple of deep breaths, I sat back down in the seat. As much as I would love to kill the nigga she's fucking, my beef was with that ho, so I would totally focus on her ass.

I watched as he got in his car and drove off. What a fucking fool. He didn't even look at his surroundings. I waited for about five minutes, and then I got out of the car, stretched, and looked around. Everything seemed cool. I crossed the street and walked into the yard. I thought about ringing the bell but decided against that. Destiny was no fool, and I was pretty sure that she knew I was free on bond.

I carefully walked around the house toward the back. Most of the windows had burglar bars on them. I continued walking until I reached what seemed like a sunroom. It was my lucky day because the window was pulled up, showing the screen.

I leaned back on the wall and listened. I wanted to make sure that there was no movement inside. The coast was clear, so I decided to jump on the chance. I grabbed the knife from my pocket and cut through the screen. Then I quickly climbed in, being careful not to make noise.

I quickly crept to the far end, where the door was located. I tried the door, and to my surprise, it was open. I looked at the table and spotted a cup of coffee. So, she must've just left the room. I pushed the door open with a gun in my hand. I was ready for whatever was waiting on the other side.

Destiny Clarke

After Spencer left, I decided to sit in the sunroom and log on to the computer to surf the web. These days, shopping had become a hobby for me. I had to admit that my favorite website was Angel Brinks. They had some nice clothes there, and I was looking for something special to wear on our honeymoon.

I had left my credit card upstairs, so I quickly went to get it. I grabbed it and went back downstairs. When I tried to open the door, it was locked. I stood there for a minute, thinking. I didn't lock the door when I came in, so why was it locked now? I knew that Amaiya was at my mama's house. I brushed it off since there was no one else in the house. I was a little on edge because that nigga was out of prison. I laughed out loud and went back to what I was doing. But for some reason, I was uneasy. That locked door kept bothering me. I just knew that I didn't lock it.

I let out a long sigh. "*Always follow your gut instinct,*" Spencer's voice reminded me in my head. I didn't waste another second. I closed my computer and quickly left the sunroom. That time, I locked the door. I looked to the left, toward the kitchen, and thought I saw the shadow of a man. I walked into the kitchen, but no one was there. I shook my head, walked out of the kitchen, and started to walk up the stairs. My nerves were messed up. Maybe it was because of my medicine. Whatever it was, I needed to lie my behind down before I fucked something up.

I turned on the TV and *Good Morning America* was still on. Ever since I was diagnosed with HIV, I'd been watching it because Robin Roberts was such an inspiration to me. She was a woman who had fought breast cancer and myelodysplastic syndrome and survived. She showed women like me that even though we were sick, we still could push forward. I lay there watching TV until I felt myself dozing off.

Just as I dozed off, that little voice popped back up in my head, reminding me that I didn't lock that door the first time I came into the house. I immediately sat up in bed, opened my nightstand drawer, and grabbed the gun that Spencer had bought me. I checked to make sure that it was loaded. Then I placed it on my chest while I lay on my back. I put my hand on it just to make sure that if anything happened, I could get to it ASAP. By now, I was feeling tired, so I closed my eyes. I needed a little nap. Maybe when I got up, I would feel better.

***

That nap was everything. I was sleeping so good until the phone rang and woke me. After I talked to Spencer, I realized that it was a little after two. It was time to get up and take some steaks out of the freezer. I was going to cook my family steak and potatoes tonight. I took the steak out and put it under the running water. Then I grabbed the ten-pound bag of red potatoes and started cutting up some of them. I wasn't the best cook, but I enjoyed cooking for my family.

"Well, hello there, love. Did you miss me?"

My body tensed up as Hassan's voiced echoed and sent chills down my spine. I was scared to turn around, to look at the bitch-ass nigga that was standing in my kitchen, breathing down my neck. I swallowed hard as my mind ran to my gun that was still upstairs.

"Say something, darling. Damn, you're not goin' welcome your husband home?"

I was no longer the dumb-ass Destiny he knew. I knew how to deal with this nigga.

"Hassan, what the hell are you doing in my house?" I quietly asked.

"*Your* house, bitch? This is *my* shit. You stole my motherfucking money and bought this shit. I told yo' ass that I would be back to pay your ass in full. Now, here I am, sugar. I'm here to get what is rightfully mine." He kissed my neck.

All the hairs on my neck stood up as I trembled inside. I had the knife in my hand, but my back was toward him. I wanted to cut out his fucking insides, then watch him bleed out, but it wasn't possible.

"Damn, bitch. You still smell good. I can imagine what you taste like. Destiny, you really thought you were gonna get away with setting me up and then robbing me? You know better than that." He taunted me while he grinded against my ass.

I was shivering on the inside as he started to fondle my breast. Tears started rolling down my face as that nigga violated me once again. I couldn't move because he had me pinned against the counter. I kept looking at the knife that I was still holding. I knew that he was armed because he kept rubbing the gun up and down my back.

"You see, bitch, you are not as smart as you think you are. How the fuck you goin' use my gun to kill my bitch and then set me up? Like I wasn't goin' find out. You a dumb-ass bitch. See, Destiny, your ass wasn't shit when I met you. You were only a means to an end. I loved Imani. I could never love your dry pussy ass." He downgraded me as he ripped my clothes off.

"God, I'm not asking for a lot. I just want strength," I whispered to God.

He pulled my drawers down and slid his cock into my asshole with force.

I closed my eyes as the pain, both mental and physical, ripped through my body.

"Noooo! Noooo!" I screamed out as he ripped my asshole apart. Pee trickled down my legs as I shook uncontrollably.

I wanted to collapse, but he had me locked in. He rammed in and out of my ass. Tears rolled down my face, and he seemed to be enjoying every bit of it. I stopped screaming because each time I did that, he went in deeper. My body was hurting, and my ass was on fire.

"See, bitch, your ass is way better than your pussy. I should've been fucking this a long time ago."

"Hassan, please don't do this to me. I'm sorry for everything I did to you."

"Shut the fuck up, bitch, and take this dick." He used the gun and hit me in the back of my head.

"Noooo! Noooo!" I screamed out.

Things started to look dim in front of me. I used all my might and tried to stay conscious, but that blow was too hard. I couldn't hold my eyes open any longer.

Hassan Clarke

That old, dumb-ass bitch thought she had all of the sense in the world. I walked up the stairs as she slept. Shit, I stood over her and watched her for a while. I could've killed her, but that would've been too easy. I planned to torture that bitch. I wanted to burn that bitch while she was alive.

I walked downstairs to look for some gasoline in the garage. While I was down there, I heard footsteps upstairs that let me know that she was awake. I wasn't tripping. Let the games begin. . . .

I stood in the kitchen doorway for a good five minutes before I walked up on her. I was so close that I could smell the soap this bitch used to bathe.

This ho jumped when I let my presence be known. I wished I could've seen her face. But the position that she was in was better for what I was about to do to that ass, and I literally meant that ass. That bitch's pussy was garbage; plus, I wasn't going to fuck her for enjoyment. I was gonna fuck her to rip out that bitch's insides. I wanted that bitch to know how I felt when my freedom was taken.

I was tired of hearing her fucking mouth, so I bust that ho in the motherfucking head with my gun. Blood spewed out of the open wound. I knew that was enough to knock that whining bitch out. I pulled my dick out of her and grabbed her as she collapsed to the ground. I threw her over my shoulder and then threw that bitch on the couch.

She was out cold, but that didn't mean the show wasn't going to go on. I dropped my pants, took out my dick, and stuck it in her pussy. I fucked her like a dog in heat. Each stroke that I put on her reminded me of what that bitch did to me, so I wasn't easing up.

"Bitch, you fucked up my life," I said as I put my hand around her neck and squeezed it hard as I pumped my dick inside of her. Her ass started to come to. I knew then that I needed to hurry and do what I planned on doing. I pulled my dick out, pulled my pants up, and walked through the house down to the garage. I was looking for gasoline because I was going to shoot that bitch and then light the house on fire. I was going to make sure that she didn't make it.

Bitch, you thought you won, but I get the last laugh, I thought as I walked away.

Chapter Thirty-two

Destiny Clarke

I started to come to. My head was throbbing so badly, and my vision was blurred. I wanted to die when Hassan kept savagely fucking me, but thoughts of my family popped into my head, and that's when I knew I had to live. I couldn't let that nigga end my life like that. And I couldn't believe that I had left my gun upstairs. There was no way that I could get away and run up there to get it. I didn't make a sound as he fucked me and spat degrading words at me.

As if that weren't enough, he put his crusty hand around my neck and started to squeeze hard. I wanted to beg him for my life. I wanted to tell him how sorry I was, but I chose not. I decided not to give that nigga the satisfaction. I kept my eyes closed as he continued pleasing himself. The physical pain was nothing compared to the mental anguish that I was feeling.

I wasn't sure what he was doing, but he pulled his dick out of me and got up. I remained still. I was scared of what he might do if he realized that I was awake. He left the room. I barely opened my eyes, so I could get an idea of where he was.

I put a gun in the living room by the couch closest to the TV.

My survival instincts kicked in immediately. I realized that I was lying on that same couch. I reached my arm underneath the cushion but found nothing. I then reached on the other side, and I found it. I quickly grabbed it and hid my hand under my leg. As soon as I did that, I heard him walking back into the room. I closed my eyes and continued holding my breath.

"Bitch, wake your ass up. I need you to look at me when I throw this gasoline on your ass," he said.

It was now or never. I brought my right hand up from my leg and fired the gun, hitting him in the shoulder.

"You stupid biiiitch," he yelled out at me.

He reached for his gun that he had laid on the far end of the couch, but he was too late. I jumped up and fired another shot in his leg. He fell to the ground that time.

"You dumb-ass bitch. I'm gonna kill you."

I stood over him as he continued to call me every name he could think of. I wiped the tears from my eyes and walked closer to him.

"Hassan, my love, you are the only dumb one around here. You should've stayed the fuck away from me, but you didn't. You just *had* to show your fucking face. You had to stick that infected-ass cock into me, and now you will fucking pay."

"Bitch, I'm fucking bleeding. You need to call the fucking ambulance."

"Shut your bitch ass up."

Blap! Blap! Blap! I smacked this fuck nigga with the butt of the gun.

Rage filled my soul as I remembered everything that fuck nigga had put me through since the day he walked into my life.

"Destiny, please, help me. Please, think about our daughter. She needs her daddy."

I stooped down beside him. "No, honey. She will be fine without your ass. You've been nothing but a fucking nuisance in our lives. Now, tell me, Hassan, how does it feel lying here, bleeding on this fucking floor, and begging me to save your life?"

"You are a wicked bitch. You're not gonna get away with this shit. You're gonna pay for this." His voice cracked as he spoke.

"I waited for the fucking day when I would have you begging like the bitch you really are. That gorilla-looking bitch should've killed your ass when she was pregnant. That would've saved a lot of fucking women you fucked over from dealing with your old, poor-dick ass. I blame myself for picking yo' old poor ass up and trying to turn you into somebody."

"Suck my dick, bitch. You weren't shit before I met you. I *made* you, Destiny. Ha-ha. Me, Hassan Clarke, made you. You hear me, bitch?" he spat.

His words cut through my skin and made me even angrier. I got up and dashed into the kitchen and grabbed the same knife that I was using to cut the potatoes, and ran back into the living room. Then I knelt beside him and tried to loosen his pants as he breathed loudly. I was going to show that fucking nigga that he didn't make shit. All he did was create havoc in my life.

"What the fuck are you doing? You crazy bitch." He grabbed at his crotch area.

"Nigga, move your motherfucking hand or die. You wanna live, don't you?" I pressed the barrel against his head. I was no longer thinking rationally. It was either him or me.

His body tensed up as he pleaded. "Please, don't do this to me, Destiny. I love you. Please, don't." That nigga sounded like a begging bitch.

I realized that he wasn't trying to let that dick go without a fight. So I pressed the barrel up against his wrist and shot him. "Let it go, fuck nigga," I demanded.

"Destiny, oh my God, you're trying to kill me. It's me, Hassan—your man. Remember us and our love?" he cried out in desperation.

I pulled the gun away from him and flashbacked on the time when I was young, and I cut my adopted father's cock off. I used my knee to put force on Hassan's groin area, snatched up that cock, and used the knife to cut it off. It didn't come off completely, so I tried a second time and made a clean cut.

"Noooo!" His scream echoed throughout the house.

I wasn't shaken. I took the limp-ass cock and stuffed it deep into his mouth.

"Now, you can suck yo' own cock, you faggot-ass nigga." I pushed it farther in.

He tried to say something, but I couldn't hear him because he was too busy sucking his cock. I used the back of my hand and wiped off the blood that splattered on my face. He couldn't speak, so he started kicking his feet.

I was still feeling angry. I didn't think that was enough torture after all of the shit he had done to me. I picked the gun up again.

"You see, Hassan, you underestimated me. You thought I was weak, but I proved you wrong. Now, tell that bitch and her son that I said hello, and I hope you all rot in hell."

Pop! Pop! Pop! I fired three more shots into his body without blinking.

Then I stood over him with the gun still aimed at him. I watched as he took his last breath after kicking his legs and shaking his hands. I knelt and rubbed his face with my hand. I then put my cheek to his. "You underestimated me, my dear husband. I am *not* the weak bitch you married years ago." I got up and wiped the tears from my eyes and left the living room.

For some strange reason, I felt relieved, like a burden was lifted off me instantly. I was no killer, but after the shit he had put me through, killing him was easy. I was enjoying him being dead so much that I forgot that I needed to call Spencer. Quickly, I ran into the kitchen and grabbed my phone. I was getting anxious when the thought of the police popped into my head.

"Hey, babe. I'm on my way to the house. I'm pulling up in two seconds."

I didn't say anything. I just hung up and ran to the door. I opened the door, and as soon as he pulled in, I ran up to the car.

"You a'ight?"

"Come with me, please." I grabbed his hand and dragged his ass into the house.

"Destiny, what the fuck's going on?" He grabbed his gun from his waist.

As soon as we got into the living room, he stopped right where Hassan's dead body was.

"Who the fuck is this, and why is this nigga dead on my motherfucking living room floor?"

"That's Hassan. He broke in here and raped me—"

"Say no more. Get your shit, get in your car, and go. Go to the city, the mall, some-fucking-where, and don't call me. I'll call you."

"Say what? I'm not leaving you. We can call the police together."

"Destiny, do as I fucking say. You want to call the police? How're you gonna explain this nigga's dick in his mouth?" he yelled.

I wasn't feeling his tone, so I stood there, frozen.

"I said, go, dammit," he yelled again.

I ran out of the living room and made my way upstairs. Once I grabbed my purse, I ran back downstairs.

I walked out of the house and got in my car. I was shaking uncontrollably as I looked at the house and then pulled off. I wanted to stay with my man, but I knew that would only anger him. I had no idea where I was going, but I had just got on the highway.

My mind ran to my baby girl. I knew that was her daddy. There was no way I would tell her the truth about what had happened. She was so young and had been through too much already, so as far as she knew, her daddy was still alive.

I decided to go to my mama's house. The entire ride there, I felt nervous. I kept looking behind me, and every time a police car drove by, it made me panic. I tried my best to keep the car from swerving off the road. Once, I pulled over to the side of the road and started to vomit. I wasn't feeling good. God knows, I just needed to get to my mama's house.

I pulled into her driveway and jumped out of the car. I rang the doorbell and waited.

"It's me, Mama. Open the door, please."

Amaiya opened the door for me. "Hey, Mama. Grandma's upstairs."

"Hey, baby." I gave her a quick hug.

I managed to make it to the bathroom and the toilet. I kept dry heaving because nothing else was left in my stomach. I lay my head on the toilet seat as I cried.

"Baby, you okay? Get your face up off the toilet," my mama said while she helped me up.

"Mama, I killed Hassan today," I cried and hugged her.

"Calm down, baby. Let me get you a glass of water." She tried to walk away.

"Did you hear me, Mama? I killed Hassan. He broke into the house, and I killed him."

She turned to face me. "I heard you the first time. What the hell do you want me to say? I wish you had done it sooner. I hope you hurt his ass as badly as he hurt you. Now, come on. Let me get you some ice-cold water. Your body is hot." Her expression was cold.

I followed her into the kitchen.

"Sit down. Here's a paper towel, so wipe your tears."

I sat down, and Mama gave me the water. I didn't want any damn water, but I knew she'd be persistent. I took a few sips so she wouldn't fuss.

"Baby, you don't look too good. Do you need me to take you to the ER?"

"No, I just need to take a shower. Mama, he raped me repeatedly. I feel so dirty right now."

"Come on. The tub is clean, and there are washcloths and towels in the closet closest to the bathroom. You know my clothes are too big for you, but I have a new pair of jogging pants that I think might fit you. I have new underwear too. They're not the ones you all be wearing, but they will cover up your behind."

As much as I was hurting, I had to smile at my mama. The words that came out of that lady's mouth were so damn funny.

I was sore from that nigga ripping my butt hole. I saw a speck of blood on my washcloth, and when the soap touched my skin, it burned. My pussy wasn't feeling any better. It hurt so damn badly, and it also burned. I started bawling as I washed the smell of that nigga off me. His dead face flashed in my mind. However, I wasn't sad. I was only crying because of the events that had transpired.

As soon as I got out of the tub, I applied some Vaseline to my ass and pussy, took some painkillers, and got dressed. Then I checked my phone to see if Spencer had called. I was disappointed to see that he hadn't. I started to feel nervous. I couldn't lose my man behind that bullshit.

I walked downstairs, where Mama was watching the news, and sat beside her. "Hey, baby. I was so caught up with what you told me earlier that I forgot to ask you if you called the police."

"Mama, I don't want to get you involved in any of this, but to answer your question, no, I did not call the police. Spencer is taking care of everything."

She didn't say a word. She just grabbed my hand and rubbed it. I rested my head on her shoulder. I was grown as hell, but nothing felt better right now than my mama's touch. "He's a good man. Take good care of him."

Mama went to bed, and I decided to lie on the couch. Amaiya was in the room on the phone, as usual. I tried to fall asleep, but I couldn't. I tossed and turned. I also couldn't stop the tears from flowing. Lord knows, I wasn't a killer, but that nigga and his bitch had turned me into one. That wasn't a good feeling at all.

I was tired of waiting on Spencer, so I finally decided to call him.

"Hey, babe, where are you? I thought you'd be asleep by now."

"I'm at my mom's, and I was waiting to talk to you. You had me worried."

"No need to worry, love. Your man has everything under control. Now, get some rest. I'll see you first thing in the morning, and remember, you see no evil, you say no evil." That was him telling me that no matter what, I didn't know anything.

"A'ight, babe. I love you."

I swear, I needed him so badly . . . just to hold me for the night, but I knew it wasn't gonna happen. I got up and walked into the kitchen. I searched the cabinet and found Mama's bottle of gin. I poured a big cup and gulped it down. I knew I wasn't supposed to be drinking because of the medications, but I needed something strong. I walked back to the couch and lay down. I cried most of the night until I finally fell asleep.

Chapter Thirty-three

Destiny Clarke

One Week Later . . .

It had been a week since all of that shit went down. Spencer kept his word and took care of everything like he said he would. Interestingly, we, unfortunately, lost our house to a terrible fire that broke out when no one was home. I was very distraught because our furniture and all of our clothes were in there. Spencer, however, figured that they were all material things that could be replaced.

I agreed since two niggas were killed in that house. There was no way I could've lived there after Hassan died in there too. That nigga was dead, but I thought that every time I entered the living room, I would see his face . . . especially what he looked like when he was dying. He looked so desperate like he wasn't ready to meet his maker. Oh well, that nigga's lights were out for good.

We decided to stay at Mama's house until after the wedding. We would go house shopping again. That would be my last time moving. It was my first time living back with my mama in a while, and I had to admit that it wasn't that bad. She gave us our space, and she cooked every day. I sure missed my mama cooking those big meals daily. If you were around Mama, you would never be hungry.

I went clothes shopping to get some clothes for us until we moved. We could do a big wardrobe makeover later. Furthermore, the house was insured, so we were going to get a fat-ass check. I was happy because I knew that I didn't have to worry about going to prison or that Hassan's ass was going to come back. That chapter of my life was over . . . I hoped. I still remembered Josiah saying something about me killing his mother. I hoped he was only assuming that because I was so done with Hassan and his whore.

I was lying on the couch, watching TV, when Amaiya walked in. She sat beside me. "Hey, Mama, can I ask you a question?"

"Sure, baby. What's up?"

"You said Daddy was out of prison. Did you ever hear from him? It's a surprise that he hasn't tried to see me."

I started coughing uncontrollably.

"You all right, Mama? I didn't mean to choke you."

"I'm fine. Give me that water. No, I haven't heard from him. Knowing your daddy, he might be laid up somewhere with some woman. I'm pretty sure that when he's ready, he'll try to see you."

"Yeah, I know everything he did to you, but he's still my daddy. Anyway, get some rest. Love you, Mama."

"Love you too, baby girl."

I felt like shit lying to my child, but I just couldn't tell her that her mama had killed her daddy. I hoped she never brought it up again because there was no way that I was going to tell her. I would have to take that to my grave.

***

My big day was rapidly approaching. However, I wasn't feeling too good. I'd been taking my medicines, but somehow, they seemed not to be working. That damn cough had gotten to the point where it kept me up at night. I was scared to go back to the hospital because they always admitted me, and God knows, I hated it there.

"Baby, you know we can put off the wedding until you feel better. I ain't going anywhere. You ain't going anywhere, so a piece of paper doesn't validate shit."

"I know, babe, but I want to be your wife. I want to wear your last name proudly," I said in between coughs.

"Well, if this fever continues, I am calling off the wedding, and I'm taking you to the emergency room. I can't lose you." He looked at me with the sincerest eyes.

"Babe, I told you that I'm good. I'm just a little tired, so I'm going to call it a night."

"Okay, great. I'm going to go down to the office, trying to get some work done because our honeymoon's coming up, and neither of us will be doing any work. It's just gonna be my baby and me."

I looked at him and smiled. I wished every woman could have a man like Spencer in her life. I pulled the cover up and dozed off.

Amiya wanted to have a bachelorette party for me, but I declined. After getting raped and going through mental and physical pain, I wasn't in the mood to see a bunch of niggas running around in their drawers and women throwing money at them. Instead, we decided to have dinner at Mama's house. Mama was fine with it because she got to show off her cooking skills.

I finally got a chance to meet Spencer's family. I tell you, his sister was very classy, nothing like the piece-of-shit sister that Hassan had. We clicked right away. I learned that she was also a registered nurse, so most of the night, she, Amiya, and I kept gossiping about hospitals and doctors. It was definitely a good feeling to see both families come together in the name of love.

The rest of the people danced the night away. I was tired, so I said good night to everyone and went to bed. I remembered back in the day when I could hang all the time. These days, my energy level was too low.

I got up early the next morning. Spencer was already up, and I heard Mama and everybody downstairs, laughing and having a good time. "I guess they didn't make it to bed yet," I mumbled to myself and laughed.

Today was my day. The day that every little girl dreamed of. I'd been down that road before, but this time was different. I could feel the love deep in my soul. I got up out of bed and got on my knees.

"Dear God, I know I don't come to you as much as I need to, but today, I'm coming to you as a sinner. Please, forgive me for all of my sins. God, you know my heart, and you know I'm tired. I try to put out the best, but I'm tired. God, I put my baby girl into your hands, so protect her from this wicked world and lead her. Also, I pray for my mama; give her strength. Wrap your wings around her for comfort. Last, but not least . . . The man that makes me smile, Spencer. God, please give him strength and courage to go on. Thank you for bringing us together and for allowing me to feel what real love is. I love you, God."

I got up and wiped my tears. As I looked in the mirror, I noticed that my eyes were sunken in, and you could see my collarbone. I looked a hot mess, but my soul was at peace.

"Baby, you look so beautiful in that gown. I know I've told you before, but I'm going to say it again. I love you with everything in me. Now, let's not keep that man waiting much longer. You know these heifers might try to snatch him up." Mama and I burst out laughing.

She walked out, and I followed close behind her. The music was blasting, and the church was packed. I could see Spencer up at the front, standing. I was ready to go to my king.

"What would I do without your smart mouth?
Drawing me in, and you kicking me out . . ."

"All of me," John Legend's song, blasted through the speakers. Spencer requested that song, and I concurred. It was beautiful, especially because, regardless of my flaws, he chose me to be his wife.

I'm not going to cry, I kept telling myself. I was too beautiful to smear my MAC makeup with tears.

I looked over at my mama, who walked beside me with her head held high. She was so proud, and so was I. I was almost there when my legs started buckling under me. I slowed down a little, but I realized that I could no longer see my Spencer. The music seemed like it was far way, and everything around me started spinning.

"Come on, baby girl. You can make it," I silently coached myself. But that didn't work. I felt my nose running, so I used my hand to touch it. Bright red blood soiled my glove. In a split second, I went down in slow motion.

"Help us!" I heard Mama scream.

"Destinyyyy," Spencer's voice echoed.

Spencer lifted me from the floor and started running with me.

"I can't lose you. Hang on, baby. I've got you." Those were the last words I heard before I lost total consciousness.

I tried to remain conscious, but I was slowly diminishing. My thoughts were confused, and I couldn't understand anything that was going on anymore. A flick of light flashed in front of me. I smiled as the pain I felt left my body.

Epilogue

Destiny Monae Clarke was rushed to White Plains Hospital but was soon pronounced dead. Although she had the AIDS virus, the cause of death was determined as pneumocystis pneumonia.

She was survived by her beautiful daughter, Amaiya, her mother, and her doting boyfriend, Spencer. After her death, Amaiya, Spencer, and her mother all moved in together so they could support one another. Amaiya finally graduated from high school and was scheduled to leave for college in the fall.

Hassan Clarke's body was never discovered, and the cause of the fire that burned the house down was considered some electrical malfunction. Spencer received a big insurance check.

Judge Morales later found out that she was HIV-positive. She was also charged with judicial misconduct and was stripped of her duties and could no longer practice law.

The bodies of Tanya and her boyfriend were later discovered, and the bullets that were used to kill them were traced back to the judge. However, she was off the hook because the gun had been reported stolen. Their murders were never solved.

After waiting on the boy's mother to return, Hassan's mom took him to DFACS and left him there. She eventually reported her son missing after she hadn't heard from him for a week.

In the end, no one really won. It's okay to have a little . . . as long as you are true to yourself.